CRITICAL ACC[...]

D0182834

'A million readers can't be wrong. Clear some time in your day, sit back and enjoy a bloody good read'
– Howard Linskey

[...] **Peter James**

'Leigh Russell is one to watch' **– Lee Child**

'Leigh Russell has become one of the most impressively dependable purveyors of the English police procedural'
– Marcel Berlins, *Times*

'A brilliant talent in the thriller field' **– Jeffery Deaver**

'Brilliant and chilling, Leigh Russell delivers a cracker of a read!' **– Martina Cole**

'Leigh Russell tells a tangled tale in which guilt catches up with the innocent. It kept me guessing until the end'
– Lesley Thomson

'*Deep Cover* is edge of the seat stuff. A highly entertaining thriller I could not put down' **– Marion Todd**

'A great plot that keeps you guessing right until the very end, some subtle subplots, brilliant characters both old and new and as ever a completely gripping read' **– *Life of Crime***

'A fascinating gripping read. The many twists kept me on my toes and second guessing myself'
– *Over The Rainbow Bookblog*

ALSO BY LEIGH RUSSELL

Geraldine Steel Mysteries
Cut Short
Road Closed
Dead End
Death Bed
Stop Dead
Fatal Act
Killer Plan
Murder Ring
Deadly Alibi
Class Murder
Death Rope
Rogue Killer
Deathly Affair
Deadly Revenge
Evil Impulse

Ian Peterson Murder Investigations
Cold Sacrifice
Race to Death
Blood Axe

Lucy Hall Mysteries
Journey to Death
Girl in Danger
The Wrong Suspect

LEIGH RUSSELL

DEEP COVER

A GERALDINE STEEL MYSTERY

NO EXIT PRESS

First published in 2021 by No Exit Press,
an imprint of Oldcastle Books Ltd,
Harpenden, UK

noexit.co.uk
@noexitpress

ISBN
978-0-85730-464-3 (print)
978-0-85730-465-0 (epub)

2 4 6 8 10 9 7 5 3 1

Typeset in 11.25 on 13.75pt Times New Roman
by Avocet Typeset, Bideford, Devon, EX39 2BP
Printed in Great Britain by Clays Ltd, Elcograf S.p.A.

For more information about Crime Fiction go to crimetime.co.uk

To Michael, Jo, Phillipa, Phil, Rian, and Kezia
With my love

Glossary of acronyms

DCI   – Detective Chief Inspector (senior officer on case)

DI   – Detective Inspector

DS   – Detective Sergeant

SOCO – scene of crime officer (collects forensic evidence at scene)

PM   – Post Mortem or Autopsy (examination of dead body to establish cause of death)

CCTV – Closed Circuit Television (security cameras)

VIIDO – Visual Images, Identifications and Detections Office

MIT   – Murder Investigation Team

Prologue

HE SPOTTED HER STRAIGHT away, leaning against the wall of a disused brewery. Once the apartment block under construction across the road was occupied, the residents would be able to see her, and she would have to find somewhere else to wait around for men who were looking for what she called a 'good time'. As it turned out, time spent in her company wasn't particularly good. Nevertheless, Thomas kept coming back. Even though he knew he should resist the urge to see her, he found himself taking the guilty detour whenever his wife was away from home. Sometimes he drove there almost without thinking.

The first time, Thomas had come across her by accident when he was looking for a pub one of his colleagues had mentioned. The woman seemed enticing because an encounter with her was forbidden and quite possibly dangerous. A violent pimp might be lurking nearby, waiting to mug him, or worse. He glanced around but there was no one else in sight. Although he loved his wife, some long-suppressed instinct in him stirred when he saw the stranger, provocative under the flickering light of a street lamp.

'Looking for a good time?' she called out.

Close up she wasn't very attractive, but he was captivated by the promise of illicit sex. It would be just the once. No one else was ever going to know.

But it wasn't just the once. He started making excuses for taking the detour even when his wife was at home waiting for him. There was something addictive about his guilt. He savoured it in secret moments. He assured himself it was harmless. No one else was ever going to find out, least of all his wife whom he loved. In any case, he told himself, the building work would soon be complete. Residents would go in and out of the new block of flats opposite, and he would no longer find the woman loitering on the street outside the disused brewery. She would have to wait for men in another street, and he would make no attempt to find her again. Although he couldn't resist coming back, he was impatient to be done with her. The guilt was exhausting.

The building work over the road was nearly finished and he knew his visits could not continue for much longer. His wife was away for the weekend and his son had gone back to university in London. His house would be empty. Knowing this was possibly the last time he would see the sex worker, he grew bold with a heady combination of relief and regret.

'Come back to my house,' he said.

She glared suspiciously at him, but softened when he offered to pay her double her usual fee.

'For your time,' he added, in case she was afraid he was going to want her to do something out of the ordinary.

As they drove off, he wondered what he could possibly dream up that would seem extraordinary to her. They reached the house and he hurried her indoors. Unless someone looked closely, they would probably think he was with his wife. As soon as they were inside, with the front door closed, she held out her hand for the promised money. Only then did he realise that he had left his wallet in the car. He hesitated, reluctant to leave her alone in his house.

'I'll pay you when we're back in the car,' he said. 'I left my wallet out there.'

'Are you fucking kidding me?' she replied, her eyes blazing with fury.

'There's no need to shout,' he said, backing away from her sudden anger.

Without warning, she launched herself at him, screeching that she would tear the flesh from his body. A stream of other equally vitriolic threats issued from her painted lips.

'You arsehole!' she yelled. 'You pay me now, you piece of shit! You promised me double and that's what you're going to hand over. Now!'

Only a few moments earlier, she had climbed willingly into his car and had let him drive her to his house without demur. Now she was reacting as though he had abducted her against her will.

'I'll see you in hell!' she shrieked.

'Keep your voice down,' he snarled, struggling to control his temper. 'The neighbours might hear you.'

'I don't give a fuck about your neighbours! Give me my money!'

As she reached for him, her scarlet fingernails curled like claws, Thomas lashed out in alarm.

'Get off me, you filthy whore!'

His first punch sent her reeling. She staggered towards him, howling, and he felt the sting as her nails scratched at his head. Terrified, he felled her with another blow. There was a loud crack as her head hit the edge of the wooden coat rack. By the time she slumped to the floor she had lost consciousness. Her arms and legs twitched convulsively, while her fingers scratched at the carpet and the breath rattled hoarsely in her throat. He watched, transfixed, as her eyes glared helplessly at him, and then she lay still.

Thomas had no idea how long he stood there, rooted to the spot, staring at the grotesque figure lying on his hall floor. His immediate reaction was relief that there was no blood to clean up. Then he began to shake uncontrollably. His legs buckled and he sank to his knees, his eyes still fixed on her, willing her to wake up. But somehow he knew she wasn't breathing. Still trembling, he clambered to his feet and stumbled up the stairs. Wrenching his shaving mirror from its bracket, he went back downstairs and held it in front of her nose and mouth. There was no sound from her and no faint mist on the mirror when he leaned over to examine the surface. He sat back on his heels and closed his eyes. When he opened them again, she was still there. Dead.

He had not actually killed her, but no one was likely to give him the benefit of the doubt, least of all the police. A forensic team would come ferreting around, picking up minute traces of evidence, and the outcome of such an investigation was inevitable. However earnestly he insisted she had accidentally tripped and hit her head while falling, the evidence would condemn him, regardless of the truth. He had no choice but to get rid of the body before his wife returned. He stared at the twisted torso, arms and legs splayed out in a macabre display, the painted face leering up at him as though she was about to scream at him to get his filthy hands off her. The sight of her made him feel sick.

His disgust rapidly turned to anger. The stupid bitch had brought this on herself. He hadn't wanted her to die, and certainly not in his house. He had just been looking for a bit of fun while his wife was away visiting her mother. Admittedly he had been a fool to bring a tart into his house. His wife could have come home early and surprised him, but somehow the threat of discovery had lent an edge of excitement to an otherwise squalid encounter. He had not expected the tart to turn on him like a cornered animal. Whether drugs or insanity had prompted her attack was immaterial. All that mattered now was getting rid of her.

Stepping over the corpse, he staggered to the bathroom and retched until his guts hurt and his throat felt as though he had rubbed it with sandpaper. The side of his head stung where she had scratched him. Fortunately she had only scraped the skin beneath his hair. Not only had he had some protection, but the injury was concealed. Doing his best to quell his nausea, he rummaged around and found an old dust sheet in the garage. With difficulty, he rolled the corpse in the sheet and dragged it into the coat cupboard under the stairs where he covered it up as well as he could. It was nerve-wracking leaving the house, knowing there was a body hidden beneath the stairs, but he had no choice. He had a lot to do, and he had to act quickly.

Using a computer in a hotel, he searched online for a second-hand van. At last he found one in a nearby village, with a telephone number to contact. He bought a cheap phone for cash and, after a sleepless night, called up on the burner phone and confirmed that the van was being sold from a private address in Heslington, not far from where he lived. Unfortunately the owner could not see him until late that afternoon. Thomas really didn't want to wait that long, but there was nothing he could do. The seller was adamant he couldn't see Thomas any earlier. After a restless few hours, he took the bus to Heslington, concealing his face as well as he could beneath a hood. He tossed the phone into a bin on his way, and bought a rusty van for cash from a man who barely glanced at him. He still had twenty-four hours to complete his mission before his wife returned on Sunday evening.

His own driveway was sheltered on both sides by high fences, and even from the road the view of what he was doing that night was obscured by the van. Even so, it was far harder than he had anticipated, dragging the dead woman out through the front door under cover of darkness. The sheet was not long enough to cover her completely, and her legs were exposed, but at least he didn't have to look at her face. She was so floppy, it was like carrying an armful of giant eels, and several times she nearly slipped out of his grasp. It seemed to take hours, but he was confident no one saw him hoisting her into the van, just as no one had spotted her climbing into his car when he had picked her up, or observed their arrival at his house. His shoulders aching from the strain of carrying the body into the rusty old van, he pulled out of the drive. He drove slowly, resisting putting his lights on until he reached the Holgate Road.

It didn't really matter where he dropped the body, as long as no one saw him, but he had been for a walk once in Acomb Wood and thought that would do as well as anywhere. There was no one around to see him carry the body in his arms as far as a small clearing, where he dropped his burden unceremoniously on the muddy ground. His next task was crucial to the success of his plan; he had to conceal the van. His wife never went in the garage so he decided that would be as good a hiding place as any until he figured out what to do with it. The longer he drove around, the more chance there was that he would leave a trail for the police to find. In the unlikely event that his wife questioned him about it, he would tell her that he was storing the van for a friend. It took him most of the rest of the night to clear enough space in the garage to put the van in there, but he persevered. He didn't really have any other choice.

Finally in the house, mentally and emotionally drained, he was desperate to go to sleep. But first he cleaned every surface she might have touched, and even wiped the carpet with a damp cloth. She might as well never have been in the house for all the signs he could see of her presence there. Thirty hours since he had spotted her loitering by the kerb, she had gone – all trace of her visit wiped out, along with her life. She was no great loss. The trauma of the past day was over and he had come through it without any lasting consequences. He doubted the police would devote much energy to looking for the killer of a sex worker. After that, he would be patient.

One day, when he was confident they had abandoned their search, he would dispose of the van. He had taken care not to touch any of its surfaces with his bare hands, and had kept the windows open while he was driving to minimise any trace of his DNA inside it. Exhausted, he staggered upstairs and took a shower before falling into bed, his horrendous experience finally over.

1

THEY CAME ACROSS HER lying face down in the slushy mud on their first walk of the year.

'Do you think she's all right?' Yvonne asked, staring at the back of the woman's head and avoiding looking at her exposed flesh.

The woman's dark hair was spread out concealing her face, but her body was on display, her skin horribly white against the mud smeared over her in uneven patches like a ghastly spa treatment. They stood gazing down in consternation and for a moment no one spoke. Despite her covering of dirt, it was apparent the dead woman had been scantily clad. One high-heeled silver sandal had fallen off and lay a short distance away from her, glistening in the mud. A second one was on her foot, a glittering fragment of attempted glamour. Yvonne wondered if the woman had liked the sandals. They couldn't have been very comfortable. Almost against her will, her eyes travelled up the woman's mud-splattered legs to her black skirt which was so short it exposed white buttocks, dimpled with cellulite.

'She's probably wearing a thong,' one of the women murmured.

'What kind of a skirt is that?' Yvonne muttered.

'She might as well not have bothered,' someone else agreed.

'She doesn't seem to be moving, does she?' another member of the walking group said.

'Well, obviously she's not moving,' Jonathan replied

irritably, crouching down and studying the woman closely. 'Her head's covered in mud. I can't see anything of her face.'

Yvonne shuddered. 'I'm glad I'm not here on my own,' she murmured, with a slight catch in her voice. 'You don't think she's dead, do you?'

'Of course she's dead,' Jonathan barked, straightening up. 'Her face is buried in mud, for goodness sake. There's no way she can still be breathing.'

'Oh my God,' another of their walking group cried out. 'What are we going to do? Shouldn't we cover her up or something?'

'How can we help her?' another voice chimed in.

'Shouldn't we turn her over?' a third one asked.

'No,' William called out loudly, waving his arms at them. 'Stand back, all of you. And stay on the path. The ground is sodden over there. Don't go anywhere near her. We mustn't contaminate the scene.'

'Do you suspect foul play?' Yvonne whispered, feeling a sudden burst of excitement, as though she was acting in a television crime drama.

Although Jonathan was officially the leader of the ramblers group, as a retired headmaster William spoke with a voice of authority others tended to obey without question.

'There's no point in discussing what we think a woman like this was doing running around the waste ground in such skimpy attire,' Jonathan said. 'We can only guess at how or why she died. She might have tripped and fallen headlong.'

'She was probably drunk,' someone added.

'Possibly,' Jonathan replied. 'We can all draw our own conclusions about what she was doing here, but what we really need to do is keep back and alert the authorities to our discovery.'

William was already on his phone, summoning the police. There was a long pause while he listened to a voice on the other end of the line. One of the women in the group began to cry loudly. Several others tried to comfort her as William explained where they were as accurately as he could, while Jonathan fed him information.

'They've asked us to wait here and to move around as little as possible,' William said when he finished talking on the phone.

'Does that mean they think she was murdered?' one of the women asked, wide-eyed.

They all stared at the body in uneasy silence. Her exposed buttocks drew their gaze like a magnet. A fly buzzed around the dead woman's bare legs and Yvonne turned away, unable to watch any longer. They seemed to be waiting for a very long time, but at last they heard voices and two uniformed police officers appeared on the path. One of them shepherded the group away from the body and back to the road, where they huddled together, shivering. Such a chilly winter day was perfect for a brisk walk, but too cold for standing around, and the wind had picked up while they had been waiting. Meanwhile, the other policeman was on his phone. Following another hiatus, a lot of people seemed to materialise at the same time, and the ramblers were herded towards the police vehicles where they were questioned by uniformed constables.

Yvonne was asked for her contact details, and a description of how the body had been discovered. Around her, she could hear the buzz of conversation as other members of the walking group recounted their experience. She caught snatches of their accounts as they described their discovery: 'horrible', and 'shocking' and 'unbelievable'. All at once, Yvonne felt herself trembling and she burst into tears.

'I'm sorry,' she muttered. 'I'm not usually like this. But that poor dead woman… lying in the mud like that…'

'Yvonne's a bit fragile. Her husband passed away a few months ago,' she heard Jonathan say.

But that wasn't what had upset her. She struggled to explain that death should not be devoid of dignity. When a person died, their body ought to be treated with respect. It was heartbreaking to think of the woman's remains lying there all alone in the woods, a prey to scavengers and insects.

'I wish we'd found her sooner,' Yvonne said. 'It doesn't seem fair. God knows how long she'd been lying here, all on her own, and no one even knew.'

'Someone might have known,' Jonathon pointed out grimly.

2

DETECTIVE CHIEF INSPECTOR EILEEN Duncan called a briefing early that morning. Looking around the room, Geraldine was surprised she couldn't see Ian Peterson, her fellow detective inspector and, until recently, her boyfriend. Although their recent split had been her decision, Ian remained constantly in her thoughts. She knew she had made a serious mistake in ending their relationship, but had not yet had a chance to discuss the situation with him. Eileen introduced a new addition to the team, Detective Sergeant Matthew Bailey. Geraldine turned to observe a tall, slim, dark-haired officer who was standing next to her. His relaxed smile slightly at odds with his penetrating eyes, his alert gaze lingered on Geraldine for a few seconds. Preoccupied with wondering where Ian was, she returned her new colleague's stare without returning his smile. As his gaze continued to travel around the room, Geraldine watched him. Clean shaven with pointed nose and chin, he had thin black brows and dark eyes, and bore himself with the confidence of a good-looking man in his early thirties.

Eileen's next words shocked Geraldine. 'Matthew is stepping in to help out while Ian is away.'

'Where's Ian?' a young constable called Naomi asked.

'Another force needed an experienced officer from out of the area to help on a specific case,' Eileen explained. 'Ian may be gone for some time.'

'Where has he gone?' Naomi asked.

A couple of officers smiled knowingly. Not for the first

time, Geraldine wondered whether Ian and Naomi had enjoyed a brief fling, perhaps before Geraldine herself had arrived in York. It was not generally known that Geraldine and Ian had been living together for a few months, although that relationship was now over. They had been very discreet, but she was sure some of their colleagues suspected they had become an item, albeit briefly. Several officers cast sympathetic glances at her and she felt her cheeks burning with embarrassment.

Wishing she had not heard about Ian's departure in full view of all her colleagues, Geraldine looked ahead steadily and hoped no one would notice her discomfort. Aware that her friend Detective Sergeant Ariadne Croft was looking at her, Geraldine focused on keeping her expression impassive. She wondered how people in other jobs coped in such situations when they had not been trained to conceal their feelings. But few other jobs would see a colleague whisked away without notice to an untraceable destination.

'I'm not at liberty to pass on any further information, other than to tell you that Ian asked me if he could go. He said he would welcome the change.'

'A nice sabbatical,' someone joked.

'How long will he be gone?' Naomi asked, with a hint of urgency in her voice.

'He agreed to come back here once his current job is finished, but I can't tell you how long he's likely to be away. Possibly until the spring.'

Geraldine hid her dismay. It was only January and spring was at least a couple of months away.

'He's been called away to serve on a special project, and I'm afraid that's as much as I'm authorised to say,' Eileen added with a tight smile. 'Now, let's get back to work. Matthew has been brought up to speed on the case. So come on, we have work to do.'

A few of her colleagues muttered that Ian must be working undercover, and Geraldine nodded uneasily. It could hardly be a coincidence that Ian had left York so soon after she had thrown him out of her flat. If he had requested a transfer, he might never return. Distracted by not knowing when she might see Ian again, she found it difficult to focus on what the Detective Chief Inspector was saying.

'We have an identity for the dead woman,' Eileen continued, pursing her lips and glaring around the room.

'She looks tense,' Matthew muttered to Geraldine.

'Don't worry, she's always like that,' she replied under her breath. 'She treats us like schoolchildren.'

Matthew grinned, and Eileen's glare came to rest on Geraldine who lowered her eyes.

'Her DNA has been on the database for years,' Eileen went on. 'Her real name is Pansy Banks, although she works under the name of Luscious.'

Someone in the room sniggered. 'Nothing very luscious about her now.'

Eileen grunted.

'Show some respect, please,' Geraldine blurted out. 'The woman's dead.'

'She was a sex worker,' Eileen went on in an even tone. 'It looks as though one of her clients lost patience with her, but until we have the results of the post mortem and the tox report, we are not going to rush to any conclusions as to whether this was an unlawful killing or an accidental death. In the meantime, we're looking for any relatives who are not estranged from her.'

'Poor woman,' Matthew murmured, and Geraldine instantly warmed to him.

'Did she have any children?' Ariadne asked.

'A daughter living with grandparents since she was born ten years ago, and a son, taken into care seven years ago,' Eileen replied. 'Probably just as well,' she added with a scowl.

'There may have been others,' she added, shaking her head.

Although she would have preferred to work with her friend Ariadne, Geraldine was not unhappy to find herself partnered with the new sergeant, Matthew, who impressed her as an intelligent and sympathetic colleague and a good addition to the team. It wasn't his fault he was there in place of Ian.

'Have you been in York long?' he asked her as they left the police station together.

'Quite a while,' she replied vaguely, adding that she had been working in London before she moved north.

He gave her an easy smile. 'Ah, London,' he said. 'It's tough down there, and from what I hear it's getting worse all the time.'

He gave a mock shudder.

'Where were you working before?' she asked.

They chatted guardedly about their circumstances as they walked to the car and she learned that he was separated from his wife who lived with their two children in Leeds.

'I decided it was time for a change, so when this opportunity came up, I applied at once and turns out I was first in line.' He smiled. 'It works perfectly for me, because I can get back to see my kids whenever I want.' He paused. 'Their mother and I didn't part on bad terms, so visiting is fairly relaxed. To be honest, she's only too pleased when I take them off her hands for an afternoon. That was part of the problem. That I wasn't around enough, you know how it is. I didn't spend enough time with the kids. Now she's found herself another partner and I still get to see my kids more or less whenever I can get away. It's not exactly ideal, not what I wanted, but we all rub along okay now we've adjusted to the new situation. How about you?'

'I've never been married,' she replied.

'Wedded to the job?'

'Like a nun,' she said tartly.

3

'YOU'LL FIND WE'RE A friendly bunch here,' Jack said with a grin.

He was a short broad-shouldered man with greying hair; the lower half of his lined face was concealed behind a droopy moustache and straggly beard, above which his eyes gazed intently at Ian. Dressed in a worn leather jacket and threadbare jeans, even sitting down he exuded energy.

'Thank you, sir.'

'It's Christian names or nicknames with us here, Ian, and senior officers are Guv or Boss. No need for formality.'

'Right you are, Guv,' Ian replied.

'We were all pleased when we heard you'd agreed to join us in London. At least one of our teams is crying out for extra manpower and we're desperately reaching out to find experienced officers to help. We've got a massive op going on and are running it on a skeleton staff, which is nothing unusual. It's a joke compared to what we need if we're to do our work properly. You've come at just the right time, and you've been highly recommended. I've seen your record and I'm sure you'll be a great asset to us.'

'Thank you very much, Guv.' Ian returned Jack's smile. 'I've got a feeling this is going to be interesting.'

His colleague grunted. 'Don't get too excited about it. Mostly it involves surveillance work. Some officers volunteer because they're looking for thrills but they soon realise it's mainly just sitting around, watching and waiting. Others have a personal reason for joining, usually on account of a friend or relative who started using. Not everyone is completely honest about their motivation for signing up.'

He glanced quizzically at Ian.

'I'm not in any way personally affected by any of this,' Ian responded quickly.

It seemed wise to keep his personal issues to himself, and he saw no need to explain why he was particularly keen to work with the drug squad covering North London.

'I want to do my bit to help protect vulnerable people,' he said. 'As far as I'm concerned, it's just another pernicious crime that needs to be stamped out, or at least kept under control to some extent. And it's not just the drugs. Addicts commit other crimes too, of course. Any officer worth his salt would be keen to clean up the streets and see the dealers and pushers behind bars.'

'Good,' Jack said. 'Officers who aren't personally affected by the fallout from drugs tend to be more reliable. But don't forget, the work isn't as dramatic as you might think, and it can be dangerous. You've been warned about what you're getting yourself into.'

Ian nodded. He had undergone seemingly endless psychological testing, as well as focused training, before being given a place on the squad. Now he hoped he wasn't making a terrible mistake.

'It's not too late to withdraw if you're not comfortable with the risks,' Jack continued. 'Believe me, they haven't been overstated. And never forget, an undercover officer who cracks is a danger to his colleagues as well as to himself.'

'When do I start?' Ian replied promptly. 'All I've been told is that I'll be working with an undercover team conducting surveillance on members of a drugs ring.'

'You'll find out the details soon enough. There's a briefing in ten minutes so get all your paperwork sorted and we can make a start.'

Ian was relieved that his superior officer had not quizzed him in any serious way about why he had joined the drug squad, because his reasons were in no way disinterested, as he had claimed. The truth was he was hoping to track down former associates of Geraldine's twin sister Helena so he could find Helena's former dealer. Only when the dealer had agreed to leave her alone could Helena come out of hiding and see Geraldine again. Ian had given up trying to glean any information from the police team responsible for spiriting her away to a new identity, where her former dealer would never find her. He hoped a network of drug dealers might leak information more readily than the police did. Until Geraldine was free to resume seeing her sister, Ian understood she would never forgive him for having saved Helena at the expense of her relationship with Geraldine. He had acted from the best of intentions, but Geraldine had been furious that she could not see Helena, who was not only her twin, but her only surviving blood relation.

'You could do with a haircut and a shave,' Jack said, gazing at Ian with narrowed eyes. 'We don't want you looking in any way memorable. And you'll have to drop your air of respectability. Have you got a leather jacket? If not, we can probably find you something here. Now follow me. Come and meet the best drug-busting outfit in the country, in fact probably the best in the whole world. We're not interested in small fry,' he continued as he escorted Ian down a long, dark corridor. 'We're the best at what we do, but we know we're fighting a losing battle. We tread a fine line here. We're not involved in seizing drugs when they enter the country. Every time the boys at Customs and Excise seize a haul, that's a win for us all. But our job is to stop the distribution of drugs once they're here to prevent the gear reaching the streets.'

'Surely it's more important to stop drugs from entering the country?' Ian replied. 'Isn't that where whatever manpower we've got should be focused?'

'Fuck off and work for Customs and Excise then. Our job is to follow the mules along the chain right to the top. We're after Mr Big, the bigger the better. So we let the couriers run and put them under surveillance, taking them out along the way, hoping they'll lead us as far up the chain as it's possible to go. But we never get to the real big boys, the international drug barons, the top players, more's the pity. We just don't have the manpower or resources to combat wealth and power at that level. They have protection,' he added cryptically. 'I'm talking more money and more corruption than you can possibly imagine. But we can and do have an impact on the charlie and smack that flood into our cities, and that's not going to happen if we only go after the little guys. There's no point in taking them out. They're easily replaced. They're like ants. No, it's the men directing the operation we're after, and they're elusive bastards. The higher up the chain we go, the more difficult it is to find them. But we have our modest successes.'

As they were talking, Jack led Ian into a large room where a group of detectives were seated at their desks or standing around chatting. They were a miscellaneous crew: men of different ages, some with ponytails and earrings, others wearing faded black leather jackets, a few skinheads, a Hell's Angel, and an assortment of bare arms, some brawny others skinny, adorned with leather bracelets and generic tattoos. The women were equally diverse: long-haired hippy chicks in flowing caftans, girls in short skirts, and girls in ripped jeans, most of them pale and thin and sickly-looking. But beneath the shoddy outward show, the carefully curated crew were all pursuing the same goal.

A very faint whiff of body odour mingled with the musty

smell of old leather and air freshener, and there was a muffled drone of many voices talking quietly. Occasionally the hum of conversation was disrupted by a burst of laughter or a voice raised in protest.

'No, you didn't,' a shrill voice cried out suddenly, laughing. 'You never did! I don't believe it. You're having me on.'

Against one wall there was a long row of cabinets. Behind glass doors various paraphernalia were visible: opium pipes, slabs of dark brown cannabis, along with syringes and spoons, leaves and plants, sheets of LSD tabs, jars of cannabis oil, packets and pots labelled Ketamine, MDMA, H and many more, all seized in drugs busts and collectively worth millions of pounds on the street.

'Here they are, the gang,' Jack said, waving at his assortment of colleagues. 'You can use the desk over by the window at the end.'

An officious-looking man scurried across the room to intercept Ian as he walked to his desk.

'Welcome to the drug squad. I deal with the team equipment.' He flourished a form and held out a black biro. 'Sign here. And here.'

'What's this for?'

'Any equipment you take off the premises. It's just a formality,' he added, seeing Ian hesitate. 'Only take what you absolutely need, and never remove anything without authorisation.'

Ian learned that many of his colleagues had been working undercover for months, trying to set up a meeting with Tod Lancaster, who had been known to the drug squad for several years as a major dealer. Despite strenuous efforts so far they had not been able to pin anything on him. Several couriers and dealers lower down the chain had been apprehended and convicted, but Tod remained at large, seemingly untouchable, running strip clubs throughout the UK as a front for his lucrative drug dealing. An undercover officer named Jenny, known to the staff at the club as Tallulah, had recently started working as a waitress at a strip club in Soho from where Tod ran his drugs empire.

The next stage in the current plan was outlined at the first briefing Ian attended. Jenny was to introduce Ian as her boyfriend and a potential bodyguard for the boss. If Ian was accepted, he would be as close to the action as anyone could be. In addition, introducing him at the club as Tallulah's boyfriend would offer her some protection from sexual predators at the club.

'I can take care of myself,' Jenny retorted when the plan was announced.

She was a dark-haired girl in her twenties, who looked as though she packed a lot of muscle into her small frame. Despite her initial reservations, she agreed it was a good plan to try and introduce Ian to a role that would take him close to the centre of Tod's operations. With detailed inside information, it was possible that a major drug dealer would be busted. A great deal depended on Tod accepting Ian as a bodyguard.

Jenny looked Ian up and down appraisingly. 'He'll do,' she conceded. 'Smarten yourself up a bit, and you could pass yourself off as a first-rate thug.'

'Flattery will get you everywhere,' Ian grinned.

'You understand what's at stake?' Jack asked.

Ian nodded. 'Perfectly.'

'Remember to behave like a member of the public any time you're out on surveillance. That means you merge into the scenery and don't do anything to get yourself noticed. Never carry your warrant card or phone, or anything else that could identify your real identity if things go wrong and the villains you're watching decide to check you out. That means you have to buy tickets when you use public transport, even if it means losing a target you're following. Get into the mindset. Protecting yourself is your priority. Once your cover's blown, you're no use to us, and you'll most likely end up with bullets for brains, or worse.'

Ian nodded, silently wondering what could be worse than being shot in the head.

4

THE DOOR WAS OPENED by a small, greasy-looking man with black hair, who looked as though he had not shaved for a few days. He started back on seeing Geraldine's identity card.

'This is about Pansy, isn't it?' he said in a hoarse whisper, lowering his head as he spoke and peering up at them from beneath wispy eyebrows. 'That girl's a slut. Was it one of her punters complained? Nothing would surprise me where she's concerned. Oh, we know exactly what she is. There's nothing you can tell us about her that we don't already know, and if you're trying to find her, we can't help you. Why would she tell us where she is? We don't want anything to do with her in this house. And that's all I've got to say to you, so you can piss off.'

He seemed reluctant to talk about the dead woman, as though he was ashamed of being associated with her, or perhaps he was uncomfortable with the police visiting his home for another reason. He hesitated to give them his name, but he must have realised there was no sensible reason for withholding information they could easily obtain without his co-operation, so he told them he was called Steven Baring, and he worked at a local MOT centre.

'Can you tell us anything at all about Pansy?' Geraldine asked, taking a step forward.

'Why? What would I know about her?' he snapped, glaring at them. 'I never even met her. What's she got to do with me?' His voice rose in sudden suspicion. 'What has she been saying about me? Whatever it is, it's all lies. She's a lying cow, that one. Go on then, what's she been saying?'

'I'm afraid she's not saying anything any more,' Geraldine replied gently. 'She died three days ago.'

'Died? Pansy died?' His eyes widened as he registered what he was hearing. 'You mean she's dead?'

'I'm afraid so.'

He shrugged. 'Well, I can't say that's a surprise. You know the kind of life she lived. So how did it happen? Was it drugs or the drink?' He lowered his hoarse voice. 'Did she do herself in? Nothing would shock me about her.'

Briefly Geraldine explained where Pansy's body had been found, and her stepfather had enough humanity to look shocked.

'The poor little slut,' he said. 'Still, she had it coming. Have you got the bastard who did her in?'

'And what makes you think anyone "did her in"?' Geraldine asked quickly.

He shook his head. 'I was speaking in general terms, you know. But it stands to reason, doesn't it? Someone must have done her in.' His eyes narrowed shrewdly. 'If she died of natural causes, you wouldn't be here asking questions, would you? Anyway, whoever it was, I hope you find him soon.'

He could have been bluffing, but Geraldine was inclined to believe he had not been involved with his stepdaughter, either in life or in death.

'We'd like to speak to her mother now,' she said, taking a step forwards.

Steven made a move to close the door but Matthew was too quick for him and had his foot over the threshold before the door shut. Forcing a smile, Steven let them in.

'Sandra?' he shouted. 'Sandra, where are you? The police are here.'

'The police?' a shrill voice replied. 'What do they want? If they're here about Pansy, you can tell them to sling their hook. I don't know where she is, and if I did know I wouldn't tell them. Oh, hello,' she said, appearing in the hall and catching sight of Geraldine and Matthew. 'Well, aren't you a sight for sore eyes,' she added, addressing Matthew with a sly grin. 'I wonder what you get up to in your free time.'

Her attempt at flirting was pathetic, given her bleary eyes and prematurely wrinkled skin. A cigarette butt lodged at the corner of her chapped lips sent up a very fine thread of smoke. She let it drop and ground it out with her heel on the floor which was pitted with burn marks.

'Give it a rest, Sandra,' Steven snapped. 'No one likes to be spoken to like that by an old woman like you, and certainly not the police.'

'Oh sod off,' Sandra replied, giving him a good-natured cuff on the shoulder. She scowled at Geraldine. 'What are you lot after, then? If you're looking for Pansy, I don't know where she is, and I don't want to know. I haven't heard from her for seven years, not since she tried to foist another baby on us. Remember that one, Steve? The stupid bitch got herself banged up again and expected us to pick up the pieces for her. Like hell we were going to be caught out like that again. Selfish cow. She's full of lies, that one. Always lying. Soon as she opens her mouth another one pops out. Lying comes easy to some people. She lies all the time, even to me, her own mother.'

'Pansy's dead, Sandra,' Geraldine said gently, interrupting the tirade. 'I'm sorry to bring you sad news.'

'Sad? What's there to be sad about?' Sandra asked, evincing no surprise at all. 'It's good riddance, if you ask me. I don't suppose anyone's going to miss her. And don't expect me to foot the bill for her funeral either,' she added with a sudden glare. 'That bitch cost me enough as it is. She's not getting a penny more out of me.'

There was no point in dragging out the visit. 'We just wanted to inform you in person about your daughter's death.'

'Yes, well, now you have so you can leave us alone with our grief,' Sandra replied. 'Good riddance,' she muttered under her breath as Geraldine turned away.

It was not clear if she was referring to Geraldine or Pansy but, either way, it made no difference. Geraldine wasn't bothered about having Sandra's good opinion. Back in the car, Geraldine and Matthew drove in silence for a few moments, each absorbed in their own thoughts.

'Some mother,' Geraldine said at last.

'Some daughter,' Matthew replied.

'What a family,' Eileen remarked when Geraldine reported back to her. 'Did you believe her when she said she had no contact with Pansy?'

Geraldine shrugged. 'I can't see any reason why she would lie about it.'

Eileen nodded. 'It's certainly true that she took in Pansy's daughter ten years ago and refused to look after her son, who would be seven now, which implies a deterioration in their relationship over the years. But beyond that, we have only the mother's word for what happened between them.'

Geraldine nodded. They couldn't ask Pansy. She wondered what her own mother might have said about her after she had given Geraldine away for adoption. Her only living link with her birth mother had been her twin sister Helena, but now they had lost contact thanks to Ian's intervention. She knew he had only arranged for Helena's identity change to protect her and Geraldine from a violent drug dealer. But she couldn't forgive him for parting her from her sister.

5

THE PEACE OF THE woods was broken by a distant hum of voices, and through the trees he could make out a distant gleam of cars. The unusual activity up ahead could mean only one thing. He cursed under his breath even though he wasn't surprised to learn the dead woman must have been found so soon after he had left her there. Having made no attempt to conceal her body, he had known that someone was bound to come across her sooner or later. It didn't really make any difference when it happened. A night in the snow would have washed away any slight trace he might have left behind, but he had been careful. The gloves he had been wearing were concealed inside a takeaway food carton in a litter bin in the centre of town. Even if they were discovered, which was highly unlikely, they wouldn't be linked to a dead body found lying in the woods a few miles away. He was confident no one would ever connect him to the body of a stranger lying in the woods.

There was a saying that murderers always returned to the scene of their crime, but this wasn't a murder scene. The woman had not been killed in Acomb Wood. She had died in the entrance hall of Thomas's house. Of course he returned to the hall every day, but not because he had murdered anyone. The woman's death had been an accident. After he had disposed of the body, the first couple of times he had walked into the house a spasm of nausea had gripped his guts, and he had half expected to see the dead woman's painted face leering up at him, her arms and legs splayed out in clumsy disarray. But he saw no such sight, because of course her body was no longer lying on his hall carpet. He knew exactly where she was, because he had put her there himself. After a couple of days, he was able to enter his house without trembling, and smile at his wife as though nothing untoward had happened. He was never going to reveal his secret, and no one would ever know about it.

He was not sure why he had come back to the wood. He just wanted to take a look at her, as if to reassure himself she was really dead. In a half waking doze that morning, before he was fully awake, he had imagined her recovering consciousness in the woods, clambering to her feet covered in mud and twigs, and staggering to the road to flag down a passing car. The thought of it made him feel sick with fear.

Now that he was in Acomb Wood, he hesitated to go closer. Through a gap in the trees he could see the top of a vast white tent and wondered if that meant the police suspected foul play. He didn't know whether a tent like that was always erected over a dead body regardless of how the person had died, or if such forensic investigations were reserved for murder victims. Almost against his will, he felt drawn towards the tent. He had to find out what was going on. It was an impulse stronger than a mere spirit of enquiry. There was a practical reason for his curiosity. He needed to find out how much the police had discovered. He was so focused on the tent and its gruesome contents he almost failed to notice a uniformed police constable standing guard by a tape stretched across the path.

'The footpath is closed to the public, sir,' the young police officer piped up. 'I'm going to have to ask you to turn back.'

Thomas's initial irritation was rapidly overwhelmed by fear.

'Oh, I'm sorry,' he replied, flustered.

The last thing he wanted to do was draw attention to himself. Questions might be asked about why he was there in the woods, so close to where a dead body had recently been found.

'I was miles away, just letting my mind wander, going for a walk. It's beautiful in the woods at this time of year.' He gave a nervous laugh. 'I didn't notice the police tape.'

Claiming to be oblivious to the police presence struck him as sensible. It made him sound innocent, if somewhat unobservant.

'That's all right, sir. It's unusual for a public right of way to be blocked,' the police officer replied.

'Yes, I suppose it is. I haven't been for a walk here for a long time,' he added.

He was aware that he was being rash talking to the police at all. He had been an idiot to return to the woods. Having managed to find a bookkeeping job with a small local business, he should have been seated at his desk in the office, quietly checking the payroll for the month. Instead, he was risking everything by talking to the police. To begin with he had said the woods were beautiful at this time of year, and now he was contradicting himself by saying he hadn't been there for a long time. He knew he ought to stop talking, turn around and walk quickly away, but he couldn't stop himself.

'What's going on here anyway?' he enquired. 'Is there a reason for the path being closed?'

'I'm not at liberty to discuss an ongoing investigation, sir.'

'Investigation, eh? That sounds serious. What happened? Was someone attacked here?'

The constable stolidly repeated that he was not free to talk about the situation. Thomas hesitated, but he was afraid of persisting for fear of alerting suspicion. He tried to think what an innocent man might do in these circumstances, and concluded that such a man would probably do just as he was asked, and turn back without evincing much interest in what was going on.

'Very well,' he conceded. 'But it all sounds very mysterious.'

'Not at all, sir,' the constable replied with infuriating stoicism. 'I'm just doing my job, sir.'

'So there's no way I can go on?'

'No, sir. The footpath is closed, sir. Do you live locally?'

Involuntarily, Thomas edged away. He had overstepped the mark, and the policeman had started asking questions. As Thomas spoke, tiny puffs of mist flew from his lips and hung for an instant in the air before dissipating. He wished he could vanish as inconspicuously.

'Not far from here. Well, thank you, and keep up the good work,' he replied, as he turned on his heel and strode away.

Terrified he had overdone his enthusiasm to discover what was happening, he expected to hear footsteps pounding along the path behind him and to feel a hand on his shoulder. It was all he could do to stop himself from breaking into a run. With an effort, he kept walking at a steady pace, away from the police officer and his tape, and the white forensic tent which covered the location where a dead body had recently been discovered. If the police wanted to know what had happened to the woman, they could have asked Thomas, instead of sending him packing. But as he walked away, Thomas was too agitated to enjoy the irony of the situation.

Back in his car, he sat behind the wheel for a few moments, shaking uncontrollably. Pulling himself together with an effort, he started the engine. He had already taken a detour to the woods on his way back from work. If he wasn't home soon, his wife might start to wonder where he was, and he couldn't afford to arouse her suspicions. Even a good-natured woman like Emily would never forgive him for bringing a whore into their home and hiding her dead body in the woods. When he thought about what he had done, he couldn't believe his own audacity. Only when he reached home did he remember that Monday was the night Emily went to her book club.

There was a note propped up on the kitchen table. His first name had been typed on white paper, cut out, and stuck on a white envelope. Puzzled that Emily had gone to so much trouble, he tore the envelope open, glancing expectantly at the oven as he did so. But the note wasn't telling him about his dinner. It wasn't even from Emily, although she must have found it and put it on the table. For a moment he stared at it, too shocked to move. The message was very simple and printed so there was no way of identifying the sender. The police would have been able to check for fingerprints or DNA, or traced where the envelope or glue had been purchased. He had no access to such sophisticated search processes, and it wasn't the kind of evidence he could take to the police. He felt himself shaking as he read and reread the message: I SAW WHAT YOU DID.

6

A BLOODY HAND ROSE in greeting from across the table as they entered the room. Behind her, Matthew coughed and Geraldine smiled in sympathy. A pungent smell of antiseptic never satisfactorily masked the foul stench of blood and decay in the mortuary. Not for the first time, Geraldine wondered at the plump pathologist choosing to work with the dead rather than the living. His jollity seemed out of place in the mortuary. Framed in wisps of ginger hair, Jonah's pale freckled face greeted her with an infectious grin. With his ugly pug-like features, she could imagine him being bullied as a child at school and becoming a recluse, yet his cheerful nature hardly suggested a man with a tormented past, and she knew he was married and had teenage sons.

'Hello,' he called out, peering across the cadaver at Matthew. 'Who's this fine fellow? It makes a change to see a new face in here that's capable of independent motion.'

'A pleasant change, I hope,' Matthew replied, equally cheerily, as Geraldine introduced him.

'That rather depends on whether you prefer your people alive or dead. But what have you done with Ian?' Jonah asked, his voice expressing mock horror like a character in a pantomime. 'Not that I'm going to miss him. He never had a strong enough stomach for the job, did he?' He winked at Geraldine. 'He's a big softie, not like us hard nuts.'

Jonah's observation was true, although Ian would have been mortified to know the pathologist had seen through his pretence at indifference to the sight of death. Even after years on the murder squad, Ian still struggled with attending autopsies.

'Maybe it was the smell,' Jonah added thoughtfully. 'He was a bit delicate, wasn't he? Not like Geraldine here.' He nodded in her direction, still addressing Matthew. 'Her guts live up to her name. Absolutely no feelings for anyone, living or dead. This woman is utterly inflexible. She knows I am devoted to her, yet she insists on spurning my advances.'

'Ignore him,' Geraldine laughed. 'Jonah's happily married to some long-suffering woman, who is blessed with the patience of a saint.'

Jonah grunted and turned his attention to the body. 'So do we have an identity for this poor creature here?'

'Yes, she was well known to the local force. Most of her dealings were with vice and drug squads,' Geraldine replied. 'Her DNA has been on the database for years and she was frequently picked up for soliciting and petty shoplifting. She was a known cocaine user and no doubt a lot more besides, but was never arrested on a drugs charge. In fact, she was never charged with any serious crime, and never given a custodial sentence. She was a sex worker,' she added, by way of explanation.

'Not looking very sexy now, is she?' Jonah responded grimly.

The three of them stood gazing gravely at the body. The woman's age was difficult to determine. Her face bore vestiges of make-up that had been wiped away: a faint streak of black in the corner of one eye, a fleck of scarlet in a crease of her bottom lip, a tiny blob of mascara on her eyelashes, while death had wiped away all trace of the anger and suffering that must have dogged her throughout her life, so that she looked almost peaceful. She might once have been attractive, with a small, thin nose and full lips, but drugs had taken their toll on her physical appearance, and her face was pock marked and prematurely lined. Even in death her skin had an unhealthy look. Her scrawny arms and legs stuck out, making her look like a giant insect with a bloated body. One of her arms was turned inward, but on the other puncture marks were visible. She had tattoos on her stomach, her thighs and her shoulders, and her nose was pierced, along with several piercings in her ears.

'How did she die?' Geraldine asked, staring at the cadaver.

Jonah pointed to the side of the dead woman's head, where her lank black hair had been shaved to uncover a large dark swelling which had been neatly sliced open to reveal a glimpse of bloody tissue under the skin.

'There was a large contusion here,' Jonah said. 'It was occasioned by her hitting her head, quite violently, due to a fall. Cause of death was the resulting internal haemorrhage which led to irreparable damage to the brain. The chances are she would have passed out quite soon after such a hefty whack and never recovered consciousness.'

'You said she hit her head during a fall,' Matthew said. 'But could the head injury have been caused by a blow from a heavy blunt weapon?'

Jonah shook his head. 'That's highly unlikely, given the nature of her other injuries. There's quite extensive bruising, mainly to her shoulder, elbow and hip, all of which bears out that she fell from a standing position. What isn't in doubt is that the head injury killed her.'

'She was found in a clearing in the woods. Could she have tripped and accidentally hit her head on a tree or something?' Geraldine asked. 'Is that a possibility, do you think?'

Jonah shook his head. 'It's hard to see how this could have been an accident, considering she was moved after she died. I would say she was killed some time on Friday night, but she wasn't moved to the woods for around twenty-four hours after that. It's impossible to be precise, since we don't know how long she was lying outside exposed to the elements, but the early insect activity suggests she was in the woods for less than twenty-four hours. In addition to that, she was found face down in wet mud, but lividity suggests she was lying on her back for some hours after she died. Look here.'

He turned the body over and indicated dark mottled patches on her back.

'So her body was definitely moved after she died?' Geraldine asked.

Jonah inclined his head. 'It must have been. I don't think we can be in any doubt she was turned over. Added to that, she hit her head on the square corner of some piece of furniture and not on the rough bark of a tree.'

'Which means that someone was either there when she fell,' Geraldine said, 'or else they discovered her body afterwards. Either way, it looks as though someone knew she was dead and didn't want anyone to find out where it happened, so they moved her body to the woods.'

'That's what it looks like,' Jonah agreed.

'It's not that easy to shift a dead body,' Geraldine went on. 'And they would have had to be careful not to be observed. Whoever it was, they went to considerable lengths to move her without being noticed. Why?'

'Isn't that obvious?' Jonah replied. 'Who wants to be found with a dead sex worker on their hands? I know my wife wouldn't be too happy if she found this body in my bed.' He heaved an exaggerated sigh and shook his head. 'And I thought you were a detective.'

'What state was she in when she received the head injury?' Matthew asked. 'Was she drunk? Or high?'

Jonah shrugged. 'The one does not preclude the other. I wouldn't be at all surprised to find she was both.' He pulled her arm back to display puncture marks from injections. 'The results of the tox report aren't back yet. As soon as I hear from the lab, I promise you'll be the first to know. And if we can get anything from the skin cells under her fingernails, of course.' Above his mask his eyes narrowed.

'So far all we know is that she had male skin cells under her nails,' Geraldine said.

'Let's hope it's enough to nail her killer,' Jonah commented, his eyes creased into a smile.

'We've not found a match,' Geraldine replied grimly, ignoring the pun. 'Not yet.'

'You get on well with the pathologist,' Matthew remarked when they were driving back to the police station.

'Yes, we've worked together before,' she replied.

'I rather gathered as much.'

'He's a good guy. I mean, it's not just that he's likeable, he's a good pathologist and helpful with it.'

Geraldine found it useful to be on friendly terms with a pathologist prepared to share his speculations with her, off the record. Several times his suggestions had led her down a useful path of enquiry. Ian had never appreciated the value of Jonah's unofficial conclusions, insisting that what they needed from Jonah was evidence, not theories. Unsure how Matthew would feel about Jonah's input, Geraldine hesitated to discuss his role further, and they drove the rest of the way back to the police station in silence.

'The fact that she was moved seems to confirm beyond any doubt that she was murdered,' Matthew said as they arrived back at the police station and reported back to the detective chief inspector.

'I have to say I'm inclined to agree, although, of course, that's not absolute proof she was murdered,' Geraldine replied.

'But why else would someone go to the trouble of moving the body if they weren't trying to cover up an unlawful killing?' Eileen asked.

Geraldine shook her head. 'To get rid of an unwanted dead body? She was a sex worker, wasn't she? Perhaps her presence was an embarrassment to whoever moved her.'

'If you say so,' Eileen replied. 'Well, come on then, let's get to work.'

Answering her phone that evening, Geraldine was guardedly pleased to hear Ian's voice on the line. He was calling from wherever he was working, so her call screening had not alerted her to his name. She noticed the number was shielded so she had no clue as to where he now was. It had taken her a long time to finally agree to live with Ian, yet now she was rejecting him against her better judgement. It was an emotional reaction, although her anger against him was not entirely unprovoked.

'Well? What is it?' she asked, agitation making her curt.

There was a faint pause before he answered. 'I want to be sure I can come home when I finish the job I'm working on.'

'Home?'

'You know what I mean,' he replied, sounding impatient.

She had the impression he was struggling to control his temper and scowled, although he was not there to see her. He would have to do better than that if he wanted to talk to her outside of work.

'No,' she lied, 'I don't know what you mean.'

'Geraldine, we need to talk. I want to talk to you.'

'Go ahead. Talk.'

'No,' he said, 'Geraldine, please, I would really like to see you when I get back and talk about what happened, face to face.'

They both knew what had happened. Ian had deliberately gone behind Geraldine's back and arranged for her twin sister Helena to be given a new identity. The upshot of his meddling was that while Geraldine's sister was now safe from a drug gang that had been threatening her life, Geraldine could never see her again without risking revealing her whereabouts. Only if Helena remained untraceable could both Geraldine and her sister remain safe. Ian insisted he had proceeded in the interests of both women, but he had acted so swiftly that Geraldine had not had the chance to say goodbye to her sister. At the time, she had been convinced she would never be able to forgive him. She had tried and had even let him move back in with her, but their uneasy reconciliation hadn't lasted long. She had spent Christmas with her adoptive sister's family and while she had been away from York, she had reached her decision to part from Ian. Now, hearing the desperation in his voice, she found herself wavering.

'You're there in your apartment all alone,' he was saying, 'and I'm here on my own, and it doesn't have to be like this. Please, can't we at least go for a drink one evening and talk about what happened, like civilised adults?'

With a tremor of self-pity, Geraldine hung up. She knew she was being stubborn, childish even, but she did not want to let Ian win her round. Not yet. If he moved back in with her again, there was a danger her resentment would fester and ruin any chance they might have of rebuilding their relationship. Ian might not appreciate her intransigence now, but it was better to walk away completely than try to resurrect a love affair that had turned sour. As things stood, they were on civil terms, and it was best they remain that way. After all, it sounded as though they might end up having to work together again. In time their relationship might improve, but perhaps friendship was the best they could hope for.

Ian rang back, as she had known he would.

'Geraldine, I never meant to hurt you,' he said. 'What choice did I have? Blame the villains who want to kill your sister, not me. This situation was not of my making, and what happened wasn't my fault. You can't keep punishing me like this.'

'I don't know what you want me to say,' she replied.

'You have to let it go, Geraldine.'

'Stop calling me. I don't want to talk to you.'

She hung up again. She half expected her phone to ring again, but he didn't call her again that evening. She wasn't sure whether to feel disappointed or relieved that he had stopped trying to contact her, at least for that evening. Many women succeeded in sustaining successful relationships with men. She was not one of them. But she had never appreciated how lonely she was living alone until Ian had moved in with her. Now he had gone and she was caught up in a wave of self-pity. Pulling herself together with an effort, she poured herself a glass of red wine and settled down to review the murder case so far. She had lived quite contentedly on her own before. She could do so again. In the end, her relationship with Ian had only ever promised a brief spell of happiness. Now she had to return to reality and focus on her work. But all the time she was telling herself that work was all that mattered to her, she knew deep down that wasn't true. Somehow she had to find a way to reconcile with Ian, before it was too late. He loved her, she was sure of that, but even he might not wait forever for her to relent. The prospect of living on her own, which had once been welcome, now seemed interminably dreary.

7

THE HUSHED ROOM WAS very quiet after the loud music, which had virtually drowned out voices raised in an attempt to make themselves heard. Just along the corridor strippers flaunted their bodies, pole dancers gyrated and swung, and scantily clad waitresses plied customers with drink, the deafening racket muffled by a green baize-covered door. In the office at the back of the premises Ian waited for the uncomfortable ringing in his head to subside. A man in a navy suit was seated opposite him behind an enormous leather-topped desk. He did not stir when Ian entered, although he must have heard the abrupt blast of noise as the door to the office opened and shut.

Ian studied the man behind the desk covertly. Tod could have been an unremarkable bank manager or senior civil servant, smartly dressed and good looking, were it not for the jagged scar that ran from his right cheek bone all the way down to his jaw, where he had been slashed in the face with a broken bottle. Such a blatant reminder of what had clearly been a violent injury would have disfigured most men, but somehow it looked almost natural on the man in front of Ian. If anything, the scar made him more attractive, a man with an interesting past. It was an odd notion to think that he wore his scar well. Black eyes flicked from Ian to his escort and back again with the lazy arrogance of unassailable power.

Conscious of the need to conceal his curiosity about the owner of the central London club in Soho, Ian lowered his gaze and stared at the carpet. Like everything else in the plush office it looked expensive, and he had immediately registered how his feet had sunk into the soft, deep pile when he stepped into the room. There were two other men present. One, who was tall and burly, was wearing a brown leather jacket. The other was skinny and wore a dark sports jacket. His arms hung at his sides, but Ian suspected he could have a gun in his hand in an instant. The first bodyguard looked about forty, while the skinny one was barely out of his teens. Jittery, fidgeting with his cuffs, his eyes flicked constantly from Ian to his boss and back again. His nails were bitten to the quick and his fingers were nicotine stained. He was so nervy Ian was afraid he could lose his self-control at the slightest provocation. Several upholstered office chairs faced the desk, but no one else sat down.

Before anyone spoke, the door opened to admit a dishevelled youth. He had shoulder-length hair the colour of dry straw and he stumbled in, eyes glazed and arms swinging loosely at his sides, the strap of a hessian satchel slung across one shoulder. His entrance was accompanied by a blast of music and shouting. The older bodyguard reached across to close the door and the noise cut out as abruptly as a radio that is switched off.

'How much?' Tod drawled, raising his dark eyes to look at the spaced-out youth who had just come in. 'How much?' he repeated, more loudly.

Seeming to hear the question for the first time, the lad emptied the contents of his bag on to the desk. A few notes fluttered to the floor and the young bodyguard darted forward to retrieve them, adding them to the fistfuls of cash the courier had already deposited in front of the boss. Ian was instantly alert, but he knew better than to let his interest show, even for an instant. He watched from beneath lowered lids as Tod counted the cash, his black eyes sparkling as they flicked from note to note, and his pink tongue flitting in and out, moistening his lips, while the boy who had delivered the cash watched anxiously. Other than the rapid flipping of money, there was no sound in the room and no one moved. Ian tried to see how much money was there, but it was impossible to watch it closely without arousing suspicion. Judging by the time it took to count, he figured there must be thousands of twenty pound notes. The club alone must have been a lucrative venture, but Tod clearly turned over a decent profit from drugs.

At last Tod nodded and dismissed the courier with a wave of his hand. The young man stuffed a bag of white powder in his pocket as he turned and shuffled from the room, grinning foolishly. Having locked the money in a safe beside his desk, Tod raised his eyes and stared directly at Ian who faced him stoically, aware that the success of a long-running project depended on the outcome of this encounter.

'So you're Archie?' Tod said, running his eyes appraisingly over Ian's broad shoulders.

Ian did not answer.

'You know Tallulah?'

'Tallulah's my bitch,' Ian replied quietly.

'Word is you fancy yourself as a tough guy?'

Ian shrugged. 'I can be handy.'

'And you had a gig as a heavy for someone else?'

'Bodyguard for my boss,' Ian replied, trying to sound proud of the job title. 'He said I was the best he ever had.'

Ian hoped he wasn't being too pushy, but if Tod decided to employ him as simply another bouncer on the door, he would be less useful to the drug squad than if he was working as a bodyguard protecting the owner of the club.

Nick, the younger of the two other men in the room scowled, perhaps suspecting Ian was after his job.

'The boss has got a bodyguard,' he snarled. 'If you're so tough, how come you got canned?'

Ian turned and glared at him. The man was younger and taller than Ian, but he thought he could take him down. It was unlikely the thug had received the kind of professional training Ian had undergone. This was a chance to prove himself to Tod. He clenched his fists and took a threatening step towards the young man who immediately responded by taking a swing at Ian. His aggression alone was enough to intimidate most assailants, but Ian was prepared. Dodging the blow, he seized his attacker's arm and twisted it up behind his back before the young man had time to react. At the same time, with his other hand, he slipped Nick's gun from his waistband and kicked it across the room.

'Fuck me,' his antagonist groaned, 'where the fuck did you pick that trick up?'

The question was more penetrating than he realised. If any of Tod's men knew the answer, Ian would be dead in the instant. But Tod's narrow face creased in an admiring grin.

'I never seen anyone jump Nick before,' he chuckled. 'Archie, you're my man.'

Ian said nothing and Tod waved a hand, slender as a girl's.

'One of my boys gave me the dirt on you,' he went on. 'Never been touched by the filth.' He nodded approvingly. 'That's lush. An ex-con's less use to me than a man with a clean record. That way they don't have your mug or your prints and all that shit. I like to avoid trouble with the filth. But you done some shit all right.' He laughed.

Ian nodded. Jack's team had been thorough in creating a fake history for Ian's new identity as Archie.

'What do you want me to do with him, Boss?' Ian asked, giving Nick's arm an extra twist so that he yelped in pain.

Slowly Tod drew a small pistol from his desk and pointed it at Nick. A few centimetres to the left, and he would be aiming straight at Ian's head. It was an effort not to flinch.

Tod shook his head. 'I'm not sure which one of you I'm going to pop,' he said with a careless shrug.

Nick began squirming violently, and Ian struggled to conceal his own terror.

'You're a cool one, no shit,' Tod said, staring at Ian with evident respect.

He flipped the gun until it was pointing at the ceiling and pulled the trigger. There was a deafening retort and Nick slipped from Ian's grasp, collapsing on the floor with a moan of terror.

'You're canned,' Tod said, scowling down at Nick. 'Get out.'

Nick shook his head. 'Fuck you,' he snarled.

It wasn't clear if he was talking to Ian or Tod, who threw his head back and laughed. Regaining his stern composure, he nodded at the burly bouncer in the leather jacket. 'Take him to the lock-ups, Frank. If he whinges, take him out.'

Whimpering, Nick was yanked to his feet and the older bodyguard dragged him from the room. There was a burst of noise before the door swung closed behind them leaving Ian alone with Tod. Eyeing the gun, Ian restrained a wild impulse to arrest him on the spot.

'Seems there's a vacancy come up now Nick's gone,' Tod said, calmly replacing the gun in his desk. 'Are you game, Archie?'

Forgetting for a moment that Archie was his new name, Ian raised his eyes and stared at the ceiling, avoiding looking at the bullet hole.

'Archie,' Tod's voice grew sharp. 'Don't make me ask you twice.'

'Yes, Boss,' Ian replied. 'Thank you, Boss. I'm your man.'

Tod nodded and looked at the ceiling. 'I need to get that fixed,' he said in a languid tone of voice.

He leaned back in his chair and closed his eyes. 'Now what are we going to do about Nick?'

'I don't suppose he's dangerous,' Ian ventured.

'Who asked you to go supposing?' Tod snapped, opening his eyes and glaring coldly at Ian. 'Obviously he must be dealt with. He knows too much. He has to be dealt with. You want his job, don't you?' He leaned back and closed his eyes again. 'Nick's waiting for you in the lock-up. It's properly soundproofed but remember to shut the door behind you when you go in. Sound carries. Frank will tell you where to find him.'

Ian understood what Tod meant before another word passed between them. This position was no ordinary case of dead man's shoes. Tod had just ordered him to kill Nick.

8

GERALDINE HAD NO OBJECTION to working with Matthew. If anything, she rather liked him. Underneath his easy-going manner, he was sharp and committed to his work. But she missed Ian, who had been her partner in her personal life as well as at work. Shortly after she had thrown him out of her flat he had left York without even telling her his plans. She had lost her life partner as well as her twin sister, and felt as though she had suffered a divorce and bereavement at the same time. Yet all the while, no one else knew anything about what had happened in her personal life. Even her friend, Detective Sergeant Ariadne Croft, had been kept in the dark. Although Geraldine was pleased that no one was feeling sorry for her, and she could mourn her losses privately, it was hard having no one to talk to.

She was relieved to be partnered with Matthew, who had never even met Ian, because she thought Ian would not come up in conversation. She was mistaken. As they drove to Pansy's flat, Matthew enquired about him.

'I hear your former partner left in something of a hurry,' he said.

Geraldine gave a noncommittal grunt.

'I was talking to Ariadne,' Matthew went on, and Geraldine looked away to hide her annoyance.

Of all her colleagues, Ariadne was the only one who had seemed absolutely convinced that Geraldine and Ian were in a relationship, despite Geraldine's equivocations.

'She thinks it was all a bit sudden,' Matthew went on. 'There's a rumour circulating that he's working undercover in London.'

'Yes, I heard that too,' Geraldine replied, keeping her tone as casual as she could. 'But I'm not in touch with him so I couldn't say.'

'Don't you think that confirms it?' Matthew said. 'I mean, if he's left without staying in contact with anyone here, it does make it sound as though he probably is working undercover. If he had just relocated, surely he would have kept in touch?'

'Perhaps,' she conceded, although she had barely spoken to her own former colleagues in London since she had moved to York. 'But he probably wouldn't have kept in touch with me.'

'Weren't you partners?'

'We worked some cases together, yes. But we weren't close outside of work.'

The lie slipped out before Geraldine thought about what she was saying. In fact nothing could have been further from the truth. Even before Ian moved into her flat, they had been good friends for years. She was not sure why she was so keen to deny that, except that she was still angry with Ian for preventing her from seeing her sister.

'I'm not very good at keeping in touch with people,' she added, truthfully.

'I heard he left in a hurry,' Matthew persisted.

'I'm sure there's a perfectly innocent reason for his relocating so suddenly,' she replied. 'Maybe he was needed somewhere else urgently, rather like you were. So, how's it going?' she asked, hoping it wasn't too blatant an attempt to change the subject. 'How are you finding it here?'

Matthew shrugged. 'New year, new job. No complaints so far,' he smiled.

'Well, let's focus on Pansy. We're nearly there.'

They spent the remaining few minutes of their journey

discussing work. Matthew seemed to have forgotten about Ian, and Geraldine was relieved not to have to talk about him any more. She did her best to convince herself that her lie had been perfectly reasonable. Her personal life was no one else's business, least of all a colleague who had only just moved to York and was effectively a stranger. She hadn't pried into his affairs or asked him why his marriage had failed. Her working life was spent uncovering other people's secrets, but she liked to keep her own life private. The irony was not lost on her.

A team of constables were questioning other local sex workers who might have known Pansy in an attempt to trace any of the murdered woman's clients, while Geraldine and her new sergeant went to have a look around Pansy's lodgings. She had rented a flat above a dingy row of shops near the hospital. A couple of the premises stood empty, which added to the dilapidated atmosphere of the street. Geraldine and Matthew agreed to split up to go into the shops, starting from opposite ends of the parade. A light snow was falling, covering the frozen grey slush on the ground as Geraldine made her way carefully along the pavement, trying to step on snow that lay between patches of slippery ice.

Her first visit was to a florist where a taciturn woman behind the counter barely glanced up. She replied to Geraldine's questions in monosyllables, but the whole exchange was pointless. If she knew anything about Pansy, she was unwilling to share her information and denied knowing anyone who went by that name or looked like the woman in Geraldine's picture. It was the same in the next shop Geraldine entered. Finally, in a newsagent's underneath Pansy's lodgings, she came across a man who seemed to recognise the picture of the woman who had lived above his shop. A thin, swarthy man with heavy dark eyebrows, he gave an uneasy smile as he saw Pansy's picture. It occurred to Geraldine that he might have enjoyed more than a nodding acquaintance with his neighbour.

'I saw her from time to time, just going in and out, you know,' he admitted. 'But I never knew her name or anything. We barely said hello.'

Geraldine wasn't sure she believed him.

'Do you know how she earned her living?' she asked.

The man shook his head. 'No,' he replied, his face twisted in a puzzled frown. 'Why would I?'

She wondered if his denial was slightly too earnest to be truthful.

'Why?' the man went on. 'Has something happened to her? I haven't seen her around for a few weeks.'

Geraldine didn't bother to tell him that Pansy had been murdered. He would find out soon enough, if he didn't already know.

'Who are you anyway?' he demanded, suddenly suspicious.

Geraldine held up her identity card and asked him where he had been on the night Pansy had died.

'I just want to know whether you might have seen anyone visiting her,' she lied.

'Last weekend?' he repeated, screwing up his face as though trying to remember. 'I was here, wasn't I? Working. But I took the Friday off.'

Geraldine held her breath. 'Why was that?'

He shrugged. 'It was my girlfriend's birthday. I took her away for the weekend to Blackpool.' He leaned forward slightly, his lips glistening moistly as the light caught them. 'Would you believe she'd never been to Blackpool?'

Geraldine breathed again. Either she was facing a very cunning killer or the man in the newsagent's was innocent. She took down details of where he had been staying in Blackpool and the times of his trains.

'Here, you don't think I'm involved in anything illegal, do

you?' he demanded, suddenly spooked by her questions.

'It will help us to eliminate you from our enquiries,' she replied.

'What happened to the girl upstairs then? I noticed a lot of police outside. Do they have anything to do with her?'

'I can't reveal any details yet,' Geraldine said. 'Thank you for your co-operation.'

Leaving the shop, she called the police station. A call to the hotel where the man claimed to have stayed confirmed his alibi. Matthew's enquiries had been equally fruitless. Disappointed but not surprised, they ascended the grimy stone staircase that led to Pansy's front door, treading with care on the slippery steps. A search team were inside, looking for evidence of Pansy's clients and acquaintances, but the pickings were meagre.

'Nothing so far,' a sergeant leading the search team told them. 'I'm afraid she didn't keep a diary of assignations with names and contact details of her punters.'

'No,' Matthew replied. 'Our girl seemed to have picked up her customers on the street.'

'All the same, she could have kept someone informed of her whereabouts,' the sergeant said. 'For her own protection.'

Leaving Matthew talking to the sergeant, Geraldine walked slowly around the flat, trying to gain an impression of the life of a dead stranger. There was a double bed in one room, covered with a miscellany of clothes strewn haphazardly over the duvet and floor. Several pairs of shoes, mostly stilettos, lay in an untidy heap on the threadbare carpet beside a tin of cigarette butts. There was no wardrobe, the only other furniture in the room being a large chest with underwear, T-shirts and wigs spilling out of drawers crammed too full to close. A dirty mirror hung on the wall above a jumble of jars and tubes of make-up on top of the chest. A case lay open on the bed, containing a few small bags of cannabis together with needles and dirty bandages, confirmation that Pansy had been a junkie. The room stank with a heavy mixture of stale sweat, drugs, alcohol, and cheap perfume. Trying not to breathe in too deeply, Geraldine stared around before checking the other rooms.

The kitchenette was predictably cluttered with dirty plates and cups, the bathroom looked as though it had never been cleaned, and a small sitting room was impossible to enter without treading on magazines or clothes or empty cigarette packets. Everywhere Geraldine looked, officers were busy combing through the detritus of Pansy's life.

'There's nothing we can do here,' Matthew said, joining her in the doorway of the living room. 'It stinks. Come on, let's go. It's too depressing.' He sighed. 'What a way to live. I ask you.'

Geraldine nodded. A few moments in the flat was enough to repel her with a combination of pity and disgust. She could only imagine how miserable it must have been living there.

'Poor cow,' she muttered as she followed Matthew back down the stairs and into the chilly fresh air. 'No wonder she felt the need to escape from reality.'

The snow had stopped, but it was icy cold and Geraldine shivered inside her parka, remembering the bare-legged corpse lying on snowy ground in the woods. Even if she had still been alive when she arrived there, she wouldn't have survived long in the freezing conditions.

9

IAN HAD NOT YET adjusted to the milder weather in London. It was mid-January but the path was as yet untouched by snow, and green weeds poked up from cracks between the paving slabs. They were seated on a bench beside a scrubby patch of grass, which a sign on the railings rather grandiloquently called a park. An elderly man was walking his dog on the far side of the grass, but otherwise the place was deserted. Not yet swept or blown away by human intervention, withered brown and yellow leaves skittered and swirled along the path with every gust of the chill wind. A dirty yellow leaf fluttered on to his shoe and settled there like a spectral butterfly. He shook his foot and it floated to the ground.

Jack brushed a stray lock of grey hair off his forehead and took out his phone. He didn't switch it on.

'You're in there, all right,' he murmured into the phone, without looking round at Ian. 'Well done. We've been trying to get close to that fucker for over a year, and you come along and snap your fingers at him and before you know it he's sharing his most intimate secrets with you.'

'What do you mean? He hasn't told me anything,' Ian replied, also talking into his phone.

Jack glanced around and lowered his voice. 'He's telling you who he wants you to get rid of, and if that isn't a secret, I don't know what is.'

Jack grinned, accentuating the lines on his face.

'Yes, I've been given instructions,' Ian replied miserably.

'Exactly. That's what I'm talking about. It's absolutely fucking brilliant. It's a sign of trust. You're a natural. You're in.'

'That's all well and good, when you put it like that,' Ian replied, frowning. 'But what now? You know what he's ordered me to do, and if I refuse, he's going to smell a rat. So what the hell am I supposed to do with this bloody secret?'

'Well, obviously you don't want to go ahead and actually carry out the order,' Jack said quietly. 'That would be taking things a step too far. Although it would certainly help to get your feet under the table,' he added.

'I thought we were supposed to be the good guys.'

'Everything's relative,' Jack murmured softly. 'It could be justified, as a means to an end. Get rid of the small fry to gain the trust of a bigger fish?'

'I'm not doing it,' Ian replied. 'No way.'

'No, better not go down that route,' Jack agreed, with a shrug. 'Pity, but of course you're right, that's not an option. Oh, for fuck's sake,' he added, with a rapid glance at Ian, 'there's no need to look so worried. I was pulling your leg. I was never really going to sanction you doing it, even though it would be no great loss to the world.'

Ian did his best to conceal his unease, but he couldn't help wondering whether Jack had actually wanted him to follow Tod's orders. There was a certain logic to it, in that seeing Nick's dead body would help to convince Tod that Ian was trustworthy. Yet if Ian murdered Nick with his superior officer's blessing, Ian and Jack would be no better than Tod. He shook his head. It was unthinkable.

'We'll just have to come up with some other way to deal with it so no one suspects you botched the job.'

'What the hell's that supposed to mean?' Ian repeated, no longer making any attempt to conceal his discomfort. 'I told you, I'm not doing what the boss wants. If that's what you're expecting, you can take a hike. It's not going to happen.'

'No, no, there's no need to be so jumpy. Jesus, what do you take me for?' Jack laughed softly. 'But come on, let's stop dicking around and be serious. What *do* you propose to do?'

Ian shook his head. 'Whatever we do, the boss has to be convinced that I carried out his orders.'

'Exactly,' Jack agreed. 'That's just what I was saying.'

Speaking in a rapid undertone, Jack explained he would arrange to offer Nick a new identity in exchange for information that would see Tod put away for a long time. They discussed how to set about bringing the discredited bodyguard in. The fewer people who knew about the plan the better. Even Jenny, who was completely trustworthy, would be out of the loop, since the team routinely operated on a need-to-know basis for everyone's protection.

'I'll make sure that fucking bastard's given a watertight new identity, even though he's probably done away with more innocent people than you've had hot dinners,' Jack said. 'Does he have any family?'

'How should I know? I've been hired to get rid of him, not to be his best friend.'

'Let's hope he doesn't, because he won't be able to contact them again after we pull him in, not without risking blowing your cover.'

'With any luck, he'll give us enough information to put his boss away for a long time,' Ian said. 'By the time anyone catches up with him, if they ever do, the job will be over and I'll be gone.'

Jack nodded. 'You were never planning on staying with us permanently, anyway, were you?'

'What makes you say that?'

'I can tell when a man is working with us because that's where he really wants to be, and when he's taking a break from whatever shit his job – or life – is throwing at him.

You're here to get away from something, aren't you? By the time we've finished nailing that bastard new boss of yours, the troubles that sent you here won't look half so bad. It's a shame,' Jack went on, when Ian didn't answer, 'you're a natural at this. Bloody hell, one meeting with the boss and you've got him eating out of your hand. Officers like you don't come along every day. Most of us have to work for months to earn trust. Must be your mug makes you look the part. You're a natural thug.' He laughed gently.

'It was Jenny really,' Ian replied. 'She was the one who put in the ground work. I just breezed in when she had established the trust.'

'Yes, she's good. One of the best in her own way. So, where's your target now?'

Ian gave him the address where Nick was being kept. 'The boss has given me the key, and told me he wants the job done by midnight tomorrow.'

'By midnight tomorrow? What does he think this is? A Hollywood B-movie? All right, all right, so we need to act fast. Best to get it over with, anyway. The longer we procrastinate, the more chance there is that it will all go pear-shaped. Sort out how you're going to do it, and bring the target to me the first chance you get tomorrow. The lock-up is probably being watched, but make sure you lose them once you've picked him up, and bring him in without anyone else knowing about it. It's crucial no one sees what you're about or your cover's blown and then you're no use to me. In fact, you'll be no use to anyone after that, because someone will have blown your brains out.'

Ian nodded tensely.

'If you think you're being watched, if there's even a sniff of a chance, drop him off somewhere you can't be overlooked, and tell him if he ever returns or contacts the boss or anyone else in his outfit, you'll finish the job properly next time. Make up some bullshit reason for not finishing him off that doesn't blow your cover. Once we get our hands on him, we won't be able to hide your real allegiance any longer, but we'll give him a clear choice: years in the nick, or freedom with a new identity and money to blow. I don't think he'll be running back to the club in a hurry, not with what we'll be offering in exchange for the boss who tried to have him dealt with. Once we've got the target, you can go back to the boss and tell him the job's done, and all the while we'll be pumping the stooge for everything we can squeeze out of him.'

In guarded language, they worked out Ian's narrative. He would say he had strangled Nick in the lock-up to avoid any mess in his vehicle while he was moving the body. He drove out to an isolated spot, weighed the stiff down with rocks, and dumped him in the Thames. It sounded plausible enough. Ian would liaise with the Metropolitan Police Marine Unit and identify a location along the river, accessible by road, where a body could feasibly be thrown into the water without risk of being observed. That was the story Ian would tell Tod, who would hopefully accept it without question.

'There's no reason why he wouldn't accept the story,' Jack said.

'What if he wants to see the proof for himself?'

Jack laughed. 'Tell him he'll have to dredge the river.'

'Do you really think this is going to work? That he'll be prepared to take my word for it?'

'Time will tell. In the meantime, you have to get going. Your boss is one of our main targets in London. We've been after him for a long time. Don't mess this up. Not now we're so close. Now go. You have a deadline.' Jack smiled with grim satisfaction and glanced quickly around before putting a key on the bench between them. 'A white van will be parked at the end of the dead end where you'll find the lock-up. Let's do this, and whatever other shit is going on in your life right now, make sure you don't fuck this up as well.'

10

Aware of the potential repercussions if his plans went wrong, Ian locked his wallet, keys, warrant card and watch in the top drawer of his desk at the police station. With nothing but the keys he had been given by Tod and Jack and around fifty quid in cash stowed in the pocket of his jeans, he set off. He took the underground as far as Great Portland Street, from where he hurried along the street towards the lock-up garage where Nick was being held captive. In all the noise and bustle of traffic, he understood the logic of killing someone in a soundproofed lock-up garage at night. Tod had thought of everything.

He did not go directly to his destination, but took a ten-minute stroll with frequent stops to look at the shop windows and buildings he passed, to check he was not being followed. The streets were not very busy and at last, satisfied he was not being tailed, he walked south down Great Portland Street, turning west into Devonshire Street until he reached Hallam Street from where he turned off through a square archway between high brick walls into Bridford Mews. It was a dingy backwater with a cobbled roadway and a row of garages on either side. At the end of the cul-de-sac he spotted his designated vehicle, a filthy white van, parked beside abandoned planks of wood and dirty cardboard boxes. It had been turned around for a speedy getaway. The mews was overlooked by high office blocks, but no one was visible at any of the windows and there were no lights on in any of the buildings. At that time of night, the place was deserted.

Ian trotted over to the van and started it up to make sure the engine wouldn't let him down. Satisfied, he took out the small key Tod had given him. The thought of Nick pacing the interior of the lock-up, waiting to be shot, was sickening. All the same, he was cautious opening the door in case Nick jumped him. He had worried unnecessarily.

'Jesus,' he blurted out, horrified by the stench as much as the sight of Nick chained to a massive metal ring on the wall, unable to sit and barely able to walk.

Nick raised his head and moaned.

'Do exactly what I say, all right?' Ian snapped.

'Fuck you, just do it,' Nick mumbled. 'I know why you're here. Get it over with, fuck you.'

'Shut up,' Ian replied, gazing around for any recording devices.

Unable to see any wires, he approached the filthy prisoner.

'Don't say anything. I'm not going to shoot you,' he muttered, fumbling with the locks on the chains, 'but I will if you start acting up. So just shut up and do what I say.'

'You think I don't know why Tod sent you here?'

'If I wanted you dead, you wouldn't still be breathing. Now shut your mouth and do as I say. I'm risking my skin to save you.'

'Why would you do that?'

'I told you to shut up. You'll find out soon enough, and you'll be grateful to me for the rest of your long life, believe me. But you have to trust me and just do what I tell you.'

Nick mumbled something about having nothing to lose as Ian released him. Nick whimpered with pain and lowered his arms to his sides. It seemed cruel to handcuff him as soon as his arms were free, but Ian was not about to take any risks. He might be injured and suffering, but Nick was a vicious and dangerous man. The handcuffs issued to Ian were generic ones that were freely available on the internet. It was possible Tod would send someone to check on him. If Ian and Nick were intercepted, no one must recognise the handcuffs as police property.

'Now get in the van,' Ian instructed Nick when the shackles had been removed from his ankles. 'If you want to get out of this stinking shithole, go! Now!'

Aware that every second they stayed in the mews they risked discovery, Ian walked behind Nick and gave him a fierce shove that almost knocked him off his feet. Slowly, Nick stumbled forwards and out into the darkness where Ian half lifted, half pushed him into the back of the waiting van and manacled his ankles together. Finally, Ian tied a gag around his mouth before running to the front of the van and leaping into the driver's seat. After taking a roundabout route out of London and back in again to ensure he was not being followed, Ian finally drove back to the police headquarters where the gate to the car park opened and he drove straight in. The first part of the plan had been accomplished. Now he just had to hope that Nick would have the sense to co-operate. Blindfolded, with his wrists still secured, he was led into the building.

An hour after bringing his prisoner in, Ian sat facing him across an interview table. Nick's blindfold had been removed, his injuries had been tended to, and he looked very different to the cowed victim Ian had discovered in the lock-up. His face was bruised and his wrists were bandaged, but he seemed otherwise unharmed. His gag had been removed and he appeared almost relaxed as he scowled across the table as Ian sat down beside Jack.

'You're fucking filth,' Nick greeted him. 'How long you been banging Tallulah then? She must be a right twat. How did you get to her?'

Ian ignored Nick's fishing to find out who else was working undercover for the police.

'You know Tod wants you dead,' Ian said quietly. 'You were there when he ordered me to kill you. Tod had you locked up in that filthy garage so I could come along and shoot you and dispose of your body somewhere rotten – dump you in the Thames perhaps, or burn your remains.'

'Why didn't you?' Nick asked.

He spoke with an air of defiance, but they could see he was interested.

Jack leaned forward. 'He could have done whatever he wanted with you. He could have hacked you to pieces very slowly, gouged your eyes out, cut out your tongue, burned you alive. It's lucky for you he's a police officer, not a vicious bastard like Tod. Now, we're offering you an escape. You give us the information we want, and we give you a whole new life. Or you go down. So, what do you say, Nick? Do you want to be locked up for your crimes and only see the light of day from a prison yard for a long stretch?'

'A very long stretch,' Ian echoed solemnly.

Nick glanced warily at Jack and back at Ian again who resumed speaking.

'Wouldn't you rather co-operate with us and have a safe home, a job, and never have to worry about where your next meal is coming from? We can give you a new identity and enough money to start over. It's your choice, Nick. But don't take too long over it. I have to get back to Tod soon, and I want to know what I'm going to tell him.'

'If you have any sense you'll listen very carefully before you refuse to work with us,' Jack said.

11

THOMAS PUT DOWN HIS knife and fork.

'That was nice,' he said, pushing his plate away and wiping his lips. 'We haven't had a proper cooked breakfast for a while. Thank you.'

Emily smiled. 'I'm popping out to the supermarket soon. We're out of milk and nearly out of tea bags. Do you want anything? You can come with me, if you like.'

He hesitated.

'You don't have to come,' she added quickly, glancing anxiously at him. 'I'm happy to go by myself. We don't need very much. It's amazing the difference it makes now Sam's gone back to uni. I can't believe how much he eats. Tell you what, why don't you stay here and take it easy? Go back to bed. You've been looking tired lately and you may be coming down with something. Are you feeling all right?'

He shook his head and blustered that he was fine. When she pressed him, he made up a lame excuse about being under pressure at work. It was easier than continuing to deny there was anything bothering him.

'I knew there was something wrong,' she said, almost triumphantly. 'You've been overdoing it lately. Well, I'll see you later. I won't be gone long. And call me if you think of anything you want.' She gazed earnestly at him. 'You take it easy while I pop out to the supermarket.'

'I'm fine, just stop fussing, will you?' He immediately regretted snapping at her, and added, 'It was a lovely breakfast.

70

And don't look so worried. Everything's all right.'

But as long as a stranger was out to get him, he knew that nothing would ever be all right again. He tried to put the whole episode with the prostitute out of his mind, but he couldn't forget about the anonymous message he had received. Not knowing who had sent the note made it terrifying. Every time the phone rang or someone knocked at the door, he was afraid the witness had decided to come forward and tell Emily everything. His initial feelings of guilt towards the dead prostitute had faded rapidly. It wasn't as though he had killed her. All he had done was move her body after she was dead, which hadn't harmed her in any way. On the contrary, leaving her corpse in the woods had led to her being found quickly. He could have hidden her away somewhere far more difficult to find, where she would have decomposed slowly so, if anything, he had done her a favour by leaving her body in the woods.

Mulling over the whole episode, he realised that he himself had been the real victim. The woman had no right to die in his house, doubtless from an overdose of drugs. He had done absolutely nothing wrong, yet he had been subjected to the most horrible ordeal. The more he thought about what had happened, the more pleased he was with himself for holding his nerve and extricating himself from an almost impossible situation. Few people would have remained so calm or been so smart when faced with a dead body. Only then the note had arrived and changed everything. Since reading it, he had felt as though he was living in an endless waking nightmare from which there was no possibility of escape.

If he could find out who had sent the note, he could try to reason with them. With luck, he might even be able to find a way to silence them. But meanwhile, he was living under the constant threat of exposure. His plight was more than he could stand, but he was utterly helpless to change it because he had no idea who his antagonist was. In his imagination, his unknown foe grew into a monstrous figure that haunted his dreams until he was reluctant to fall asleep at night and lay in bed, sweating and cursing his fate. He had done nothing to deserve this, and raged in silence against his anonymous enemy who was causing him so much distress.

For the past week, since the woman's death, he had been increasingly tetchy with his colleagues at work. Although he had done his best to hide his agitation, at times he had been unable to control himself. On Friday morning he had shouted at a secretary for sending him the wrong file. He had never raised his voice at work before. He was not surprised when the boss summoned him and gave him a dressing-down.

'I'm sorry,' he muttered, and said something about having troubles at home.

'Well, keep them at home where they belong,' his boss had snapped. 'Don't bring your personal problems into the office again. Sharon was very upset by your language. I'm issuing you with a verbal warning.'

Thomas had been sufficiently shocked by the reprimand to watch himself from then on. He had even apologised to the secretary, who had assured him it was all right. But she seemed wary around him after that, and avoided meeting his eye. He didn't mind her reticence. On the contrary, he was happy for his colleagues to keep their distance from him. Whenever he interacted with them, he felt he had to watch what he said. And he couldn't ignore the possibility that one of them was somehow responsible for his ordeal. He knew he was being crazy. His paranoia at the office was uncalled for. No one he worked with could have witnessed him disposing of the prostitute or written that note. Nevertheless, he began to watch them all, wondering if they were secretly aware of his recent night-time activity. Suspicion plagued him. Even when he was alone, he was afraid the phone might ring and a stranger would accuse him of committing murder.

Whatever happened, he had to keep the truth from Emily. More than anything, he wished he had never seen the prostitute, and he bitterly regretted having taken her back to his home. Looking back on it, he could hardly believe he had been so stupid. There were so many ways in which the situation could have gone horribly wrong. The thought of Emily coming home and discovering him with a whore was too distressing to contemplate, although at the time the risk had seemed exciting. But he could never have foreseen what had actually happened, and could see no possible way out of his predicament.

12

IAN FOLLOWED JACK INTO the interview room and sat down opposite Nick. Tod's former bodyguard had been locked in a police cell for several hours to think about his situation and was already looking distressed. His face was ashen and he was trembling. Whatever adrenaline had been buoying him up on his arrival at the police station had clearly deserted him, and he looked very young and scared.

'You've had time to consider our proposal,' Jack said. 'You have to admit it's a good offer, and far more generous than you deserve. In fact, I'm beginning to think we must be insane to even consider letting you walk out of here, when you should be facing a trial for at least one murder.'

'Murder?' Nick repeated, sounding shocked. 'Who said anything about murder?'

'You were Tod's bodyguard?' Jack asked him.

'What the fuck?' He glared at Ian. 'You bloody well know I was. You were there.' He muttered something insulting under his breath. 'But I never popped anyone. So what the fuck am I doing here? What do you want with me?' His voice rose in agitation. 'I'm innocent, I tell you. Whoever's been handy with a shooter, it wasn't me. I'm the victim here! He wanted me shot. You know that. You heard him. I haven't done anything. You can't keep me here. I want a lawyer. I don't even know why I'm here. I don't get what's happening. You should be after Tod, not me.'

Ignoring the outburst, Jack continued. 'You haven't been

arrested. You're free to walk out of here any time you like. Go on, be my guest. But if you leave here, how long do you think it will be before Tod catches up with you, once he knows you escaped? Or my colleague here might decide to slug you like Tod wanted to protect his own cover. He can do that. Why should he risk falling out with Tod? For what? For you?'

'But if you prefer to walk away from this in one piece,' Ian said, 'you need to start helping us with our enquiries. We can protect you from Tod. Don't be a moron. Do you want to end up at the bottom of the river?'

'Oh yeah? I can walk out of here, can I? And I can go back to the boss and tell him you're filth,' Nick retorted, glaring at Ian.

Despite his attempted bravado, he was obviously terrified.

'My colleague isn't from around here,' Jack said quietly. 'No one apart from me and one other trusted colleague knows his real identity. Once this is over, he's going away and Tod will never find him, not with the protection we can offer him. But you... well, you're a different matter altogether. Quite honestly, with the pitiful resources at your disposal, I don't think you'd last five minutes now Tod wants you dead. You can take your chances if you like, but you'll be on your own out there, just you against the wealth and power of your former boss. He'll start by paying off all your friends and associates, then he'll find your family. Only he won't treat them so well. Or you can co-operate with us and we'll protect you and make sure nothing happens to you or anyone close to you. What's it to be, Nick? Only time's running out and I need an answer now.'

'OK, OK, I'll co-operate. But I can't help you. Tod didn't exactly confide in me.'

'You must have seen or heard something,' Ian said.

Nick shrugged. 'Like what? What do you want to know?'

'How long were you working for Tod?'

Nick drew in a deep breath before answering. 'About three months, but after a couple of months I wanted out. I'd been employed as a security guard before, but working for Tod was very different to what I was used to.'

'How was it different?'

The young man was sweating, although the room was cool. Ian watched him closely as he replied.

'What he was after was a heavy. Protection, you know? He hadn't asked me to silence anyone, not yet, but I knew what was going down. I'm not a complete donut, though it was dense of me to go and work for him, I see that now. But how was I supposed to know what was going on there?'

'What *was* going on?' Ian asked.

Nick grunted and scowled at Ian. 'You know. You were there. He wanted you to put a bullet in my head, didn't he? That's what he's like. He's brutal. Look, when I went to work for him, I took on the job as his bodyguard, not as an iceman.'

'Why would he need a bodyguard?' Ian asked.

'I don't know, do I? I didn't ask him. I just took the job. He was minted and generous and it was double what I'd been getting as a bouncer.'

'And you didn't find that suspicious?' Jack asked.

'What do you mean, suspicious?'

'That he was willing to pay you so much? Didn't you stop to wonder what he wanted for his money?'

'No. I thought he wanted protection, and it made sense that a rich guy would be prepared to stack the decks for that if he was feeling threatened.'

'Who was he being threatened by?' Jack pressed him, but Nick shook his head.

It was becoming apparent that Nick knew very little about Tod's operations.

'Who were his associates?' Ian asked.

'I only saw the runners who brought the charlie and smack

into the office. I wasn't involved in meeting and greeting the mules and body packers who brought the stuff into the country. And I never saw any of the big players apart from Tod. I couldn't even tell you who they are.'

'Did you ever hear him talking on the phone in the three months you were working there?' Jack asked.

Nick shook his head. 'Most of the time I was outside his door, just waiting there in case any shit went down.'

'Who were you waiting for?'

'I don't know. No one in particular. When the runners arrived, it was my job to search them for weapons before they went into the office. I had to check their bags and give them a shakedown before I let them past me.'

'Did you see any drugs inside their bags?' Ian asked.

'Yeah, I saw plenty. Mostly charlie but smack too, and plenty of dope and pills. You name it.' His eyes softened. 'He had a right mother lode right there in his office. But the product was never there for long. He shifted it out as soon as it came in. I wasn't involved in that part of the organisation and I don't know where he sent it. He had a lot of runners working for him, as well as a lot of hustlers, and that's all I can tell you.'

'Either he doesn't know anything or else he's a very cool customer,' Jack said when Nick had been returned to a cell.

'He seemed pretty rattled to me,' Ian replied.

'Ah yes, but was he scared of us or of Tod? Is it possible this whole business of telling you to kill Nick is a set-up to flush us out? Think carefully, Ian. Was there any reason for Tod to become suspicious of you?'

Ian shook his head. 'I don't think so. But there's only one way to find out for sure.'

Jack nodded to show he understood. 'What if we're wrong and he knows who you are?'

Ian shrugged. 'That's a risk we'll have to take.'

Jack stared at him. 'It's a huge risk,' he said at last. 'If we're wrong, they're not going to treat you gently when you return and we may not get to you in time. If they move you before you have a chance to alert us, you'll be dead... or worse. You do understand what I'm saying? These characters will tear you apart, piece by piece, inject you with mind-altering drugs, and I won't be able to help you.'

'All right, enough. I get the picture. But are you ever going to have another opportunity like this to get inside Tod's organisation and bust him? If I can convince Tod I killed Nick, he'll trust me and then I can start listening in and gathering evidence so we can make a watertight case against him when we raid the club. But he has to be convinced that Nick is really dead, which means that he can't surface again, ever.'

'Leave that to me. We'll mock something up so you have evidence to prove Nick's dead. A splash of tomato ketchup on his chest and some white powder on his face – that should do the trick. Don't look so worried. It'll look convincing. I'll send you an image to show Tod. We'll do it in the back of a van. And after that we'll keep Nick behind bars until this is all over.'

Ian nodded. 'Is that really fair on Nick? Locking him up without a trial?'

'What's not fair about it?' Jack replied. 'We're saving his life, aren't we? I just hope it won't be at the cost of yours,' he added softly.

13

EILEEN GLARED AROUND THE room with her customary ferocity.

'Is she always this dour?' Matthew muttered to Geraldine who was standing beside him.

Geraldine didn't answer. Matthew's light-hearted comments reminded her of Ian when they had first met, before his disastrous marriage to his childhood sweetheart. In those days Ian had been young and carefree and his laidback attitude had irritated her. After all, dealing with serious crime, their job was not to be taken lightly. But she had come to understand that Ian's cheerful exterior masked a deeply sensitive and loving person. With an effort she turned her attention to the detective chief inspector who was addressing the assembled officers.

'We cannot possibly trace all the men who had relations with Pansy,' Eileen was saying. 'Most of them were probably casual encounters, and goodness only knows how many of them there were over the years. We don't even have any way of finding out if she had any regular punters, anyone she might have had a relationship with.'

'Didn't she have a pimp?' a constable asked. 'Most working girls like to have someone looking out for them.'

Another constable cracked a joke about how his male colleague seemed to know a lot about sex workers.

Eileen ignored the interruption. 'We've been in contact with the vice squad, and they managed to uncover a name for us,' she said. 'It's not certain, but they believe her pimp was a man called Borneo. Unfortunately, he died from an overdose last month, since when Pansy seems to have been operating independently as far as we can ascertain. Someone else has just moved into Borneo's flat now, but we still went in, and luckily we were there before the bins were emptied. The search team found a list of names that had been thrown out which could be useful.'

'Was it a coincidence she was murdered so soon after her pimp died?' Matthew asked.

'It's possible one of her regular customers knew she was unprotected and took advantage of her solitary status,' Eileen said, 'or they could both have been killed by someone who wanted them dead, perhaps to protect their own identity. Who knows? Without more information, this is all speculation. We don't even know if she had any regular customers. So far, we know very little about her life. And very little about her death,' she added miserably.

'What about the other names on Borneo's list? Might they know something?' Geraldine asked.

Once again, Eileen could only shrug her shoulders.

Geraldine went to question other sex workers on Borneo's list, although they might not have known Pansy, and it was doubtful whether any of them would be able to help. The vice squad supplied Geraldine with a list of names and addresses with which to begin her enquiries. She drove along Gillygate, her wipers working furiously against the icy sleet that had begun to fall, and stopped outside a large house allegedly shared by a number of sex workers who had all enjoyed the protection of Pansy's former pimp. The door was opened by a statuesque woman in a magenta kimono. Geraldine imagined Cleopatra might have looked something like the woman who stared imperiously back at her with dark eyes ringed in heavy black kohl. Her hair had been scraped back off her face, emphasising her prominent cheek bones and pointed nose, and there was something magnificent about her.

'Yes?' she said, in a surprisingly deep voice. 'What do you want?'

Her expression darkened when she saw Geraldine's identity card and she took a step back, her haughtiness crumbling.

'Did you know a woman called Pansy?' Geraldine asked.

The woman's eyes narrowed. 'Why? What's happened to her?' she demanded.

A voice called out from somewhere inside the house, and the woman on the doorstep shouted back. 'It's the police here, asking about Pansy.'

'I'm afraid Pansy's dead,' Geraldine said quietly.

'Bloody hell. What happened? And,' she went on, sounding frightened, 'what are you doing here? What do you want with us?'

A slight blonde woman appeared at her side.

'Pansy's copped it,' the statuesque woman said.

'What's she doing here?' her companion asked. She looked at Geraldine. 'Are you the police?'

'We're investigating the circumstances of Pansy's death,' Geraldine explained, displaying her identity card again. 'We're afraid it might not have been an accident.'

'You mean she was murdered?' the blonde sex worker asked, a frown creasing her face. 'Bloody hell.'

'Occupational hazard,' the other woman said sourly. 'I hope you get the bastard who did for her.'

'We're doing our best,' Geraldine assured them. 'We were hoping you might have some information for us.'

'You'd better come in then,' the blonde woman said with an uneasy glance at her companion. 'You can't stand out there all day. You'll freeze to death. And we're losing heat with the door wide open. I'm Honey and she's Morag.'

They stood aside to let Geraldine enter a hall that smelt of air freshener and perfume.

'We'll do what we can to help you track down whoever did her in,' Honey volunteered. 'But she wasn't really one of us. She liked to keep to herself.'

'It could be one of us next,' Morag said.

They led Geraldine into a well-furnished living room, where they sat down on comfortable armchairs. Without going into any details, Geraldine explained where Pansy's body had been discovered, face down in the mud.

'We're not sure yet what happened to her,' she concluded. 'In fact, we have very few leads, but we suspect she might have been killed by a violent customer.'

There was no need to reveal that Pansy's body had been moved after she died. Given that someone had been keen to cover up the location of her death, it was fairly safe to assume she had been murdered. But the details of her death had not yet been disclosed, and there was no way of knowing how discreet these two women would be.

'Do you have any idea who might have been regular customers of Pansy's?' she asked.

The two sex workers shook their heads. 'No, I'm sorry,' Honey replied. 'We didn't really mix with Pansy. We only knew about her through our pimp.'

'He would have known about her,' Morag said. 'But he's dead. We don't talk much about our work with girls we don't really know. Pansy wasn't one of us,' she added, repeating what her companion had already said. 'We didn't spend any time with her, and she wasn't much of a one for socialising. In fact, I think I only spoke to her once, when she wandered into the club where I work.'

'I don't think I ever spoke to her,' Honey said. 'I used to see her on the street sometimes, but we never spoke. I'm sorry we can't be of more help.'

'Can you recall seeing her last week? On Friday?'

The blonde woman nodded. 'Oh yes. Don't you remember, Morag? I told you.' She turned back to Geraldine. 'I noticed her because she was completely off her head that night. She often used to stumble around, totally out of it.'

'Did you see what happened to her?'

Honey shook her head. 'A car pulled up, she got in, and they drove off. That's all I saw.'

Geraldine questioned her, but Honey couldn't remember the make or colour of the car. She wasn't even able to say whether it had been a large car or a small one.

'It was at night,' she apologised, 'and I wasn't really looking. I only caught it out of the corner of my eye, and then they were gone.'

'What time was that?'

Honey shrugged. 'I've no idea. It was dark, if that helps.'

It was the same story from everyone who might have been in contact with Pansy: her mother and stepfather, her fellow sex workers, and the police who patrolled the streets at night in an attempt to keep them safe, although in this instance they had failed miserably. No one the investigating team spoke to had any idea who might have killed Pansy. Despite all their efforts, they were no further on with the investigation.

'We knew it might take a while to get anywhere with this one,' Geraldine said as she sat over a coffee in the canteen with Ariadne. 'Most murder victims have friends and relatives who can point us in the direction of their killer, but in this instance it was most likely a random stranger who picked her up in the street.'

'And they wonder why we don't like them soliciting at the roadside,' Ariadne muttered. 'How the hell are we supposed to find some random stranger? She's been dead for over a week and we still have no leads at all. Seriously, how can we be expected to protect people who put themselves at risk like that? As if we don't have enough to do.'

'You surely don't think we should stop trying to find out who did this?' Geraldine asked.

'No,' Ariadne replied slowly, 'but I just think we're wasting a lot of resources on a case that we're unlikely to resolve, and perhaps our time could be spent more usefully elsewhere.'

Geraldine shook her head. 'Honestly, Ariadne, I don't know how to begin to answer that. A woman has been murdered. It doesn't matter what her job was, or how she chose to live her life, she's been murdered. And it's our job to find out who did it and see them brought to justice. It's as simple as that. You're probably right that we won't get anywhere, but that doesn't mean we shouldn't keep trying. No one is above the law, and we can't pick and choose who we go after.'

'Yes, of course, I know you're right,' Ariadne agreed. 'It's just going to be a difficult case, that's all.'

Geraldine sighed, knowing that Ariadne was right. The chances of them tracking down this killer were slim.

14

THE SEARCH TEAM HAD come up with a list of phone numbers retrieved from Pansy's phone, and CCTV footage of the area where Pansy had picked up her punters. Several of the men were impossible to identify, having never stepped out of their cars or faced the cameras, but a few had been filmed clearly enough for sophisticated facial recognition software to match them with a particular individual, and a few more had been captured with their car registration numbers visible. Even then, some of the identifications were unreliable, but the police were steadily working their way through them all. It was likely to prove a thankless task that could take months, but they could not afford to neglect any potential source of information.

Geraldine was part of an extensive team questioning Pansy's identified contacts. Her first subject was believed to work in a butcher's shop in town. She glanced in the window on her way in, noting different kinds of sausages along with a variety of burgers and offal. The cuts of beef were mostly cheap strips, and the store was clearly not upmarket. Entering the shop, Geraldine called the number the police had registered for the person she wanted to question, and a spindly young man behind the counter pulled a ringing phone from his pocket and glanced at the unlisted number. As he answered the call, Geraldine stepped forward and approached him.

'Nigel Waring? You can put your phone away.'

He looked at his phone, and then back at Geraldine, a puzzled expression on his face.

'Hello,' he replied, glancing at his colleague who was busy serving another customer. 'Can I help you? Is there a problem?' He frowned. 'Do I know you? Was that you calling me just now? How do you know my number?'

Geraldine held up her identity card and he drew back in surprise.

'I'd like a word with you please,' she said.

'I can't, not now, I'm at work,' he stammered, glancing at his colleague who had finished serving his customer and was now watching them with some interest.

Another customer came into the shop and the other man behind the counter reluctantly went to serve her.

'Is there somewhere we can talk?' Geraldine asked quietly. 'We can do this in private if you prefer.'

'In private?' Nigel repeated, looking over at his colleague who was still busy with the customer. 'What's this about?'

'I'd like to talk to you about a woman called Pansy.'

'Pansy? I don't know anyone called Pansy.'

'You may have known her as Luscious. We have reason to believe you knew her intimately,' Geraldine replied.

Nigel gave a guilty start on hearing the name and lowered his gaze. Geraldine had given him as clear a description of the relationship as he needed.

'Is there somewhere we can talk without being overheard,' Geraldine asked again, 'or would you prefer to accompany me to the police station where we can have a chat?'

Nigel fidgeted nervously with his large heavy gold watch which was almost certainly fake. He shook his head and his greasy black combed-over hair fell forward over his face, to reveal a bald patch on top of his head.

'This way,' he muttered, leading Geraldine through a small door marked 'Staff'.

Nigel's pale face turned even pastier when she showed him a photograph of Pansy's face, cleaned of mud but obviously dead, and explained the police were investigating the circumstances in which she had died.

'I didn't know she'd passed away,' he muttered, refusing to meet Geraldine's eye. 'We didn't have a relationship or anything like that. I don't know anything about her. I mean, I guessed Luscious wasn't her real name, but I only saw her the once and we didn't even do anything,' he added, with a surge of courage.

'We both know that's not true,' Geraldine replied evenly. 'We have you on CCTV meeting her, and if you hand me your phone, I think we'll find you called her number on more than one occasion.'

Geraldine's guess was rewarded when Nigel slipped his hand into his pocket as though seeking reassurance his phone was still there.

'We can easily check your call history remotely if necessary,' she added, holding out her hand.

Nigel seemed to sag. 'Oh, very well, yes, I did see her. Not regularly, but from time to time. It suited us both. There was never any funny business, and she didn't do anything she wasn't comfortable with. And I didn't harm her,' he added, with a sudden flash of energy. 'Why would I? She was – she helped me, you know. She was nice to me. She understood a man has his needs. Oh, I know she was a tart, but she suited me. She understood what I wanted. She let me pretend it was more than that, you know.' He sighed. 'I suppose it was the drugs. She knew they would get her in the end. I never hurt her,' he assured Geraldine earnestly. 'I wanted her to be happy.'

'I'm sure you did,' Geraldine said, taking care to keep her tone impassive.

Nigel claimed he had not seen Pansy for at least three weeks, and admitted he used to see her in his car.

'I saw her once a month or so,' he added. 'There or

thereabouts. I'd be about due for a visit now.' He sighed. 'What am I going to do without her?'

Geraldine didn't retort that she couldn't care less what he did, but she was convinced he hadn't killed Pansy. All the same, she had his phone records checked to confirm when he had last spoken to Pansy to arrange a meeting.

Geraldine's next interviewee was Pansy's landlord. She found him at home in a tidy little house off Bootham. Monty Belmont was a corpulent middle-aged man with a jovial smile who could have been anything from thirty to fifty: his exact age difficult to determine on account of his size.

'Yes, Pansy Banks is a tenant of mine,' he wheezed, as he sat down in a wide red armchair opposite Geraldine. 'She's no problem, not like some, although she dresses like a slut.'

Appreciating the warmth of his home after the freezing temperature outside, Geraldine waited to hear what he would say next.

'Not that I'm in any position to criticise what other people choose to do with their bodies,' he added, ruefully patting his huge belly, 'but she had tattoos you could see halfway up her arse, and a ring through her nose. Why do young women do that?' he asked, a hint of outrage in his voice. 'As though they want to look like animals. Still, like I said, I'm not one to criticise. Live and let live, that's my motto. It's still a free country. So what brings you here? If you're looking for accommodation, I might just be able to help you, officer.' He leaned forward slightly in his chair which creaked under his weight. 'I had a police officer as a tenant once before and he was no trouble. No trouble at all. A real gent, he was. That's all I want, a tenant who pays up when the rent is due and doesn't cause any trouble.'

When Geraldine explained the purpose of her call, Monty sat back and gaped at her.

'You mean she's dead?' he said. 'But it's nearly the end of

the month. She owes me–' He broke off, realising his outburst was inappropriate under the circumstances. 'That is, I'm very sorry to hear the poor girl has died, but I don't suppose anyone's going to pay me for the three weeks rent she never paid, are they? She never did set up a direct debit. I had to phone her to remind her every month to let her know the rent was due. Can you believe it? And she was often late with her payments. And now this.' He shook his head, looking vexed. 'Gone, without any notice.'

A quick check of Pansy's phone records seemed to bear out what her landlord had said.

'You don't suppose it was all an elaborate charade to put you off the scent?' Ariadne asked when Geraldine reported her findings.

'He certainly made it sound as though he was only interested in getting his rent, and he seemed genuinely irked by losing her as a tenant near the end of the month,' Geraldine replied. 'Unless he's a very good actor, I really don't think he's our murderer.'

The rest of the team had drawn similar blanks. Having questioned more than twenty people who had been in close contact with the dead woman, they were no closer to finding her killer.

15

A WEEK HAD PASSED since the white envelope had been posted through his door. As soon as he read the message, 'I saw what you did', Thomas had known exactly what it meant. He still shivered with fear at the thought that Emily might have opened it. They were both pretty careful not to open each other's mail, but mistakes did happen occasionally. In a way, he supposed the cryptic nature of the message was reassuring. The writer of the note had not wanted to reveal Thomas's secret to anyone else. If Emily had chanced to open the envelope by mistake, she might well have been intrigued, but she wouldn't have had any idea what the message meant. At least he hadn't faced the problem of trying to explain it to her.

The use of his first name suggested it had been written by someone he knew, but anyone could have looked up his address online and done enough research to discover his name from the electoral role, or even paid a private investigator to find it. With a thrill of fear, it occurred to him that his unknown blackmailer might even be a police officer. He hesitated over destroying the note but, under the circumstances, he could hardly take it to the police. He had hidden the note at the bottom of his toolbox. After some deliberation, he concluded there was only one thing to do. It was the work of a moment to tear the note to shreds, hide the scraps of paper in an empty cereal box in the rubbish bag in the kitchen, and dispose of the bag in the bin outside. No one would find it there.

Before long, the slip of paper would be shredded by the refuse collection lorry, along with the rest of the household waste. The note would be completely obliterated, but there remained the question of who had sent it, and what they had seen. A neighbour peering out of an upstairs window or an unseen passer-by could have witnessed his struggle to drag the body into the back of the van. The anonymous witness had evidently not gone to the police. Not yet. Unless they were planning to blackmail him, he could not imagine the reason for the note, which made no demands and issued no explicit threat. The writer had simply advised him that he had been seen. It was intensely frustrating not being able to confront the writer of the note to find out what they intended to do. He couldn't even be sure that this was about his guilty secret. In many ways it would be a relief to discover what lay behind the note, and end this uncertainty. In the meantime, he could do nothing but wait.

He assumed he was dealing with a blackmailer. However he thought about it, nothing else made sense. Yet still the writer of the note remained silent. Whoever was behind the message wanted Thomas to speculate about what was going to happen. Presumably once his antagonist was confident that Thomas was in such a state of trepidation that he would agree to absolutely anything, the blackmail would begin. The threat of bankruptcy was less terrifying than the fear of exposure. Agitated though he was, being ignorant of his enemy's identity rendered him powerless to resist or fight back. He grew increasingly desperate to discover who was behind it.

'Are you sure you're all right?' Emily asked, when she was about to leave for her book club that evening, as she did every Monday. She gazed earnestly at him, her blue eyes solemn. 'You look a bit pale. I don't have to go out, you know. I can call Maisie and tell her I'm not going tonight.'

In the week that had passed since the note had been posted

through the door, Thomas had been doing his best to conceal his growing anxiety from his wife, but it was difficult. In addition to the need to hide his anxiety, there was the question of money. When the blackmailer issued his demand, Thomas had to have enough cash available to pay his enemy off. Whatever else happened, there must be no trail that could link him to his blackmailer. But he was proceeding in the dark. He didn't even know whether he would be faced with a demand for money. He tried not to think about what might happen if the blackmailer asked for more than he could afford, although that was quite likely. He wondered how much a stranger might consider it would be worth to him, to keep his guilt a secret. Perhaps he would be expected to sell his house to pay the blackmailer off, and how would he explain that to his wife? He tried to hope for the best, but worry plagued him and he couldn't sleep. Although he didn't think he was eating any less, and he was certainly drinking more, his trousers were becoming loose. He was sure Emily had noticed.

Fortunately, he had a pension fund which was worth about ten thousand pounds. He thought he would be able to redeem that without anyone else knowing. One day Emily might learn what he had done, but he would deal with that problem when it arose, if it ever did. For now it seemed to be his only chance of getting his hands on some money swiftly and discreetly. He was sure blackmail was a crime, but he could hardly go to the police, and nor could he afford to ignore what was happening. If only his blackmailer would show himself, or herself, Thomas might be able to convince them that he simply didn't have any ready money. Admittedly he had a house, but that was already mortgaged to the limit of what he could afford. He would have to persuade his blackmailer that he was asset rich and cash poor. For now, his only course of action was to wait until he was contacted again and then insist that he could only manage to hand over a small amount of cash each month, a sum that Emily wouldn't even notice. Somehow he was going to have to convince the blackmailer that he couldn't stump up a significant amount in one payment.

The more he thought about it, the angrier he became, and the firmer his resolve grew not to touch his pension fund. There was no way his blackmailer could know about that, and Thomas was going to make sure things stayed that way. He had worked hard for what little he had and the thought of having to hand it over to a vile stranger made him feel as though he was suffocating. It was so unjust. The prostitute's death had been an accident. He didn't deserve to be punished like this. He almost regretted not having gone to the police as soon as the woman had kicked the bucket. He might have been able to convince Emily that her presence in their house was completely innocent. Even if she hadn't believed that, and he had been forced to come clean, she might have forgiven him eventually, if he had been sufficiently contrite.

'It was the first time,' he could have told her. 'It was awful. We didn't even do anything. I'll never be that stupid again.'

But it was too late for that now. A prostitute had died in his house, with no witnesses to confirm what had really happened, and he had been seen moving her body. No one was going to believe he hadn't killed her now he had covered up the truth.

'Are you sure you're all right?' Emily asked again, still staring at him.

'Yes, yes, stop pestering me, will you?' he snapped.

He immediately regretted his outburst. None of this was Emily's fault. But it wasn't his fault either. If he had suspected for an instant that stupid tart was going to collapse and die in his hall, he would never have brought her back to the house. Now he was in serious trouble just because of one silly mistake – no more than an error of judgement.

'Have a good time,' he told his wife, forcing himself to look and sound relaxed about her outing. 'What are you reading this time?'

She told him the title and he nodded, not really paying attention as she trotted out a summary of the story. He was wondering which of his neighbours' windows overlooked his drive at the correct angle for someone looking out to have seen him behind the van, where he had thought he was hidden from view. Another thought struck him. He might have been spotted in the woods as he carried the body through the trees to the clearing. He had wanted to leave it hidden among the trees, ideally propped up in a sitting position against a trunk, but the body had been too difficult to manoeuvre. He had been forced to let it drop to the ground in an open space in the woods.

Frantically he tried to remember whether he had checked carefully to make sure no one was around to observe what he was doing, but he was afraid he had been too wrapped up in the challenge of moving the corpse to be vigilant. He hadn't been aware of another vehicle following him home from the woods, but he was unused to driving the van and that, combined with his exhaustion and shock, meant he had not been looking out to check if he was being followed. The truth was, a complete stranger might have seen him in the woods, and followed him home to find out where he lived. The note could have been written and delivered by anyone at all, and Thomas had no way of finding out who he was up against. All he knew was that, one way or another, he had to put an end to the situation before anyone else discovered the truth.

16

ONCE AGAIN IAN EMPTIED his pockets of personal possessions before picking up a worn leather wallet containing Archie White's credit card and driving licence which he slipped in his pocket, along with a false set of house keys and a rigged mobile phone, a cheap lighter, a packet of cigarette papers, and a small quantity of weed. He made sure he carried no clues to his real identity apart from a minute tracking device concealed in the waistband of his jeans, and an emergency button on his phone which was programmed to alert his colleagues at the police station if he needed rescuing.

'Remember to call in every evening so we know you're still alive,' Jack said with a lame attempt at sounding lighthearted. 'And don't forget to delete the call history straight away. And whatever you do, don't lose that phone because if we don't hear from you, we'll have to come and get you. Good luck.'

Ian took the train to Camden where he strolled along the crowded high street and on through the busy market. He stopped frequently, ostensibly at first to look in shop windows and then to view the wares on display at the stalls: leather boots, T-shirts with skulls and other cult designs, studded bags, Gothic jewellery, and all manner of commercial bric-a-brac purporting to be alternative. In reality, his interest in the goods was as sham as they were. He was stopping only to check that he wasn't being followed. The market was bustling with people, mostly young, many with tattoos and piercings and coloured hair, shoppers mingling with tourists.

As he walked, Ian kept his hand on his waistband, comforted by his invisible tracker, although if anything kicked off he would have to deal with the danger alone, at least until his colleagues arrived. Having walked around the market a few times and reassured himself that he was not being tailed, he made his way to the club. It was a pleasant walk. The sun was shining and he felt curiously uplifted as he strode along the street, convinced he was embarking on a worthwhile mission. Confident in his own mental and physical agility, he felt like a warrior in days gone by, risking his life to fight for his country and protect the woman he loved. If he succeeded, Geraldine would be able to see her twin sister again, and he and Geraldine would be reconciled.

But as he reached the club, his self-assurance faded and, for the first time, he seemed to see clearly what he was doing. A police officer entering the control centre of a major criminal outfit risked more than his life if his cover was blown. It was easy to tell himself that he was mentally strong enough to withstand physical torture. The truth was, he had never been tested in that way and had no idea how he might hold out. Hesitating as he drew near, he was tempted to turn on his heel and walk back the way he had come. But Jack knew where he was and what he was doing and a sense of shame prevented him from leaving without finishing the job.

Frank was lounging around in the street outside, as though he was a punter waiting for the club to open for the evening. Ian recognised him immediately, leaning against the wall, his eyes almost closed against a thread of smoke rising from a cigarette butt lodged in the corner of his mouth. He straightened up at Ian's approach, and shifted so that he was blocking the entrance.

Nodding at Frank, Ian spoke as boldly as he could. 'I'm here to report back to Tod.' He paused before adding in a low voice, 'Nick's been dealt with.'

With a grunt of exasperation, Frank flicked his cigarette to the ground, and the end glowed orange for an instant. Unsure whether the bouncer was about to let him pass or attack him, Ian tensed, ready to defend himself, although he suspected the other man was armed and would not hesitate to shoot him, perhaps to avenge his former colleague's death. Just at that moment, Jenny appeared on the pavement right behind Frank. For a second, Ian didn't recognise her behind her lurid make-up: kohl circles around her eyes and lips the colour of blood. Her jeans had been replaced by a denim skirt that barely covered her knickers, and her upper body was swathed in a fake fur jacket. Stepping forward, she flung her arms around Ian and he stifled a cough at the overpowering scent of her cheap perfume, cloying in its sweetness.

'Don't show him you're scared of him,' she warned Ian in a barely audible whisper, as she nibbled at his ear. 'I could smell your fear from halfway up the street.'

'Later, Tallulah,' Ian replied loudly.

He wanted to thank her for intervening, but Frank had edged closer and Ian was afraid of being overheard. A man who needed the protection of a woman was easy pickings. Pushing Jenny away roughly, he turned to Frank and clenched his fists, scowling as ferociously as he could.

'This way,' Frank said.

He led Ian through the public area of the club, now eerily quiet: roulette tables stilled, deafening music silenced. Chairs stood neatly arranged at tables, and a uniformed waiter stood behind the bar, polishing glasses and humming softly to himself. He barely glanced up as Frank and Ian passed, unlike Tod who fixed his eyes on them as they walked through the baize-covered door. The scar that ran down Tod's cheek looked more livid than Ian remembered it, perhaps because the light from the window fell directly across that side of Tod's face, but his dark eyes stared with the same cool authority. Dressed as smartly as before in a dark suit and tie, apart from his scar he looked like a respectable businessman. It was hard to believe that the last time Ian had seen him Tod had casually ordered Nick's execution. Now he looked at Ian, his eyebrows raised in tacit enquiry.

'It's done, Boss,' Ian said quietly.

Tod nodded. 'Where is he?'

'Fuck knows,' Ian replied airily. 'You'll have to send a team of divers into the Thames if you want to find him. All I know is they'll find him at the bottom somewhere. I filled his pockets with rocks before I tossed him in. He sank like a stone.' He grinned.

'How do I know you're not bullshitting me?' Tod snapped, leaning forward in his chair and staring at Ian. 'What's to say you didn't bottle it?'

Frank grunted appreciatively and took a menacing step towards Ian as though itching to finish him off. It occurred to Ian that Frank might have a soft spot for Tallulah. That could complicate matters. On the other hand, if it was the case, they might be able to exploit it to their advantage. Making a mental note to ask Jenny about her relationship with Frank, he took out his phone. It had been carefully prepared to deal with such a response from Tod, and was pre-set with appropriate links and images, mostly pornographic, together with a few contacts, such as a violent thug like Archie might keep on his mobile. Scrolling through, he found an image of Nick playing dead, and held it up. At a nod from Tod, Frank snatched the handset and handed it over to his boss. Ian held his breath, knowing that he would be in trouble if Tod examined the phone too closely, or refused to return it. Ian gave a nonchalant yawn, while Tod studied the screen. He seemed to look at it for a very long time. At last he nodded and held the phone out to Ian.

'Why did you put the body in the river?' he demanded.

'What did you want me to do with him?' Ian replied breezily. 'Send him to you in the post, gift wrapped? Somehow I didn't think you'd want him back. Was I wrong?'

To Ian's relief, Tod burst into noisy laughter. 'Way to go, Archie,' he said. 'Way to go.'

Ian shrugged, more relieved than he dared to show. He swallowed hard, tasting sour vomit in his throat, and had to fight to control his shaking.

17

IAN DARED NOT MAKE a move until he was on his own with Tod, but Frank continued to hover nearby. At the periphery of his vision, Ian was aware of Frank scowling suspiciously at him. Ian pretended not to notice the thug fingering his gun and licking his lips.

Tod nodded at Frank. 'Stay cool,' he said. 'Archie's my man.' He stood up and came around to their side of the desk to slap Ian on the back. 'Isn't that right, Archie?'

Ian smiled. Without a word, he lowered his head deferentially. Afraid his voice would betray his fear, he couldn't trust himself to speak.

'I ain't got no faith in this fucker,' Frank growled, taking a step towards them so that he was almost touching Ian. 'And I don't think you should either, Boss. You know nothing about him. He just tips up from nowhere, and all at once you're acting like he's family. He's a stranger. What the fuck is he doing here anyways?'

'Well, he's not going to do me any harm while you're around, is he?' Tod replied, laughing. 'And he didn't blow in from nowhere. Tallulah introduced him.'

That was true. But Ian was growing increasingly anxious. If his cover was blown, not only would he end up in the river with a bullet in his brain, but Jenny would too, for having introduced him to the boss. Somehow Ian had to get Tod on his own. He was tempted to try and orchestrate a distraction, but it was difficult to see how he could arrange a disturbance that would result in Frank being ordered to sort it out. Tod was far more likely to send Ian to help the bouncers deal with a fracas in the club. Frank needed to meet with an accident, not fatal, but enough to render him useless as a bodyguard. While Ian was speculating about the best way to achieve that without drawing attention to himself, events overtook him.

A skinny bouncer rushed into the office, his face sweaty. 'We got a situation, Boss,' he announced.

'What the fuck?' Frank growled, eyeing the man suspiciously.

Ian was faintly reassured to discover that Frank distrusted everyone.

'Pipe down and let the man speak,' Tod snapped and Frank subsided, scowling.

'Word is there's a snitch, Boss.'

Frank turned to glare at Ian who ignored him, and kept his gaze severely on the speaker.

'What do you mean? Who's squealing?' Tod demanded.

His face looked flushed, and he punched the palm of his left hand with his right fist, clearly agitated.

'Who's the snitch? Who the fuck is it?' Tod repeated with growing fury.

The bouncer shrugged. 'Fuck knows who it is. I told you what I heard, that's all. There's a snitch on the staff here.'

'Who told you?' Ian asked, taking a step forward. 'Find out what they know. They must know something.'

He had an uneasy feeling that Jenny might be in trouble.

'If you ask me, it was Fat Neddy,' the bouncer replied. 'He helped the filth bust that fucker who was trying to move in on us.'

Tod nodded. 'Stupid fucker,' he muttered. 'Thought he could take over my turf.'

'Anyway, Fat Neddy said he was given a heads up there's a snitch right here at the club,' the bouncer said. 'He seems a bit too friendly with the filth if you ask me.'

'No one's asking you,' Tod replied.

'You leave Fat Neddy out of it,' Frank said. 'Am I the only one to see what a coincidence it is, hearing about a snitch just when Archie pitches up?' he added, not unreasonably.

'Don't be stupid,' Ian retorted, deeming a counter attack to be the best course of action. 'You think they'd want to advertise a grass as soon as he arrived? It's more likely to be someone who's been here a while, someone who's been attracting attention because he acts like a dick.'

'No one's advertising it,' Frank replied. 'It was a narc who passed on the info.' He turned to Tod. 'Can't you see, we've had nothing but trouble ever since Archie pitched up? Nick never screwed up before he joined us.'

Frank took a step towards Ian, his face dark with anger, his fists clenched.

Ian stood his ground and snorted in disgust. 'Funny sort of filth who murders a bodyguard on the orders of a...' He hesitated, reluctant to call Tod a criminal to his face. 'Of his boss,' he corrected himself. 'The filth aren't going to kill people because someone like Tod tells them to.'

'Says who?' Frank asked. 'How come you know so much about the filth?' But he didn't sound so certain. He turned to Tod. 'Fat Neddy's been with us for years. If you ask me, Boss, Archie's the fucking grass.'

'Well, he didn't ask you, so shut the fuck up,' Ian retorted, raising his fist.

Tod frowned. 'You can both shut it. I need to think. Now, about this heads-up about a snitch at the club – we need to find out more.'

'Send Frank,' Ian said promptly. 'He knows Neddy, and I'm sure Frank is ace at getting people to talk.'

He gave Frank a respectful nod and the bodyguard grunted his assent. The threat seemed to have fizzled out for the moment, but Ian knew that time was running out, and it wouldn't be long before Frank rumbled him.

'Well, go on then,' Tod snapped. 'Sort it out, Frank. Archie, you stay here with me.'

'Watch your step, fucker,' Frank warned Ian as he went out, followed by the skinny bouncer.

Ian looked over at Tod, sitting behind his desk, and smiled. He had to act quickly, and his lies had to be convincing. This might be the only chance he got to speak to Tod alone.

'Here's the deal, Tod,' he said, approaching the desk. 'Don't move until you've heard me out. I said don't move, if you want to walk out of this office alive.'

Tod glanced at the door. They both knew Frank wouldn't be gone for long.

Ian continued, speaking rapidly. 'I'm working for the drug squad. Everything you've said to me has been recorded and transmitted to a remote site. If I fail to report to my chief remotely every hour, and see him alone and in person, at a predetermined time every day, the recording will be retrieved. It implicates you in drug dealing and murder.'

'But you popped Nick–' Tod stammered.

'Of course I didn't.' Ian laughed. 'That was a sham. All you saw was some pretty pictures of Nick holding his breath. It was all a set-up. Now listen, if Frank comes back, send him away. If you make any attempt to interfere with my carrying out my duty, I'll have the DS here in force and it'll all be over for you. Remember, one missing contact and the alert goes out to my boss. My real boss.'

Tod's eyes flickered all over Ian, searching for the device that would alert the drug squad.

'You can't afford to let anything happen to me. If I don't

contact my chief on the hour, he'll be all over this place like a rash. Do you understand me?'

'All right, all right. I hear you. I hear you and I'm not a fucking moron.'

'Well, you are if you believe my story about a secret recording device,' Ian thought.

But Tod was looking pensive. 'Why haven't you sent in the black suits then?' he asked, glaring shrewdly at Ian. 'If it's true you've got enough to bang me up, what are you waiting for?'

It was a fair question. Ian knew his next step was a gamble, but he had no choice if he wanted to retrieve Geraldine's sister from her enforced change of identity.

'No one's listening to us right now, because there's a deal of my own I want to make,' Ian replied quickly. 'A deal that's just between the two of us. It could save your skin if you give me what I want.'

Tod visibly relaxed. This was the kind of language he understood. 'Go on,' he said softly. 'I'm listening.'

Just then the door burst open and Frank entered, red-faced and agitated.

'I can't find out a bloody thing, Boss,' he blurted out.

'Sod off,' Tod replied quietly.

'What?'

'Go. I need to kick something around with Archie.'

'But, Boss–'

'Did you hear me?' Tod asked, his voice rising in anger. 'I told you to sod off!'

'Straight up, Boss, Archie's a grass. Stands to reason. We had no grief before he pitched up and now Nick's gone and word is there's a snitch in our crew. It's all happened since Archie arrived. We need to ditch him.'

Frank's hand slid inside his jacket, fingering his gun. Ian stared at Tod, willing him to send Frank away, afraid that he was going to order the bodyguard to shoot him. Within the hour, Ian himself might be at the bottom of a river, where Tod believed Nick was now.

18

THE TOXICOLOGY REPORT WAS finally in. Geraldine let out a low whistle as she scanned through the details on her way to a briefing. Ariadne, who was walking beside her, glanced at the document.

'No wonder it took them so long to complete,' Ariadne said. 'It's the longest tox report I've ever seen by a mile. It's going to take me the best part of a day just to read it.'

'It must have taken days to write it, let alone the time it would have taken to analyse all the substances floating around in her bloodstream,' Matthew agreed, as he caught up with them in the corridor. 'It's a miracle she managed to walk around with that cocktail of drugs floating around inside her.'

'Maybe that's what really killed her,' Geraldine said thoughtfully.

'And which of the drugs do you suppose moved her body to the woods?' Matthew asked. 'Did the LSD enable her to fly there? Or perhaps it was Red Bull that gave her wings.'

Geraldine laughed.

'Well,' Eileen announced grimly, when the team were assembled. 'We have a real smorgasbord here.' She turned and reeled off the list from the toxicology report displayed on the screen behind her. 'She must have been high as a kite.'

'I've never even heard of some of them,' a young constable said.

'She would have been completely out of it, and hallucinating, if she was even conscious,' Eileen said. 'It's a miracle she was able to function at all with that lot inside her. The tox report certainly makes interesting reading. You've all had a chance to study it.'

'Hardly,' Ariadne muttered.

'Apart from that, I called you in to share some further information.'

Everyone listened intently as the detective chief inspector announced that the analysis was back on unidentified skin cells discovered under the dead woman's fingernails. Examination of DNA revealed the source of the cells to be a male Caucasian adult, with brown hair and brown eyes. It wasn't much to go on, but it was a strong indication that before Pansy died she had been involved in some kind of physical encounter with a man. It was not a great leap from that to surmise that he might have been her killer.

'It's amazing she could even stand upright, looking at the number of drugs that were in her system when she died,' Eileen said.

Geraldine nodded. 'Given the tox report, her head injury could have been accidental.'

'Her injuries confirm that she hit her head when she fell over sideways,' Matthew said.

'But someone was with her when it happened, someone whose skin cells were under her fingernails when she died,' Ariadne said.

'And that someone didn't report her death, but moved her body and hid it in Acomb Wood,' Geraldine added.

Eileen grunted. 'It's quite likely she was deposited in Acomb Wood by the man she scratched. We need to find him.'

'He didn't want her body to be found in the place where he'd killed her,' Geraldine said slowly, thinking aloud. 'That means it's unlikely she died on the street, or he wouldn't have risked being seen moving her. He would have just left her there and done a runner. Given the nature of her injuries, it looks as though she must have fallen from a standing position, because she badly bruised her shoulder, elbow and hip when she hit her head. So she couldn't have been in a car when she fell, and she wasn't out in the woods, because she hit herself on smooth surfaces, not on a tree. So even if she wasn't actually killed by the man she scratched, he was probably there when she died and was probably the one who moved her body. She was a sex worker, so he might have picked her up and taken her home with him. That would explain why he had to move her body without reporting it. He didn't want it to get out that he had taken a prostitute home with him.'

'And he didn't want to be tried for murder,' Ariadne added.

Eileen nodded. Geraldine's theory made sense, but they couldn't be certain of anything until they found the man who had been with Pansy before she died.

'If only we had a match for the DNA found under her nails,' Eileen sighed.

'All we need to do is test the DNA of every brown haired man in York,' Ariadne muttered.

'At least we know he lived in York,' a constable pointed out. 'He must do, if he took her home.'

'He could have taken her to a hotel,' Matthew said.

Geraldine shook her head. 'It would be more difficult to remove a dead body from a hotel than from a private house.'

'He might have followed her into a public toilet,' Ariadne suggested.

'Let's not waste time speculating about the many places the encounter might have taken place,' Eileen snapped. 'We need more information.'

She instructed Matthew to organise a team to contact hotels and B & Bs in case Pansy had been taken there instead of to a private home. At the same time CCTV from Saturday night was being checked, to see if anyone had stopped a vehicle near the clearing where Pansy's body had been abandoned.

'You've got to admit this is a waste of time,' Ariadne grumbled as she and Geraldine were given lists of guest houses to visit. 'No one could move a dead body from a B & B without being spotted. No one. Even moving it from a private house without being seen would be tricky. And now we have to go round every little guest house in York, asking the same questions. Why did I ever think police work would be exciting?'

'It's necessary though.' Geraldine replied, smiling. 'Someone's got to do it.'

'You sound like you actually enjoy traipsing around, asking questions of people who obviously won't have anything useful to say. Honestly, you take the most pointless task seriously.'

'I guess I just enjoy my work,' Geraldine replied.

'We all do, but that doesn't mean we have to like every boring minute of it. I bet you were enthusiastic about all your lessons at school. Your teachers must have loved you.'

'Any seemingly useless piece of information might prove invaluable,' Geraldine began.

'Oh, spare me the pep talk, for Christ's sake.'

As she drove to Bootham, Geraldine thought about Ariadne's jibe. It was true, Geraldine was conscientious over the most apparently tedious aspects of her job, but any particular line of enquiry might prove unexpectedly worthwhile. A seemingly trivial question put to an unlikely source had sometimes thrown up a lead resulting in an arrest. She wasn't ashamed to admit that she loved her job. She knew that Ariadne did too, and wondered what had happened to upset her friend. Usually cheerful and good-natured, lately Ariadne had become quite crabby. Geraldine had been too engrossed in her own problems with Ian to pay much attention to anyone else. She resolved to question her friend at the first opportunity, and find out what was troubling her.

They spent the day with the team visiting bed and breakfast

premises along Bootham. Wherever she went, Geraldine heard the same response.

'Did a couple stay here for just one night? I don't think so. When did you say? Let me check the book.'

So far no one had a record of a one-night booking on the Friday night Pansy was murdered, but the enquiry continued rigorously.

'If he killed her in his own house, we're going to struggle to find the place without a match for the suspect's DNA,' Ariadne said to Geraldine when they met up in the canteen later that day.

'We just have to keep looking,' Geraldine replied. 'Sooner or later something will turn up. Ariadne, you seem a bit down lately. Are you all right?'

Ariadne shrugged. 'It's just this place,' she said. 'This work. It gets to me sometimes. I mean, I know we do a good job and all that. And I know someone has to get out there and do it. I don't need to be reminded that we're the ones who are holding back the tide of violence, and that without our protection society would descend into chaos, and so on. I know all that and I know it's all true and most of the time it's enough. But sometimes it just isn't.' She sighed. 'I mean, I can't help wondering, is this all there is? It might be enough for you, but...' She broke off with a shrug. 'Nico thinks I should pack it in, find another job. He's always on at me about it. He says he doesn't like the idea of me working with dead bodies.'

'That's no way to talk about your colleagues,' Geraldine said.

Ariadne laughed, but she quickly grew serious again. 'Nico doesn't understand. Do you think someone who doesn't work for the police could ever understand why we do it? What it's like for us?'

Geraldine shook her head. 'I don't know.'

'Maybe we can only have a successful relationship with another cop,' Ariadne said.

Thinking of Ian, Geraldine shook her head, more vehemently this time. 'I'm not sure that's such a good idea,' she said.

19

'GO ON THEN, I'M listening,' Tod said, affecting to study his fingernails.

Tod glanced up and saw Ian scowling at Frank.

'Beat it,' Tod said.

Frank turned to his boss, looking concerned. 'Me?' he replied.

'Well, obviously.'

Muttering darkly, Frank obeyed, casting an evil look at Ian as he left the room. Tod took no notice of Frank's dismay but continued staring at his fingers.

'You don't look like you're listening,' Ian said.

He had taken the initiative in the conversation and was keen to retain control of it. Tod leaned back in his chair and looked up. He appeared to relax, but his sharp black eyes never left Ian's face, and his long fingers tapped a rapid tattoo on the desk.

'I'd feel more comfortable if you'd come out from behind there,' Ian said, standing with his back to the door.

'Comfortable? Why don't you cop a seat if you want to be comfortable?'

'Get out from behind that desk,' Ian snapped.

He couldn't afford to allow Tod to dominate him. He took a step towards Tod and felt his feet sink into the deep pile of the carpet.

'Why? You scared I'm going to call in my boys?' Tod drawled, but despite his defiant words he complied with Ian's request.

While Ian frisked him for weapons, Tod stared straight ahead and his scar twisted the angry sneer on his lips into an ugly smile.

'Now go and lock the door,' Ian said.

'What makes you think I've got a key?'

'Just do it.'

Tod walked slowly over to the door. Ian was afraid he might leave the room, locking the door behind him, but it was a gamble he was prepared to take to be alone with Tod. Drawing a bunch of keys from his pocket, Tod did as he was instructed.

'You have clocked that you're now shut in here with me?' he said, turning to Ian with a faintly puzzled smile.

'Sit down.'

Tod took a seat on one of the upright office chairs facing the desk, while Ian remained standing, gazing down at him.

'Well? What's this about?' Tod demanded in a futile attempt to wrest back his power.

Slowly, Ian explained the position, and Tod listened without interrupting. He didn't show any surprise, but when Ian finished, he frowned and shifted in his chair.

'So what you're saying is you want me to ask around and find this bitch's former dealer?'

Ian nodded. The room was beginning to feel uncomfortably warm, and he could feel a bead of sweat crawling down his forehead. He dashed it away with an impatient gesture.

'What makes you think I'll be able to come up with a name?'

'You'll find him, because you know what's going to happen to you if you don't.'

'Let me get this clear. If I find this dealer for you then you'll leave me alone, but if I don't, you'll get me banged up?'

'Exactly, and with what I've got, you'll go down for life,' Ian replied steadily. 'If anything happens to me, the recording goes straight to my chief. At the moment I'm blocking the transmission but it's all there on the cloud, waiting to go.'

What Ian was saying was a complete fiction, but Tod was listening.

'I'd say you're being more than a trifle shady, considering who you are, using one dealer to track down another. I'd say that's not how a policeman should be carrying on. What are you after anyway? Payback? If you want this fucker dealt with, maybe I can sort that out for you, and there'll be no mess for you to clear up?'

Ian glared at Tod. 'My reasons are no concern of yours. I'm not interested in any help from you other than exactly what I asked for. I want you to track down this dealer and tell me where I can find him. Me and him, we've got business that doesn't concern you.'

'Do you want me to deliver him to you laid out or breathing?' Tod asked with a half-smile.

'Alive. He's no good to me otherwise. I need to find him. You stand a better chance than me of doing that, and doing it quickly.'

He did not explain that he was impatient to arrange for Geraldine to see her sister again. Since he had ultimately been responsible for her separation from her sister, he was desperate to do everything he could to reunite them. Now a way seemed to have opened up for him to do just that. If he was successful, there was a strong chance Geraldine would forgive him. He and Geraldine had been good friends for a long time before they became lovers, and he missed her more than he would have thought possible. With Geraldine, he had begun to see a future where he could finally be happy; only now that dream had been snatched away from him by someone very like the man now sitting in front of him.

The situation was complicated. The dealer who had been

behind Helena's drug habit had been arrested, and would no longer be interested in one random user, but now Ian needed to persuade the middle man who had delivered the drugs to Helena to leave her alone so that she could see Geraldine again without fear of reprisal. He could have arrested Tod there and then, and felt a brief sense of relief at getting some revenge for his troubles, but he was playing a longer game. In order to succeed, he had to work with Tod, however repugnant that was.

'Why don't you ask your boys to find this fucker for you?' Tod asked. 'You got the whole of the filth to do your dirty work. Why do you need me to hook you up?'

'Do you think I want to come to you for help? I've asked around, but none of my colleagues knows where he is. I'm guessing you do, and if you don't yet, you can find out. Besides,' Ian said, 'it's complicated. I've had to be fairly discreet in my enquiries because I don't necessarily want all my colleagues to know what I'm doing, so this needs to be done quietly.'

Tod grunted. 'Well, I can't say as I'm on terms with your mates, so you don't need to sweat it that I might blab to them. I have to say, Archie, the way you're carrying on doesn't sound at all shady.' He grinned at his own sarcasm.

'I don't give a toss what you think of me or my actions or my motives, I just want you to find this dealer for me.'

'And then I'm free of you?'

Ian nodded. 'That's the deal. And from where I'm standing you don't have any choice in the matter.'

'So you and Tallulah?' Tod asked. 'You just used her to get to me?' He shook his head, watching Ian closely. 'Poor bitch is going to need some consoling when I spill the beans to her.'

'You leave her out of it,' Ian began and then thought better of it. Any attempt to protect Tallulah might make Tod suspect she was another undercover cop. 'At least until I get what

I want,' he added. 'A tart who works for someone like you deserves whatever she gets.'

When Tod said he needed time to think about the proposal, Ian shook his head. 'I want his name and address by tonight or it's game over for you. There'll be no second chances. I can give you details of where he was in prison and when he was released, and his real name, although he may be using an alias. That should be enough for you to find him.'

Tod nodded. 'Very well. Give me the dirt on this dealer and I'll see if I can discover where he's at.'

'Good,' Ian said. 'I'll be back in here tomorrow, and you'd better have something for me when I return. Otherwise, you know what's going to happen.'

'Yeah, yeah, you've told me more than once. Chill. Didn't I just say I'll do what I can? But I'm not a bloody miracle worker. I can't make any promises.'

'Neither can I,' Ian thought.

20

'THE KILLER MUST HAVE left some trace behind,' Eileen fumed. 'People don't just vanish, especially not if they're carting a dead body around. How did he get her to the woods without leaving any trace?'

They knew from the carpet fibres in the dead woman's hair and clothes and from the regular shape of the injury where she hit her head, that she had most likely been killed indoors, somewhere with a carpet and furniture.

'If she wasn't killed in the woods, how the hell did her body get there?' Eileen repeated her question.

'In a van?' a constable asked.

'Yes, obviously, in a vehicle of some description,' Eileen replied irritably. 'I didn't imagine he flew her there on a magic carpet. But what vehicle? And where is it now?'

A team had been tasked with checking CCTV in the areas surrounding the woods, and later that morning Eileen called a meeting. A van had been spotted near the woods where Pansy's body had been found. Peering at the screen, Geraldine saw a grey van driving along the road leading away from the woods.

'We saw it going in the other direction, towards the woods, about half an hour before this,' one of the visual images and identifications detection officers said. 'It was driving really slowly on the way there, as though the driver was searching for a particular place. Unfortunately we haven't been able to trace the vehicle's route to and from Acomb Wood Drive. It appeared from a maze of side streets where it disappeared again afterwards, and we don't know where it came from, or where it went after this. But we did get a shot of the registration number.'

There was a muted buzz of excitement at this news.

'Good work,' Eileen said, flashing a smile that softened the contours of her square face.

'The van is registered to a Bill Riley,' the visual images identifications detection officer said.

She read out an address near Heslington, and Eileen immediately sent Geraldine and Matthew to bring the suspect to the police station for questioning. No one dared voice the hope that they had found Pansy's killer, but Eileen seemed quietly confident. Geraldine and Matthew drove to Bill Riley's lodgings in silence, accompanied by a patrol car and enough officers to surround the house and prevent the suspect from slipping away. A stout woman in a white apron came to the door.

'Bill Riley? Yes, he's my lodger,' she replied when Geraldine asked for Bill.

'Is he in?'

The woman nodded warily before turning and yelling out Bill's name. A thickset man with a mop of tousled mousy hair came trotting down the stairs to join them. He looked scared when Geraldine and Matthew introduced themselves, but rallied quickly and challenged them with an air of defiance.

'What do you want with me?'

'We'd like you to come with us to answer a few questions,' Geraldine said.

Bill shook his head and reached to slam the door, but Matthew put his foot out to prevent him from closing it.

'You need to come with us,' Matthew said sternly. 'It will be better for you in the long run if you co-operate with us and, in any case, we're not leaving here without you.'

Even Geraldine felt mildly intimidated by her colleague's gruff authoritative air, while Bill quailed and turned pale. 'I'll just get my keys,' he murmured before shuffling away down the corridor, followed by Matthew.

By the time they were all back at the police station, and seated in an interview room, Bill appeared to have recovered some of his earlier defiance.

'I know what I did, right? I just hadn't got around to notifying anyone yet,' he admitted. If that seemed like a strange turn of phrase under the circumstances, his next grumble was even less appropriate. 'I never realised it was such a big deal.'

'Not a big deal?' Matthew muttered, frowning. 'What planet are you on? We're dealing with a nutter,' he added under his breath to Geraldine. 'Or else he thinks he can plead temporary insanity.'

'Bill Riley,' he said, 'I am arresting you for the—'

'Arresting me?' Bill interrupted him, sitting very upright and glaring at Matthew. 'What the hell for? You're having a laugh, aren't you? What? Need another arrest to meet your targets? Listen, you muppet, whatever it is you're trying to pin on me, you're making a big mistake.' He leaned back in his chair and folded his arms, looking thoroughly shifty. 'Go on, then, arrest me, but don't be surprised when you get sued for wrongful arrest.' Bill's eyes narrowed suddenly. 'What's this all about anyway? You haven't brought me here because of what happened last weekend, have you? We told the police at the time it was an accident. I mean, we were all over the limit, but my mate's already admitted he was driving. It's not as if anyone was hurt. In any case, it's not a crime to be a passenger when the driver is over the limit. How was I supposed to know? He said he was all right to drive and I believed him. We all did. Shit, even he didn't realise he was over the limit. How was anyone else supposed to know?'

'Where were you the Friday before last?' Matthew asked.

'Hanging out with my mates,' Bill replied promptly.

'You seem pretty certain of that. Most people don't find it so easy to remember where they were ten days ago,' Matthew said.

'Well, you asked about Friday night, didn't you? That's what I do on Friday nights. Last Friday was at Beezo's in Leeds. The week before we were all up in Northallerton at Harry's. The week before—' He screwed up his eyes trying to remember. 'Ask Beezo. He'll remember.'

'That's enough,' Matthew snapped, but he didn't sound sure of himself. 'Who are Beezo and Harry?'

Bill gave them details of his friends, one of whom lived in Northallerton, the other in Leeds. Bill insisted on having a lawyer present before he said anything else, so they returned to their desks and kept him in a cell while they waited. In the meantime, Eileen contacted the police in Northallerton and asked them to check out Bill's alibi for the Friday when Pansy was murdered.

'Even if he was in Northallerton, it's only forty minutes' drive away,' Matthew pointed out. 'All he's done is prove he was out on the road that Friday night. He could quite easily have spent the evening there and picked Pansy up on his way home.'

'Depending on what time he left Northallerton,' Geraldine said. 'He could have been back here in York at any time.'

'So unless he stayed there all night—' Matthew began and broke off with a frown. 'Well, that's hardly likely, is it?'

At last the duty brief turned up and they resumed questioning Bill.

'Has my client been charged?' the lawyer demanded as soon as they sat down.

Bill threw an approving glance at the lawyer, a smartly dressed man in his twenties, clean shaven and earnest looking. As he spoke, the young man fidgeted with the knot on his sober grey tie, as though he was unused to dressing formally.

'Not yet,' Geraldine replied. 'We just want to ask him a few questions.'

'They're trying to arrest me!' Bill blurted out indignantly. 'I'm telling you, it's a bloody joke. What happened to citizen's rights?'

'We're interested in your van,' Matthew said reciting the registration number.

'Oh Jesus, now you really are taking the piss,' Bill said. 'So I forgot to notify the DVLA as soon as I sold my old van. Well, if that's your game, I can tell you, I'm not even going to be paying a fine, mate, because the DVLA give you time to notify them – at least, I think they do.'

He glanced at his lawyer, who murmured a response. 'When you sell a vehicle it's advisable to notify the DVLA straight away. Not only is it an offence not to do so, but until you do so, you remain liable for the vehicle.'

'Well, all right, so I forgot, but I'll get on to it as soon as I get home. For fuck's sake, it's not even two weeks since I sold it. So why are they talking about arresting me?'

'When exactly did you sell your van?' Geraldine asked, doing her best to hide her dismay.

Bill frowned. 'It was on Saturday afternoon, soon after I got back from Harry's. Some geezer had phoned up asking about it, and he came round an hour or two later and drove it away.' Bill shrugged. 'And if it's him put you up to this, I can tell you, there was nothing wrong with that van when I sold it. He could have checked it out first, but he just bought it on the spot. If anything, he was the one in a hurry to take it off me. I sold it, fair and square, and he's not getting a penny back from me. It was dirt cheap anyway. He knew he had a bargain. That's why he was in such a hurry to conclude the deal. But I'm no mug. It was no use to me and I was pleased to be rid of it. But there was nothing wrong with it when he drove it away.'

'Caveat emptor,' the lawyer murmured. 'My client was not aware of any problems with the vehicle when he parted with it and cannot be held in any way liable for any problems that subsequently arose.'

Geraldine and Matthew exchanged a glance. It made sense that someone might have been in a hurry to acquire a van the day after Pansy was killed.

'Who did you sell it to?' Geraldine asked, hardly daring to listen to the answer.

If Bill was able to give them details of the purchaser, they could have Pansy's killer behind bars within the hour. But Bill shrugged. The purchaser had been in a hurry. He had paid cash, four hundred pounds, and Bill was unable to describe him.

'It was all over so quickly,' he said. 'I scarcely glanced at him. I was too busy checking the cash.' He frowned. 'All I can remember is that he was wearing a jacket of some kind, with the hood up. I wondered about that, because it wasn't snowing, but it was freezing and in any case, to be honest, I wasn't that interested. He bought my van. That's all. I wouldn't know him from Adam.'

Geraldine tried not to feel deflated. Once again she had been optimistic about a lead that turned out to be a dead end.

21

WHILE POLICE AT NORTHALLERTON questioned Bill's friend, Harry, the Leeds police were busy looking for Beezo. The report from Northallerton was fairly conclusive.

'He arrived at Harry's flat early Friday evening, and left after a late lunch on Saturday. According to Harry, the three of them get together most Friday evenings to get wasted and watch films, and they usually stay at each other's houses. Sometimes they spend Saturday evenings together as well, but Bill wanted to get home because he'd received a call that someone wanted to buy his old van and he was keen to get rid of it.'

The report from Leeds confirmed what the police at Northallerton had already been told. Both Harry and Fred Beasley – known as Beezo – confirmed that Bill and Fred had stayed with Harry in Northallerton on Friday night.

'Is it possible we were wrong about the time of death?' Matthew asked.

But they had to admit it was looking unlikely that Bill had killed Pansy. Bill's alibi checked out, meaning there was no way he could have been in York killing Pansy on Friday night.

'Unless the pathologist miscalculated the time of death by twenty-four hours,' Matthew suggested.

'That's always a possibility,' Eileen agreed. 'After all, estimating the time of death is just that, an estimate. But Jonah Hetherington's very experienced and he was happy to confirm what the doctor said at the scene. Jonah hasn't been proved wrong yet.'

'Is it possible the suspect killed Pansy earlier and deposited her body in the woods before going to Northallerton on Friday, and then sold his van as soon as possible after he returned to York? It would explain why he wanted to sell the van, wouldn't it?'

'But she wasn't left exposed in the open air until Saturday,' Geraldine pointed out.

'He could have killed her on Friday, kept her in his van all the time he was in Northallerton, and then deposited her in Acomb Wood on his return to York, just before he sold the van,' Ariadne suggested.

'Honey said she saw Pansy getting into a car on Friday night,' Geraldine said. 'And Bill doesn't own a car.'

'If you think she's a reliable witness,' someone muttered.

'I do,' Geraldine replied, slightly irritably. 'She may be a sex worker but she still has eyes, and she wants to help us discover who killed Pansy. Why would she lie about it?'

There was silence for a moment and then Eileen dismissed them.

The following morning, Eileen reported that Pansy had not been stored inside the van while Bill was in Northallerton. Eileen had gone back to Northallerton and Leeds to check whether anyone had seen inside the van over the weekend. On further questioning, Harry and Beezo had both independently revealed that Harry had a neighbour he thought might be interested in buying Bill's van. Harry had invited his friend over, and they had all gone out to look at the van, inside and out.

'That was convenient,' Matthew muttered.

'It seems that Bill's no longer a suspect,' Eileen said, scowling around the room as though her officers were responsible for his innocence.

Before Bill was released, Geraldine asked him whether he

had a photograph of his van, and he nodded and told her he had a picture of it on his phone.

'I took it for the online advert, listing the van for sale. Although why I should show it to you, I don't know,' he said irritably. 'You come to my house, drag me here, lock me up for the night, and question me like I'm a criminal, and now you expect me to show you what's on my phone. I've a good mind to delete the photo.'

Geraldine spoke gently, although her words were harsh. 'There's no point in deleting the photo, because we'll only take your phone and restore the photo from the cloud. You'll just end up with no phone until we're ready to return it. And in any case you're going to show me a photo of the van, because we need to speak to whoever bought it, and you'll be helping us to find him. Unless you want to obstruct a police enquiry?'

Bill scowled and showed her the image which she had him send to her before he was released. An appeal was then made to the public, asking anyone who thought they might have seen the van to come forward. It was a long shot, expecting someone who had spotted the van to not only see the appeal but also to recognise the particular vehicle and recall where they had seen it, but it was possible a witness might come forward. And as long as there was even the faintest chance they might discover some new information, they had to try. As Eileen was fond of saying, they would 'leave no stone unturned' in the pursuit of this killer.

That evening, Geraldine left work punctually at the end of her shift. More often than not she would linger at her desk, working until late, but on this particular night she was tired. There was nothing for her to do at work that couldn't wait until the morning, so she went home, ready for an early night. She had just showered and was sitting in her living room in her pyjamas and dressing gown, remote control in one hand, and glass of wine in the other, trying to relax, when her phone rang. It was quite late for a social call, so she guessed it must be work. With a sigh, she reached for her phone, wondering what was so important it couldn't wait until the morning. It flashed across her mind that this could mean that a second murder victim had been discovered.

The voice on the line startled her. 'Geraldine?'

'Ian? Where are you?'

'Never mind that.'

'There's a rumour you're in London.'

'Don't worry about where I am. I've got tied up with something, but it's a temporary move and I'll be back in York before anyone notices I've gone.'

'Don't be daft. Everyone's noticed your absence. You can't just bugger off like that, without so much as a word about where you're going, and think no one's going to ask questions. Where are you?' Geraldine repeated her question, her anger towards him returning.

'I can't talk now,' Ian said, suddenly lowering his voice. Geraldine had the impression he was no longer alone. 'I can't tell you – I can't tell anyone – where I am,' he muttered. 'I'll try to call you tomorrow. Same time. Don't tell anyone I called.'

He rang off leaving Geraldine shocked and disappointed. Automatically she made a note of the time. Ian had said he would call back at the same time the next day. Furious with him for playing stupid games, she phoned him back, but the number from which he had called her was unobtainable. She tried again with the same result. After her third attempt, she gave up, telling herself fiercely that she didn't want to speak to him anyway. He had called her and then hung up without saying anything. She didn't know what kind of stupid games he was playing, but wherever he was, he could stay there as far as she was concerned. She told herself she didn't care if he never returned to York. But deep down, she knew she was lying to herself.

22

EVIDENTLY TOD HAD TAKEN Ian's threat seriously, because the next day he came up with the information Ian was looking for. Ian was with him in the office when Tod sent Frank away on an errand.

'Leaving you with him again?' Frank muttered crossly. 'What the fuck? I hope you know what you're doing. I don't trust him. Who does he think he is anyway?'

Tod glared. 'Don't you fucking call me out,' he growled.

Ian turned and watched Frank stalk out of the room, while Tod grumbled about him being 'uppity'.

'What the fuck indeed,' Tod went on, after Frank had gone. 'If he knew who I'm with, he'd completely lose it. But we can't keep up this pillow talk much longer, Archie, if that really is your name.'

Ian didn't reply. Once the deal was complete, he would return to York and Tod would never see or hear from him again. There was nothing to connect Archie, member of the drug squad in London, with a detective inspector working in York where Tod and his henchmen would never track him down. But before he was ready to leave London, he had a task to complete, and he had only just begun.

'So what is your name?' Tod asked.

Ian shrugged. He was certainly not about to reveal anything about himself beyond what Tod already knew.

'Well?' he said instead. 'What have you got for me?'

'This dealer you're after, his moniker's Jammie,' Tod replied.

'Jammie? What kind of a name is that?'

'No one uses their real name, do they?' Tod replied. 'You don't, do you, Archie? Why should anyone else?'

'I suppose he thinks he's lucky?' Ian said.

Tod laughed. 'Jammie. You know what that is, don't you?'

Ian felt a cold shiver as Tod mimed shooting him. No doubt the name had been chosen to inspire fear in anyone who grasped its meaning. He wished now that he had come up with something more intimidating for himself. Tod meant death; Jammie referred to a gun. Archie was a bit lame, really. He comforted himself with the thought that Frank was worse, unless it was ironic, which seemed unlikely. Frank wasn't capable of such subtlety. Even Nick had another meaning, now he thought about it, although that had been his real name.

Ian answered Tod with a question of his own. 'Where can I find him?'

Tod laughed. 'You sure you want to meet him?'

Ian took a step towards Tod, trying to look menacing rather than afraid. 'I said, where can I find him?'

'Chill.'

Tod reached into a pocket and Ian tensed as he drew out a filthy scrap of paper.

'This dealer you're after, you'd better stay on point. He's a right smackhead.'

'Are you sure he's the one I'm looking for?'

'Sure. I got the word he was her pusher all right. According to what I heard, he was more than that. Helena Blake. That was the moniker you gave me. He supplied her junk until she got his boss nicked, and then she disappeared.'

Ian snatched the piece of paper and stuffed it in the back pocket of his jeans.

'Has her dealer tried to find her?' he asked.

'Sooner or later a junkie's going to croak. There's always others waiting. That's how it goes. But word is Jammie was mad when Helena disappeared. She was more than just another punter to him. He was furious when she ditched him. You'll steer clear of him, if you know what's good for you.'

Ian scowled.

'Anyway, you want to keep your cards close to your chest or you'll be napping in dirt yourself before long. Jammie's boss is the business. Do you think he's out of action because you've got him banged up?' Tod shook his head. 'I'm telling you, Archie, compared to Jammie's boss I'm small time.'

Without a word, Ian turned and stalked out of the office. Frank bared his teeth at him as he hurried past. Ian made his way to the station by a roundabout route around the market, constantly checking that he was not being followed. Aware that he was playing a dangerous game, he trusted Tod as much as he would trust a poisonous toad that had found its way into his bed. For all he knew, Tod had already sent a message to Helena's former drug dealer, warning him that Ian was on his way to confront him. And Ian was on his own. Jack knew nothing about his plans to warn Helena's drug dealer to leave her alone. Ian was taking a crazy chance, risking his own life, just so that Geraldine could see her sister again. If he failed, not only would Geraldine never see Helena again, but she wouldn't see him again either. Perhaps no one would find his body. Geraldine would never know the sacrifice he had made for her.

He walked fast, driven on by the hope that he might succeed in warning Helena's enemies off, and so enable Geraldine to be reunited with the sister he had stolen away from her. After all, he was the one who had requested that Helena be given a new identity, meaning that Geraldine could never see her again without compromising her sister's safety. At the time, it had seemed like the only way to protect them both. Ian still considered his actions had been justified, but Geraldine's obstinacy was both a strength and a weakness.

The address Tod had given to Ian was in Catford. Sitting on the train, Ian turned over in his mind what he was going to say to Jammie when he found him. Jammie was not a major player, but a runner for the dealer who was now behind bars. Still, the dealer would not want Jammie co-operating with a maverick police officer. Tod had warned Ian that even from his cell the prisoner had influence. Only fear, or the promise of a lot of money, could possibly convince Jammie to leave Helena alone if he ever discovered she was still alive. Jammie's boss believed Helena had been responsible for his arrest. He did not know that Geraldine had stood in for her twin in a desperate attempt to protect Helena. No one apart from Jammie would recognise Helena. Living under a new name, she would not be at risk if she met with Geraldine, as long as Jammie was prepared to keep silent if he ever came across her. But it would be risky for Geraldine to see Helena without the assurance of Jammie's co-operation.

As the train jogged along, Ian came up with a plan. It was a long shot, but he couldn't think of anything better. With a sigh, he turned to gaze at the ugly buildings of south London passing by the smeared window of his carriage. It was possible all his apprehension would be for nothing. This could well prove to be his last journey, the grimy urban landscape his last view of the world outside. Jammie might shoot him before he even had a chance to utter a word. He closed his eyes and tried to relax as the train jogged onwards, rushing him towards whatever fate might be waiting for him.

He found the address with some difficulty, in a maze of dirty side turnings on a council estate where the grimy buildings were all identical, with peeling paintwork on the windows and doors and brickwork in need of repointing, interspersed with ugly concrete blocks whose walls were already showing cracks. Weeds grew along the pavement and in the tiny front yards, as though seeking to fill the vacuum created by the absence of nature. The few scrubby wild plants were a poor substitute for trees and grass. Ian rang the bell to number sixty-three but no one answered. He tried the next bell by the front door and a crackly intercom buzzed.

'What?' a muffled voice fizzed in response.

'I'm looking for the tenant at number sixty-three,' Ian shouted back.

'This is sixty-four,' the voice replied and the intercom fell silent.

Ian tried again but this time no one answered. Cursing, Ian pressed the next bell and went through the same charade.

'This is number sixty-five,' the next voice said.

'Yes, I know,' Ian replied quickly, before the woman could end his call. 'Do you know where your neighbour from number sixty-three is?'

'Number sixty-three? How the fuck should I know?'

He heard a man's voice in the background calling out, 'Who is it?'

'Who are you anyway?' the woman asked.

'It doesn't matter.'

Ian decided not to pursue his search any further that day. It wouldn't do for Jammie to hear that someone had come looking for him. Ian would have to return and hope for better luck the following day.

23

TEN DAYS HAD PASSED since Thomas had received the message warning him that he had been seen. He knew as well as the writer of the note what it signified, but without knowing who had written it, he was powerless to respond. All he could do was wait. He no longer thought of the writer of the note as a witness to his guilt. He – or she – was The Enemy now. Thomas had never intended to kill anyone. All he had been after was a bit of fun. But now he found his mind drifting into violent thoughts. There was really nothing he could do to prevent his enemy from exposing him. They could hardly sign a contract: 'I pay you however many thousands of pounds and you promise to tell no one that you witnessed me dispose of a dead body.'

It might be better if Thomas simply removed the blackmailer from his life altogether, rather than handing over money he couldn't afford to lose. While he didn't begrudge what Emily had spent on putting her mother into a private care home for the last year of her life, he had been secretly relieved when his mother-in-law had died. She had been little more than a vegetable towards the end of her life anyway. And now there were Sam's university expenses to fund. His job was reasonably well paid, but money was still tight.

Thomas was no murderer, but there was no knowing what any man might do if he was desperate enough, even one who had never set out to hurt anyone. The truth was clear in his mind. Thomas's crime had been inadvertent. He hadn't even killed the stupid whore, for goodness sake. She was the one who had attacked him, fatally injuring herself in the process. That was hardly Thomas's fault. But the police would never see it like that, especially not now he had dumped the body in the woods. They wouldn't understand that he had been determined to prevent his wife finding out he had brought a prostitute back to their house. Not for the first time, he regretted not having buried the body. That way, if his blackmailer went to the police, Thomas would at least have had a chance to deny all knowledge of the accusation. There would have been no reason for the police to search his house for evidence that an unknown woman had ever been there because, without a body, the whole accusation would fall by the wayside. He could say he had been seen throwing out an old carpet. But it was too late for that now.

With hindsight, he realised that he ought to have called the emergency services as soon as the woman had collapsed, and claimed that the tart had knocked on his door uninvited. He could have said she had told him she was being pursued by an assailant, and he had stupidly let her in out of concern for her safety. If he had gone straight to the police, without going anywhere near the body, the police might have believed that he was innocent, and he might have convinced his wife that he had not been involved with a sex worker, but had simply tried to help a woman in need. Calling the police himself would have confirmed his innocence.

At the time the woman had died, getting rid of the body had seemed the safest course of action. Now that he risked exposure, he realised he had been a fool to have gone anywhere near the body. Having behaved like a guilty man, there was no way he could plead ignorance. The stupid part of it all was that he hadn't actually been guilty of a crime until he had taken steps to conceal his behaviour from his wife. On the other hand, the police could have found evidence that the dead woman had been a passenger in his car, which would have disproved any claim he made that she had turned up unannounced on his doorstep. The truth was he should never have brought a prostitute back to his house. He had done so more than once, and had always known he was asking for trouble. Well, now trouble had found him, and he had only himself to blame for the awkward situation he found himself in. But he hadn't killed the woman. That had been sheer bad luck. All he could do now was keep his head down, avoid trouble, and make sure he gave the police no reason to take a sample of his DNA.

With every passing day, he grew more apprehensive, until it became difficult to conceal his agitation from his wife. He barely slept at night, and struggled to keep his temper under control during the day. He never became violently angry. That wasn't in his make-up. But he grew increasingly irritable, both at work and at home until he barely recognised himself any more. He used to be an easy-going sort of bloke. Now he was a nervous wreck, jumping every time the phone rang, and scouring the newspapers every day for any report about a murder in York.

'Are you sure you're all right?' Emily asked him on more than one occasion.

He mumbled vaguely about being under pressure at work. He realised this was his enemy's plan, to make him suffer unbearable anxiety, to the point that he would be prepared to agree to almost anything, just to make it stop. But there was nothing he could do about it. His sense of helplessness was the worst aspect of his situation. Instead of being reassured as the days passed without a word from the witness, he grew more and more stressed, not knowing when his enemy might contact him again. He realised no one had reported him to the police or they would have been knocking on his door by now.

That meant his enemy must be planning to blackmail him. He wished he or she would get on with it, and put an end to this unbearable suspense.

By the time ten days had passed since he had received the note, he began to dare to hope it might have been a stupid hoax. For all he knew, the writer had not seen him with the body at all. 'I saw what you did' could refer to just about anything. He might have dropped some litter, or parked badly. Perhaps the writer had forgotten all about it, or was already dead, having suffered a stroke or a heart attack, or been knocked down by a car, leaving Thomas worrying for nothing. He was not a religious man, but he found himself praying that the witness had met with a fatal accident.

He was on his way to his car at the end of a working day when his phone rang. He answered without thinking, not bothering to check to see who was calling him. Expecting to hear his wife's voice, he was caught off guard by an unfamiliar one.

'Hello,' the stranger said.

Thomas waited, wondering if it was a scam.

'I know you're there.'

The sound was curiously husky, as though the caller was trying to disguise his voice.

'You must have the wrong number,' Thomas said.

'I don't think so,' the caller replied, his voice deeper than before.

'Who are you?' Thomas asked, with a growing suspicion that he was talking to the writer of the menacing note.

'You don't need to know who I am. What's important is that I know who you are, Thomas. Thomas Hill.'

There was a pause after the speaker recited Thomas's address, as though he expected a response. Thomas didn't answer. He couldn't trust himself to speak without betraying his terror.

'You know why I'm calling you,' the voice resumed.

Thomas remained silent.

'It's about the money you're going to pay me. Five thousand pounds.'

'And what if I don't agree to your ridiculous demand?' Thomas blurted out, shocked into responding.

'The police put out an appeal on TV,' the voice went on. 'I expect you saw it? They're looking for a grey van with your registration number. It would be very easy for me to come forward in response to their appeal, and inform them that I'd seen that same van in your drive. No doubt they'll come knocking on your door to ask you a few questions. And once they start, they won't leave you alone. They'll have a search team around, looking for evidence of a dead body in your house. They can find a single drop of blood, and they have dogs that can sniff things like that out, long after the body's gone. You don't want your wife finding out what you did, do you? All I have to do is describe how I was cycling past and saw you carrying a large heavy bundle out to the van, the night after a sex worker was killed. Of course, I'll tell them, it never occurred to me at the time to question what you were doing. Who would suspect someone of disposing of a dead body at night? The police are bound to take it seriously. They'll drag you off for questioning, and they'll probably want to question your wife, too. And who knows what evidence they might find in your house?'

Thomas thought of the grey van, still in his garage. He had been waiting for the fuss to die down before cleaning every surface he might have touched with bleach and dumping it. He knew he really ought to have disposed of it straight away, but the fear of being seen had held him back. At least in his garage it was safely out of sight – unless the police came calling.

'Think about it, Thomas. Five thousand pounds and this

will all go away, as though it never happened. Leave it in a bag below the tallest tree on the waste ground by the railway at seven o'clock on Saturday morning. I'll be there to collect it. You won't see me. If the money's not there, you know what will happen. Five thousand pounds is a small sum to ask for in exchange for your freedom, don't you think?'

Thomas had expected to be asked for more, but he was still shocked. In his wildest imaginings he had been afraid he might have to sell his house, but now that the blackmail had become a reality, he balked at the amount demanded.

'If you think I can get hold of that kind of money, you're out of your mind,' he blustered. 'There's no way I can find anything like that. And I'm not going to pay you a penny. Do your worst!'

He could hear his voice trembling, rising to a shrill crescendo as he finished speaking. The blackmailer must have noticed how he lost control of himself.

'Do you think I care how you get it? Rob a bank, if you must. You're a fool if you think you can haggle with me. You don't have any say in this. I set the amount and the terms. You simply do as you're told. Otherwise, your wife's going to know all about you and your dirty secret. Everyone will know.'

'What guarantee do I have after I pay you that you won't come back and ask for more?'

The caller laughed and hung up.

24

IAN SAT HUNCHED MISERABLY on the train, wondering if he was misguided in hoping to negotiate with Jammie all by himself. There was only a slim chance that a junkie could ever be persuaded of anything. To start with, Ian revealing that he was a detective inspector would be risky. Convincing Jammie that Helena had special police protection was going to be even more difficult. He had probably been fed a story that she was dead to stop him ferreting around looking for her. Jammie was unlikely to believe a word Ian said and, even if he did, there was no reason why he would accommodate a request from a police officer. A lot was at stake for Ian, so it was with a dry mouth and slightly sweating brow that he walked along the street on trembling legs and approached Jammie's front door again. A steady sleet was falling, making the scene look even more miserable and grey than on the previous day.

This time, as soon as he knocked the door was opened by a bleary-eyed tousled-haired man in scruffy jeans and a grey T-shirt. He stared blankly at Ian, his lips moving wordlessly.

'Who sent you?' the man asked at last, his eyes seeming to focus with difficulty.

'No one sent me,' Ian replied.

It was the wrong answer.

The man's face twisted in temper. 'Fuck off then. You're not welcome here. I don't give a damn who you are.'

The door slammed.

Ian knocked again, repeatedly. Finally the door opened a fraction, barely sufficient for a sudden shove to allow Ian to get his foot through the gap. The man inside resisted but was not strong enough to withstand the force of Ian's shoulder pushing against him.

'Fuck off!' he yelled. 'Whoever you are, fuck off!'

After a few moments, the door shifted and Ian stepped across the threshold to be hit by a heady aroma of incense and weed, mingled with tobacco and other pungent smells. Someone had recently been eating curry. Ian sniffed and struggled to maintain an impassive expression.

'Who the fuck are you?' the householder demanded, his voice shrill with alarm.

Shivering with agitation and briefly pumped with indignation, he was clearly too stoned to sustain his anger for long. After a few seconds his rage subsided and he stood helplessly staring and mumbling under his breath, his skinny arms hanging loosely at his sides.

'Is your name Jammie?' Ian asked, kicking the front door shut behind him. 'Don't fuck with me. Is your name Jammie?'

The man nodded without speaking. All at once, he seemed to wake up and fumbled to take a switchblade from his pocket.

Ian reached out and calmly twisted the other man's wrist until the knife fell from his grasp. Ian kicked it away and placed his foot on it.

'I wouldn't try anything else if I were you,' he said quietly, without releasing the other man's arm. 'I'm not here to bust you. I just want to make an arrangement with you.'

Jammie scowled. 'Fuck off,' he snarled. 'I don't have no truck with filth.'

'You're right, I'm a police officer. One of my colleagues knows where I am and she's ready to send a truck load of drug enforcement officers along, in the unlikely event of anything happening to me. But I don't think you want that sort of trouble, do you? Do you?'

Ian twisted Jammie's arm slightly, and the dealer shook his head, wincing and mumbling about 'police brutality'.

'Good,' Ian said, still gripping Jammie's arm. 'Then I suggest you pay very careful attention to what I'm saying.'

Jammie's fists clenched and he glared around wildly.

'On the other hand,' Ian continued in an even tone of voice, 'if you're stupid enough to change your mind and decide to attack a police officer, you're never going to walk out of a prison cell alive – if I don't break your neck myself first. Because if any harm comes to me, you'll never be free again. Never. And that's a promise. Now, wouldn't you like to listen to me?'

What Ian had said was a lie. None of his colleagues had any idea where he was, nor did they care about Jammie, who was one of a host of unimportant runners who kept their heads below the radar, delivering smack for dealers. He wouldn't be much of a catch for Ian's colleagues on the drug squad. If they took Jammie off the streets, in no time at all there would be a clutch of other runners eager to take his place and pocket their cut. The drug squad were after the big dealers, the ones who brought consignments of heroin and cocaine across the border into the country, and flooded the cities with them. In the meantime, all that interested Ian was that Jammie be stopped so that Helena could come out of hiding and see Geraldine again.

Jammie hesitated before nodding at Ian. 'Go on then,' he muttered. 'I'm listening.'

'Shrewd move,' Ian said, smiling to conceal his relief. 'You're doing the right thing. Being sensible. This way, no one gets hurt and no one ends up in trouble. Now, let's talk. I want to cut you a deal just between us.'

'What you after?' Jammie asked, his eyes sharp, his manner suddenly slick. 'You name it I can get it. I'm not shitting you.

Crack, crystal, poppers, ganja, angel dust, whatever you want.'

Listening to the list of drugs Jammie supplied, Ian wondered if he should reconsider his plans and see the dealer put behind bars after all.

'Charlie, smack, acid, skunk, uppers, downers, whatever you want, dude,' Jammie went on, growing affable in the belief that he had found a lucrative new source of income, as well as a potentially useful ally. 'Anything. All pure, no crap. I got good sources. Come on, dude,' he went on, wheedling, 'we can cut a deal, just like you said, just between us. And seeing as who you are, I'll give you a special price. Trust me, cheap as chips for you.'

'Not that sort of deal,' Ian snapped. 'Shut up and listen.'

Jammie's eyes widened in surprise as Ian outlined his demands, in exchange for which he undertook to protect Jammie from his colleagues. That wasn't true, but Ian was fairly confident Jammie swallowed it. He had no compunction about lying to someone like Jammie, who made a living from causing untold misery and suffering.

'You want this bitch left alone?' Jammie repeated, frowning. 'What the fuck? What the fuck?'

'You don't need to know why this is important,' Ian replied.

'I reckon I can take it,' Jammie said, with a sudden leer.

Ian didn't bother to try and explain himself. The less Jammie knew about his reasons, the better.

'I've told you all you need to know,' Ian said. 'If you don't want to play nice, you'll be behind bars before you know it. In fact, I'll throw you in a cell right now.' He took out his phone. 'One call and this place will be surrounded. What's it to be, Jammie? You lay off Helena and you walk free, or you refuse to help me and get banged up for your bloody mindedness. Hardly worth it, I'd say. Well? Do we have a deal, or are you an even bigger fool than I thought?'

'Okay, okay, chill,' Jammie replied. 'I'll get off her. She's nothing to me. Fucking boiler.' He clicked his fingers. 'You fuck off and pound her, if that's what you're after. Unless you want me to find you a real lulu,' he added, with a hopeful leer. 'I can get you any number of bitches.'

Ian shook his head to hide his disgust. 'Just guarantee this one will be left alone,' he said. 'That's all you have to do. But I'll be watching. If anyone touches a hair of her head, you'll be inside before you know it.'

'You got it real bad,' Jammie laughed.

25

ALTHOUGH BILL WAS NO longer a suspect, he remained a possible link to the killer. It wasn't much, but so far he was the only lead the police had. It was frustrating knowing Bill had probably seen the killer, face to face, yet despite that they were no closer to finding out the identity of whoever had purchased the van from him. Questioning Bill further, Geraldine confirmed that he had placed an advertisement for his van online, and the buyer had phoned him, impatient to make the purchase straight away. The site advertising the van could not necessarily trace people who looked at any specific item, and in any case there was no guarantee the purchaser had been using a personal computer with a private IP number. There were internet cafés and libraries in York, where anyone could have logged on and scrolled through the site. Unless he was a complete moron, a man looking for a van in which to transport a dead body was unlikely to use a traceable private IP address. Even so, a team set to work checking out the private computers from which the van had been viewed. There were not many of them and they were all followed up, without producing any useful leads.

Questioning Bill further, Geraldine struggled to discover anything definite about the appearance of the man who had bought the van. Bill thought the man was about the same height as him, somewhere under six foot and he had been wearing a dark jacket, with the hood pulled right forward.

'Did you get the impression he was trying to hide his face?' Geraldine asked.

Bill shrugged. 'Maybe he was. I couldn't see much of him but, to be honest, I wasn't really looking at him.'

Bill could not recall the exact colour of the man's jacket, only that it might have been navy or black, and he thought the man had been wearing blue jeans.

'What about his shoes?' Geraldine asked patiently.

Bill shook his head and his mop of hair flopped from side to side. 'I mean, I'm sure he was wearing shoes. I'd have noticed if he wasn't,' he said, evidently trying to be helpful.

'Was he wearing trainers? Or leather shoes?' Geraldine prompted him, but he shook his head again.

'Like I said, I didn't really look at him very closely. I was too focused on watching him count out his money.'

'Don't worry, I know you're doing your best,' Geraldine assured him.

'There's no need to patronise me, lady.'

She stifled a sigh. 'What about his hands when he was giving you the money? You must have noticed if he was black or white.'

'No, you just reminded me, he was wearing gloves.'

'What sort of gloves?'

'Black gloves. I seem to recall they were leather, and they might have been new. There was a scratch on his wrist,' he added suddenly.

'A scratch?'

'A long scratch on the back of his left – no, his right wrist, as though someone had...' He broke off as the significance of his words struck him.

'Can you think of anything else?' Geraldine asked.

'Like a tattoo or a piercing, you mean?' Bill said. 'Or a scar?'

'Anything you can remember would help us with our enquiry,' Geraldine replied steadily.

She waited, hardly daring to hope that Bill would describe

an unusual distinguishing feature he had noticed on the man who had purchased the van. But he merely shook his head once again, and confessed he was unable to recall anything else about a man he had barely seen.

'What about his voice?' Geraldine asked.

'Oh Jesus,' Bill replied, seeming to tire of the questions. 'I've told you everything I can remember about him. I don't have a photographic memory or anything.'

'Can you remember what his voice was like?' Geraldine repeated.

'He spoke with a normal local accent,' Bill told her. 'Like mine. Not like yours. And his voice was – well, he sounded like you'd expect a man to sound.'

'Can you be more specific?'

'His voice was quite deep, not that unusually deep, and – well, that's it. He didn't lisp or stammer, or have any kind of speech impediment that I can recall.' He shrugged. 'He sneezed a couple of times,' he added.

'Did he use a tissue or sneeze into his sleeve?' Geraldine asked.

'I don't know. I can't remember. He just sneezed. I think he used a tissue.'

Geraldine made a note of everything Bill said, but it wasn't much to go on. A man who occasionally sneezed hardly narrowed it down.

'When can I have my money back?' he asked, when they were finished and she stood up to leave. 'I've answered all your questions and done everything I can to help you, and I'd like to take my money and go home now. You said I'm free to go.'

Geraldine smiled gently. 'Yes, you can go home. But I'm afraid we need to hold on to the money for now. It's been sent away for testing.'

'Testing? What the hell does that mean?'

'You can pick it up tomorrow.'

Geraldine didn't add that the police would be keeping some of the notes as evidence. Bill would be unhappy when he discovered that until the case was over he was only going to receive back around two hundred and fifty of the three hundred pounds he had handed in. The other hundred had already been spent before the police caught up with him. An unknown man's DNA had been found on Pansy's body, mostly concentrated on superficial injuries that had been inflicted post mortem, no doubt when her body had been moved after she died. Traces of the same DNA were found on most of the notes Bill had been paid for his van. If it had matched Bill's DNA, the case would have been resolved, but there was no sign of Bill's DNA on Pansy's body. Nevertheless, they now had confirmation that the killer had handled the notes paid for Bill's van a day after Pansy's death.

'It's one more tiny piece of the puzzle,' Eileen said sourly.

'It's very tiny,' Geraldine agreed, and Eileen glared at her.

That evening, Geraldine went home as soon as her shift ended, and waited impatiently for her phone to ring. Ian didn't call. She tried to tell herself she didn't care, but she couldn't help worrying that he had met with an accident.

26

'BEAT IT,' TOD SNARLED at his thickset bodyguard. 'Archie and me, we got business together.'

His feet making no sound on the thick carpet, Frank shuffled towards the door, a thin trail of smoke dispersing slowly in his wake. A whiff of smoke caught Ian as Frank passed him, and he suppressed a cough. Being indoors with so many smokers was one of many aspects of his new role that disgusted him, but there was nothing he could do about it.

Reaching the door, Frank hesitated. 'Boss—' he muttered, turning to glare at Ian. 'Boss, trust me, you got it wrong. I think you should listen to me.'

'Don't you start bleeding thinking,' Tod snapped. 'That's all I need, opinions from a numpty like you. I got my own philosophy, thank you very much. I just told you to beat it.' While he was speaking, Tod's voice rose in pitch.

His elevated tone could have resulted from anger, but Ian suspected the hike in his tone was due to nerves.

'Archie and me, we got business together. Scram.'

Frank made one last attempt. 'If you ask me, Boss—'

'No one's asking you,' Tod replied. 'Now get the hell out of here.'

Frank left the office, slamming the door behind him. Beneath Ian's feet, the floorboards quivered at the violence of the impact. He stood gazing at Tod, their eyes locked across the large leather-topped desk. For a moment neither of them spoke. The scar on Tod's face seemed more prominent than Ian remembered it.

Tod finally broke the silence, as Ian had hoped he would. 'So you got to your slanger, like you wanted?' he asked, lowering his eyes to study his long fingers with an affectation of nonchalance. 'And that's all thanks to my kind nature.'

Ian was only slightly reassured to know that Tod was nervous in his presence. Every step of the way, Ian had to work hard to ensure he remained in control of the uneasy relationship they had established. Whatever happened, he couldn't afford to let his guard down, even for an instant. The slightest slip and Tod would turn on him, like a shark scenting blood. But if Ian played it right, he could continue his pretence of working for Tod, and Jack would be none the wiser. The problem was that Tod's moods were volatile, and he was not to be trusted. Frank was no doubt standing just outside the door, waiting for a signal to come in.

'Step away from the desk,' Ian commanded.

'I know, I know, no need to tell me again, your people got your back,' Tod said. 'You don't need to keep banging on about it. Like I'm gonna plug you and land myself knee-deep with the filth. Like I'm not screwed enough as it is.'

Still grumbling, he came around the desk and perched on one of the upright chairs.

'What is it?' he demanded. 'I done what you wanted. So what's your beef now? Not got the grit to take the slanger out after all? Not as hard as you make out?' He threw his head back and laughed very loudly, without taking his sharp black eyes from Ian's face. 'You bottled it, didn't you?' he asked, leaning forward, suddenly serious. 'So what's the deal? You in need of someone to clean up for you? Thing is, buster, I found this slanger for you, like we agreed. And now I'm done with this. Done with you.' He stood up. 'Spill it to Frank to get his arse back in here on your way out and don't bother coming back.'

'Sit down,' Ian growled.

For a long moment, Ian was afraid Tod wouldn't comply, but at last he sat down again.

'The thing is,' Ian spoke very slowly, 'I want in.' He didn't take his eyes off Tod for a second.

Tod frowned and shook his head, looking perplexed. But he was interested.

'Just listen to me for a minute,' Ian went on, doing his best to hide his trepidation. 'I can be useful to you. Very useful. I want–' He paused. 'The thing is, I need more money if I'm going to impress Tallulah. The chief sent me to sweet talk her, as a way to get to you. But…'

He gave what he hoped was a helpless shrug. With a flash of inspiration, he thought about Geraldine.

'You got the hots for the bitch all right,' Tod said, leering at Ian. 'You got it bad. I guess your chief never meant for that to happen.'

He rubbed his long fingers together and laughed quietly, while Ian studied him covertly. There was nothing to indicate Tod doubted what Ian had said.

'The bitch is hot,' Tod went on, nodding his head. 'So you get smitten. And that makes you my boy now.'

Ian nodded, with a show of reluctance. 'Like I said, I can be useful to you. But my services don't come for free,' he added quickly, aware that it would be a mistake to appear too eager. 'If you don't play fair and square with me, I'll leave and I'll take Tallulah with me.' He gave what he hoped was a fierce frown. 'I'm not leaving without her.' That much, at least, had some element of truth to it.

'Fair and square?' Tod replied, with a snigger. 'What a thoroughly decent chap you are, to be sure,' he added, mimicking an upper-class accent.

'I want you to double my wages,' Ian said, before he lost the advantage he had gained from taking the initiative. 'And make sure no one gets fresh with Tallulah.'

'That's for you, innit,' Tod replied. 'I see what you cop out of this. You get the dough and the honey, solid. But what's in it for me?'

'Information,' Ian replied promptly. 'The police won't come near you. I can protect you and, if they ever do start sniffing around, you'll know about it straight away. You'll be safe. Invincible.'

Tod clenched his fists. 'No one touches me,' he growled.

'Not yet they haven't,' Ian said, aware that he was playing with danger.

Tod grunted and shouted for Frank who burst into the room so promptly Ian wondered if he had been listening from the corridor outside. One of Frank's brawny fists was raised, clenched, but Ian was more concerned about the thug's other hand, which was out of sight in the bulging pocket of his jeans. Ian guessed he was holding a gun.

'Yes, Boss,' Frank said gruffly.

Tod walked around his desk and took his seat behind it, leaning back and watching Ian and Frank.

As his gaze came to rest on Ian, Frank licked his lips, like a man eyeing a tasty morsel of food. Tensed for a blow, Ian forced himself to stand his ground and keep his expression impassive.

27

THOMAS WAS PHYSICALLY SHAKING as he walked along the street towards the path of waste ground beside the railway. It wasn't only the cold that was making him shiver. An old khaki rucksack slung over his shoulder held just over five hundred pounds, withdrawn from his personal account. It was all he had been able to get hold of at such short notice. He had already paid out four hundred for the old van. With this new withdrawal, he was dangerously close to his overdraft limit. He had bought the rucksack that morning from a charity shop, and had been careful to wear his leather gloves while handling it. Whatever happened, he intended to leave no evidence of his dealings with his blackmailer. It was to be a quick handover with minimal contact.

The street was deserted that early on a freezing Saturday morning, but he remained vigilant. He kept his hood up as he scurried across the road as quickly as the icy ground allowed, casting furtive glances around to make sure no one was watching him. The only sign of life he encountered was a fat pigeon that hopped on to the pavement in front of him and immediately took off again. Thomas was so jumpy he nearly cried out as the bird flapped away.

Despite his agitation, he was almost excited to be finally meeting his blackmailer. The waiting had been driving him crazy. Desperately hoping this would somehow signal the end of their dealings, he was afraid his blackmailer would not let him off so easily. Even if he managed to stump up the remaining four and a half thousand pounds the blackmailer had demanded, it would probably not be over. Still, he had no choice but to go along with the payment as far as he could. Cursing the stupid whore who had got him into this mess in the first place, he glanced over his shoulder before turning into the patch of waste ground. The surface was uneven and more slippery than on the road, and he had to advance carefully.

Reaching the tall, overgrown shrubs and trees at the side of the winding path, he went to the tallest tree, which the blackmailer had specified as the drop-off point, and slipped his bag off his shoulder. Having lowered it to the ground, he took a few steps back. Without really thinking about what he was doing, he manoeuvred his way into the bushes behind the tree and stood there, shivering and watching the path to make sure the bag was collected. A muffled hum of traffic barely impinged on the silence which encompassed him like a shroud as he waited concealed behind a thick tree trunk.

After a few moments, he thought he heard someone shuffling across the frozen ground towards him. The footsteps were so quiet he wasn't sure whether he was imagining the noise. It could have been a whisper of a breeze in the branches above his head. As he stood trembling behind the tree, a figure came cautiously into view. Without moving from behind the tree, it was impossible for Thomas to see the blackmailer's face. All he could see was one side of a long hooded coat. From the stranger's build, Thomas judged it to be a woman, but the figure could have been a small man. The stranger halted near the tree and glanced around without seeing Thomas, who remained hidden from view behind the tree, scarcely daring to breathe in case he exhaled a puff of mist to alert the blackmailer to his presence. Unaware that Thomas was watching, the blackmailer leaned forward to grab the bag of cash, pausing to unzip it and take a peek at the contents.

Anger welled up inside Thomas as he saw his enemy take

hold of the bag, sling the strap over their head before turning to walk away with the bag clutched against their chest. That was Thomas's five hundred pounds, and he was about to lose it, just because a drunken tart had happened to knock her brains out inside his house. On a sudden impulse, he lunged forward and seized the bag, only dimly aware that he was being stupid. The strap tightened around the blackmailer's throat, dragging them backwards, choking, before Thomas managed to pull it free. Caught off guard, the blackmailer lost their footing and fell, hitting their head on the trunk of the tree. The impact made such a loud thwack, Thomas was sure it would be heard from the street and people would come running. Seizing the bag in a panic he fled, slipping several times as he ran and nearly falling over, while his blackmailer lay on the ground, dazed by the blow.

Thomas had acted in retaliation, having been pushed beyond any reasonable level of endurance. When the blackmailer contacted him again, he would insist he had left the bag of money where they had agreed. If someone else had come along and taken it after Thomas had gone, that was nothing to do with him. He had done exactly as he had been instructed: left the bag on the ground by the tree and gone. The blackmailer hadn't seen him retrieving the bag. As he trotted away as fast as he could, he realised that things had actually worked out for the best. He would say he had left all five thousand pounds in the bag, and it had cleaned him out.

'There were five thousand pounds left in a bag by the tree,' he would say. 'Just what you asked for. I left the money in good faith. It's hardly my fault if someone else came along and stole it from you.'

There was no sound of pursuit as he rushed away across the waste ground towards the road without looking back, his bag securely over his shoulder once more. Reaching the street, he slowed down to a brisk walk and made his way around the block and back to his own house, making sure he wasn't being followed, and avoiding passing by the waste ground, for fear his blackmailer was waiting for him there. As he reached his own street, he kept looking around, but there was no sign of a short person in a long hooded coat, and he reached his house without further incident. Somehow, the sight of his enemy, if only from behind, made them seem less frightening. The blackmailer had been small and probably out of their depth, hoping to make some easy money. Well, it turned out Thomas wasn't as easy to outmanoeuvre as his enemy had expected. The blackmailer would think carefully before taking Thomas on again. With luck he would hear nothing more from his enemy. Smiling, he let himself back into the house. The nightmare situation was finally over.

28

FRANK STARED BACK AT Ian, his eyes dull as a shark's, and just as cold. Ian watched Frank's pale tongue sliding over his lips, leaving them glistening, and heard his hoarse breath wheezing in his barrel of a chest. Without thinking, Ian felt his own hands clench into fists, and he took a step back, automatically weighing up his chances. There was no point in sizing up his enemy if Frank pulled out a weapon. Neither physical force nor reason would provide any defence against a psychopath with a gun. Nevertheless Ian stood his ground, poised to withstand an attack if at all possible. Whatever happened, he was not going to give up without a fight.

His thoughts spun around wildly. He wondered whether he had time to reach Tod before he was shot. With Tod to shield him, Ian might manage to escape from the room, but Frank would whip his gun out before Ian had time to reach his boss. Any attempt to reach Tod would only provoke the bodyguard to shoot. In some ways Ian thought he might as well make his move and get it over with, yet he clung to his life and stood perfectly still, paralysed with fear.

The sound of Tod snapping his fingers broke the heavy silence. 'Fetch Tallulah.' He was talking to Frank. 'Jump to it.'

'Yes, Boss.'

Casting an evil look at Ian, Frank swung his huge bulk around and left.

The exchange between Tod and Frank reached Ian as if from

a great distance and he blinked, struggling to comprehend what they had said. A wave of relief swept through him and he felt his eyes water as he understood that he was not about to die. Not yet. For some reason, he had been granted a reprieve. As his mind cleared from a fog of terror, he recalled Tod telling him that he did not intend to kill a cop.

'Like I'm gonna plug you and land myself knee-deep with the filth. Like I'm not screwed enough as it is.'

Realising the threat to his life had been a product mainly of his own fears, Ian concentrated on breathing deeply. Meanwhile Tod returned to his seat behind his desk, where he was studiously avoiding looking at Ian. Perhaps he had genuinely forgotten about him. Once he had processed that he was out of immediate danger, Ian turned his attention to what Tod wanted. Before he could come to any sensible conclusion, the door burst open and Jenny strode in. She looked striking in her thick black make-up, with rigid strands of dark hair fanning out from her face. She was wearing a short denim skirt Ian had seen before, black thigh-high boots, and a skimpy red tank top.

'What's going down, Boss?' she asked, barely glancing at Ian.

'I take good care of my girls,' Tod said, nodding at her. 'So, Tallulah babe, dish the dirt on Archie.'

Jenny's eyes flicked to Ian, and he sensed uncertainty in her hesitation. It shouldn't have mattered that she was unaware Tod knew Ian's real identity. But Tod's question suggested he had discovered, or at least suspected, something about Ian. At the same time, if Jenny revealed Ian's secret, it would be tantamount to admitting that she was in league with the police, if not a cop herself. Tod would not look kindly on her withholding information from him. But her dilemma was that she didn't know how much Tod already knew. Ian hoped she would trust that he would never have disclosed her double life, but they barely knew one another. Jenny was a tough woman with a mind of her own. She had no reason to trust Ian, just because Jack did.

'What d'you wanna know?' she asked, all wide-eyed and innocent.

Ian had to admit, she carried it off well. She looked Ian up and down with a sly grin, playing for time, while he thought frantically of how he could make sure she understood he had protected her fake identity.

'He's fit,' she said at last. 'He's my fella.' She darted a look at Tod. 'Why? What's he done, Boss? What do you want me to do now?'

Tod grunted in satisfaction. Tallulah had clearly passed a test in deferring to him. Whatever her feelings for Archie might be, she had made it clear Tod was her boss and she took her orders from him.

'Keep your cards close to your chest,' Tod advised her. Neither of them looked at Ian. 'Don't trust anyone.'

'Not even you, Boss?' she replied, blatantly flirtatious.

'You got the hots for him, I get that. But stay sharp is all I'm saying.' He frowned suddenly and turned to Ian. 'You, scram,' he said. 'I got business with Tallulah.'

Ian hesitated.

'You heard the man. Piss off,' Jenny said. 'Tod and me, we got business,' she added, as though that was something to boast about.

Tod nodded and smiled. Clearly Jenny knew how to dance around him.

With a shrug, Ian left the office. He was worried about what Tod might do to Jenny but, after all, she had been working for him at the club for over a year. If anything was going to happen to her, it would probably have happened by now. He just hoped he would not be the catalyst for trouble. Still, he told himself, Jenny had made her own decision to work undercover, and she was capable of taking care of herself. Now that he had been introduced to Tod, he was as powerless to protect Jenny as she was to help him. Accustomed to working in a team, he felt horribly isolated, knowing that he and Jenny were each on their own at the club and he might have compromised her safety.

That night, Jenny called him on their secure line.

'How did you get on?' Ian asked, hoping Tod had not told Jenny that he knew Ian was an undercover cop.

'He doesn't seem happy with you, for some reason,' she replied. 'Did you do something to piss him off?'

'I don't think so. What did he say? Does he suspect?' he asked, unable to restrain himself from touching on the question that was weighing on his mind.

'I don't know, no, I don't think so,' she replied, and Ian breathed a sigh of relief. 'But he warned me off you. He said you might not be around for much longer.'

There was a pause.

'Frank's taken against me,' Ian said at last. 'Could that have anything to do with it?'

'It might, I suppose,' she replied. 'Yes, that's probably it. Tod wanted to warn me not to get too close to you because he thinks something's going to happen to you soon.'

'What were his exact words?' he asked.

'He said you might not be around for much longer,' Jenny repeated.

'But he didn't say why?'

'No. I'd have told you if he had.'

The idea that Ian might not be around for much longer was ambiguous. Hopefully Tod was thinking nothing worse than that Ian would leave the club and carry on his police work somewhere else. But he was afraid his life might be in danger if he stayed in London.

29

THE COMMON APPROACH PATH had been established along the far edge of the waste ground. A few straggly tufts of grass poked up through the dirty snow, a splash of green at intervals in the slush. No one had walked along there at the edge of the waste ground before the police turned up, so it had been adopted straight away as the best route to the site. In her slippery protective overshoes, Geraldine struggled to make her way across the row of plastic stepping stones that had been positioned alongside the bushes.

'The dead woman's name is Vanessa Slattery,' a scene of crime officer greeted Geraldine, when she arrived at the site where a body had been discovered at the foot of a tree. 'We found a wallet in her pocket.'

Behind his mask the officer looked very young. He held up a credit card and Geraldine leaned forward to read the details. A quick check revealed that Vanessa had been forty-one and single, living in a street that ran at right angles to Holgate Road, not far from the waste ground.

'So what happened?' Geraldine asked, gazing around the area of open land where several white-coated scene of crime officers were already busy searching the ground and bagging potential evidence.

The young officer gesticulated at the body, which was covered with a dusting of fresh snow.

'Look,' he murmured eagerly, his eyes shining.

Seeing his nervous excitement, Geraldine wondered if

this was the first serious crime scene he had attended.

'We reckon she's only been here a few hours,' he went on.

Geraldine searched the scene with her eyes and nodded. There was noticeably little insect activity near the body; even the flies had not yet gathered, but that was probably due to the cold. She shivered and approached the body. The dead woman was lying on her back, mud-coloured eyes staring up at the sky, her small mouth half open as though she was about to speak. Apart from her extreme pallor, at first glance there was nothing remarkable about her appearance except for the flakes of snow that had landed on her and not melted. Other than that, she could have been resting, about to clamber back up on her feet and continue on her way.

'If this was India, there'd be vultures by now,' the young scene of crime officer said, jumping from foot to foot in an effort to ward off the cold. 'I was there on my gap year and made the mistake of falling asleep on a deserted beach. When I woke up, there were three bloody great vultures circling in the sky right above my head. They were almost close enough to touch. They vanished as soon as I moved, of course. They were just waiting to find out if I was still alive.' He shook his head. 'You can't be too careful.'

'I'll remember not to fall asleep on a deserted beach next time I go to India,' Geraldine muttered. 'Now if you don't mind, nice as it is to chat, I'd like to focus on this body.'

A medical officer was crouching down beside the corpse. Although his light brown hair was thinning on the top, he too looked very young. Stifling a sigh Geraldine tried not to dwell on the thought that she had reached an age where all of her colleagues were starting to look young. After a moment, the doctor straightened up, and Geraldine saw a tall and spindly young man wearing an open-necked blue shirt beneath his thick black winter coat. He peered at her through rimless spectacles.

'Are you in charge here?' he asked in a thin reedy voice.

'What happened?' she replied, holding up her identity card.

For answer, the medical officer pointed at streaks of blood in the dead woman's fair hair, and at traces of blood faintly discernible on the tree beside her head.

'So she hit her head on the tree,' Geraldine said.

'Yes,' the medical officer agreed. 'That's certainly how it appears initially. But you also need to take a look at this.'

With a frown, he pointed at a few long smudges on the dead woman's throat that could have been caused by dirt or bruising.

'Those look suspiciously like there was something around her neck,' he murmured, as though he was sharing an embarrassing secret.

'Are you saying you think someone strangled her?' Geraldine asked bluntly, staring down at the marks and frowning.

'Strangled her or tried to,' the doctor replied. 'You'll have to wait for the post mortem to be sure. But yes, it does look as though someone else might have been involved here.'

The scene of crime officer overheard and chipped in. 'We found disturbance in the grass and weeds behind the tree, and a thread of fabric caught in the bark. Someone might have been hiding there, waiting for her to arrive before they pounced.'

Geraldine shook her head. 'Let's not get distracted with speculation while we've yet to gather all the evidence. If she died from the head wound, it could have been an accident.'

'It's hard to see how she could have attempted to strangle herself,' the medical officer remarked drily.

'The woman is dead, but how she died is not yet clear,' Geraldine replied firmly.

It was hard not to begin drawing conclusions before all the proof had been gathered and scrutinised, but it was important not to pre-empt the evidence. With a sigh, she turned her attention to the body. The woman's expression was calm. She was lying slumped back, her head propped up against the trunk of a tree, her arms flung wide. Pale, fair hair covered her ears, a few strands stained with blood on one side of her head. Her dowdy navy jacket was speckled with snow, and half unzipped, with the hood thrown back. Below that her black trousers were similarly flecked with snow, and she was wearing flat brown moccasins with little tassels. There was something poignantly human about the style of the dead woman's shoes. Geraldine wondered whether she had been pleased with the tassels, or if she had tolerated them because the shoes were particularly comfortable or cheap. Either way, the shoes were not very practical in the snow, which might explain how she came to slip over and hit her head. The sight of death always brought Geraldine a deep sadness, along with curiosity as to how the victim had died. Slowly, she turned and made her way back across the plastic stepping stones to the street. Geraldine's colleagues would already be knocking on the victim's door to inform anyone who had lived with her of her sudden and unexpected demise.

Back on the street, she saw a young woman wrapped in a silver sheet, talking to a female constable. Geraldine went over to listen.

'I was just on my way to work,' the girl was saying anxiously. Her teeth were chattering with the cold or shock.

'Where do you work?' the constable enquired.

'At Tesco. I looked up because a train was passing and caught sight of her out of the corner of my eye, just lying there. At first I thought she must be ill, or drunk, you know? She looked so pale. I went over to find out if she was all right because she was lying in the snow, but she just lay there without moving, and her eyes were open, not blinking, just staring up, and I kind of knew, really, so I called 999 and told them I thought she was ill or dead or something, I couldn't tell which. They asked me if she was breathing and I said I didn't know and then the police arrived and–' She broke off with a helpless shrug. 'She's dead, isn't she?'

Geraldine nodded. 'I'm afraid so.'

The girl let out a low whimper. 'I knew it.'

'Did you know her?' Geraldine asked gently.

'No. But it's just so horrible,' the girl replied.

'I'm sorry you had to find her like that,' Geraldine said. 'It must have been a shock, but you did the right thing to call us. The constable will finish taking your statement.'

As Geraldine turned away, the snow began to fall more thickly, covering the dirty pavement in a layer of pure white. She wondered how long it would be before the snow turned to ugly grey slush and sighed. People made the world a horrible place in so many ways.

30

'SHE DIDN'T HAVE A bag with her,' Eileen said at the briefing later that morning. 'At least, not one that was found anywhere near the body. Why was that? Was it stolen in the attack? Could this have been a mugging that went wrong?'

'It seems highly unlikely her bag would have been stolen but not her wallet,' Geraldine pointed out.

'She was found only a few hundred yards from her house,' Ariadne said. 'She'd probably just gone out for a walk.'

'Maybe she'd gone out to post a letter,' a constable suggested.

'Yes, well, let's not indulge in idle speculation about irrelevant details,' Eileen snapped and the constable looked down at the floor, abashed. 'Whatever her reason for going out, whatever her reason for walking on the waste ground beside the railway line, all she appears to have had on her was a set of keys and a wallet containing a credit card and around thirty pounds in cash.'

'If this was a mugging, she wouldn't still have thirty pounds in cash on her,' Geraldine said. 'It just doesn't stack up.'

'Unless her mugger was frightened off,' Ariadne suggested. 'It looks like she might have fought back and fallen over in the struggle.'

'She could have been attacked at home and run out to escape,' a constable suggested. 'Isn't domestic violence just as likely as a mugging?'

'The disturbance on the ground suggests the attack took place where she was found,' Geraldine replied.

They were still awaiting the results of the post mortem, but there was little doubt in anyone's mind that Vanessa had been attacked on the waste ground. Even if she had been killed by slipping over on the icy ground and injuring her head on the tree, the marks around her neck appeared to be contusions, not dirt, in which case they could only have been made by someone else. If that proved true, the police needed to find her unknown assailant urgently. In the meantime, while waiting for the results of the post mortem, they had received a preliminary report from the forensic team examining the crime scene.

The grass had been partly covered by a recent light snowfall which would have concealed any tracks. Around the tree, however, the ground had been somewhat protected by branches, and the churned-up slush that had been there for a few days told a different story. A layer of slushy mud behind the tree had recently been trampled by large feet. The size of the prints suggested they had been made by a man wearing trainers. They had definitely not been made by Vanessa's shoes. At one point the indentations were slightly deeper, indicating the man had been standing still behind the tree for some time. The picture built up from the footprints was further borne out by a thread of cotton caught in bark behind the tree which didn't match anything Vanessa was wearing. The thread could have been there already, so the evidence didn't prove beyond doubt that a man had been standing behind the tree when Vanessa had arrived, but it was a distinct possibility. That suggested that whoever he was, he had been waiting for her. Geraldine recalled the young scene of crime officer's speculation that someone might have been hiding behind the tree, concealing his presence until she arrived. It seemed he might have been right.

Eileen set up a team to check all the CCTV footage in the area, but Vanessa had lived only a few doors from where her body was found, and there was no CCTV along the street facing the waste ground. Another team was tasked with carrying out door-to-door questioning in case anyone living along there had seen someone entering or leaving the waste ground. So far no one had come forward with any information at all. It was as though Vanessa and her attacker had been invisible.

While Vanessa's neighbours were being questioned, Geraldine was sent to inform Vanessa's sister about her death. For Geraldine, sharing news of the death of a loved one was the worst part of any investigation. She found it far more difficult than dealing with the dead, who were beyond grief and suffering. At the same time, she was keen to discover as much as she could about the dead woman. Louise Gibson was married, living with her husband and two children out towards Driffield. Geraldine approached the front door across a small but neatly cultivated garden. The bell chimed loudly when Geraldine rang, and a woman opened the door and peered warily out. Three years older than Vanessa, Louise looked so much older than her forty-four years that Geraldine wondered if she was ill.

'Yes? Can I help you?' Louise asked.

'I've come to speak to you about Vanessa.'

'Is my sister up to her tricks again?'

'What makes you say that?'

Louise shrugged. 'Just that she's always on at me for money. She can't hold a job down, can't get on with people. If she's not been paying her rent, that's not my problem. I'm sorry, but I can't keep bailing her out, you know. Whatever mess she's got herself into, she'll have to get herself out of it. That's just how it is.'

She began to close the door, but Geraldine held it open with the flat of her hand. Louise looked faintly worried but she didn't resist.

'Can we go inside?' Geraldine asked, introducing herself.

'The police?' Louise asked, her frown deepening. 'You're from the police? Why? What has she done?'

Geraldine was interested to note that Louise immediately assumed her sister had broken the law, rather than fearing she had met with an accident. That possibility occurred to Louise next before Geraldine could answer, because in her next breath, Louise asked if her sister was all right.

'Can we go inside?' Geraldine asked again, more gently this time.

'What is it? You can tell me here.'

Once she heard that Vanessa was dead, Louise's demeanour altered completely. No longer angry and defensive, she broke down in tears. Her shoulders slumped; she flapped her hand at Geraldine, gesturing for her to enter. Standing in the narrow hall, she spoke in jerks between her sobs.

'Dead? She's dead? Vanessa dead? But I don't understand. I spoke to her yesterday and she was perfectly fine. She was talking about taking me on holiday.' She broke off to wipe her eyes and blow her nose. 'Was she run over?' Her eyes gleamed suddenly. 'Did you get the bastard who did it? Was he drunk?'

'She wasn't run over.'

'Then, what–? Oh my God, it wasn't – did she–'

'Did she what?'

'Was it – suicide?'

Geraldine shook her head. 'No, it was nothing like that.'

She wondered what might have prompted Louise to suspect that Vanessa had killed herself.

Louise drew in a deep, shuddering breath. 'Then what happened? Tell me. Please, I want to know.'

'We're investigating the circumstances of your sister's death,' Geraldine said slowly. 'We don't yet know what happened. Did Vanessa suffer from depression?'

'No, no, nothing like that.'

'What made you think she might have taken her own life?'

But Louise just shook her head, too overcome to speak. 'I don't know,' she muttered at last. 'I don't know. I mean, you never know, do you? You never really know how someone else is feeling, do you? She was always so up and down, I was always afraid something like this might happen.'

'Something like what?'

'I mean, I was afraid she might take her own life.'

'I don't suppose it's much comfort to you to know that she didn't,' Geraldine answered helplessly.

'We were never that close,' Louise sobbed. 'But she was my sister. I wish I'd told her.'

'Told her what?'

'How much I love her.'

Watching Vanessa's grief, Geraldine felt a spasm of guilt about her own adoptive sister with whom she had not spoken for several weeks. She resolved to call her that evening to ask how she was. Although they had been brought up together, they had never been really close, but they were still sisters. She couldn't imagine life without her.

31

'SO WHEN'S THE WEDDING?' Geraldine asked when she and Ariadne were settled with their drinks. 'I need to make sure it's in my diary.' She smiled at her friend. 'I've never attended a Greek wedding.'

'Don't worry,' Ariadne smiled back. 'You'll be there. In fact, I promise you'll be one of the first to receive an invitation. I wouldn't want to get married without you there to witness the ceremony. You've always been there for me,' she added, becoming serious. 'I want you to be at my wedding.'

'Well, as long as you don't expect me to be a bridesmaid and wear a frilly frock.'

They both laughed. It made a change from talking about the murder investigation. They were having a quiet drink together in a pub just outside the town centre, where they were unlikely to run into any of their colleagues.

'It's not that I don't want to see anyone else from work,' Ariadne had explained, when she had invited Geraldine to join her for a drink. 'It's just that it would be really nice to have a private natter once in a while. I miss our chats.'

Before Ian had moved in with Geraldine, she and Ariadne used to go out together quite regularly. Somehow, once Geraldine had no longer been living alone, her socialising with Ariadne had lapsed. Now Geraldine was on her own again and she had been pleased when Ariadne had suggested going out together.

'So,' Geraldine repeated, 'when's the happy day? Are you getting excited?'

Ariadne smiled uneasily. 'We haven't agreed when it's going to be yet,' she admitted. 'My mother keeps on at me, asking me if we've fixed a date and whether we've started looking at venues, and have we settled on a caterer, and chosen a photographer and a florist, and God knows what else besides, and she's desperate to come with me to choose a wedding dress.' Ariadne sighed. 'The trouble is, we really only want a small wedding with immediate family and a few close friends, but my mother's set on our having a huge traditional affair, with all my aunts and uncles and cousins. There are nearly fifty of them. Fifty! Can you imagine? And that's without Nico's family and any friends. I hardly even know some members of my extended family, and I don't like most of the ones I do know. In any case, Nico and I don't want to have anything like such a huge affair, but my mother's impossible. She's always been overpowering to say the least, but honestly, since I told her we're getting married, she's gone completely mental. She keeps sending me wedding magazines and brochures. Honestly, Geraldine, she's determined to wear me down. It's really hard, because she's got these really fixed ideas about what we ought to be doing, but it's not what I want.'

'It's your wedding,' Geraldine said firmly. 'It's up to you what you do.'

'I know, I know. I'm a forty-year-old detective sergeant. Direct me to make an arrest, and I'll be as fierce as you like. No one puts one over on me, no one throws me off balance. You know it's true, Geraldine. Whatever needs to be done, I'm there and I'll do the job, whatever it takes. But when my mother gets started, I'm like a child, and she takes charge of my life. I know she means well, and I don't want to upset her, but she's making this whole wedding thing impossible.'

She lowered her voice. 'I think she's been sending out invitations.'

'You have to talk to her.'

'I've tried, but she won't listen. And when she does listen to me, she cries. I know she's just being manipulative, but what am I supposed to do? She's completely set in her views. "This is what we've always done in our family," she says. It's true, actually. There are family traditions that go back generations. But so what? You'd think I was committing treason, the way she goes on about it.'

'You're happy with Nico, aren't you?'

'Yes. Yes, I am. He's a good man.' Ariadne paused and stared earnestly at Geraldine. 'You miss Ian, don't you?'

Caught off guard, Geraldine took a gulp of her pint and fidgeted with her glass, aware that Ariadne could see she was procrastinating.

'No, not especially,' she replied untruthfully. 'I mean, I do miss him, of course. We're good friends. We've known each other for more years than I care to remember.'

'So do you know where he is right now?'

'Me? No, of course not. Why would I?' Conscious that she was sounding defensive, she added, 'As far as I am aware, no one knows where he's gone. Do you know?'

Ariadne shook her head. 'There was a rumour he'd gone to London.'

'Listen,' Geraldine said, keen to change the subject.

Ariadne sat forward. 'Yes?'

'Are you sure about Nico?'

'What do you mean, sure about him? He's a hundred per cent committed.'

'Yes, but I meant you. I mean, you had a fling, didn't you?'

'Which lasted one night,' Ariadne replied, looking worried and shifting uncomfortably on her chair. 'And I ended it straight away. It was a mistake, Geraldine, no one else knows about it. You mustn't ever say anything to Nico. Not to anyone. You have to promise me. If Nico ever found out, it would be over between us, I know it would. It's not like he's weirdly possessive or anything, he's just old-fashioned.'

'I understand,' Geraldine assured her. 'I'd be just the same. But don't worry. You know you can rely on me to be discreet.'

'Which is why I don't know whether to believe you when you say you don't know where Ian is.'

They sat in awkward silence for a minute, each absorbed in their own thoughts.

'There's more snow forecast,' Geraldine said at last, doing her best to sound nonchalant.

'Yes, it's supposed to get worse. We're lucky Vanessa was found when she was,' Ariadne replied.

'Yes, the footprints might have been completely covered if we'd got there a few hours later,' Geraldine agreed. 'It's been snowing on and off all day.'

They engaged in desultory chat about the case while they finished their pints. Wistfully, Geraldine realised that Ariadne had reached out to her, but somehow the opportunity to be close again had faltered. They had made each other feel uncomfortable. Ariadne clearly regretted having confided in Geraldine about her fling with a colleague, while Geraldine couldn't bring herself to share details about her own private life with anyone, not even Ariadne. It wasn't much of a friendship, really, with neither of them comfortable confiding in the other. They speculated idly about Vanessa's killer, but it was more to fill the silence between them than for any other reason, and their remarks were vacuous.

'It could have been someone she knew, or a random stranger,' Geraldine remarked.

'Whoever it was, he appeared to have been hiding behind a tree,' Ariadne replied. 'Was he waiting for her specifically, do you think?'

They finished their pints. Neither of them suggested another one.

'Well, I have to be up early,' Geraldine said.

'Nico will be waiting for me.'

Hearing Ariadne's words brought home to Geraldine how lonely she was now Ian had left her. Somehow, the faintest hint of intimacy and she seemed to shrivel up inside and feel a need to escape. She got on well enough with her adoptive sister, but they lived two hundred miles apart and only saw one another occasionally, and in any case Geraldine couldn't speak freely to a sister who didn't understand her work at all. Ian was the only person she had ever felt able to be completely honest with and now he had gone, driven away by her reluctance to get close to anyone. By the time she reached her empty flat, Geraldine felt like crying. The evening had been a harsh disappointment. Telling herself she was just hungry, she made an omelette, and had an early night, but she couldn't sleep. Thinking about Vanessa, dying alone on the snowy ground, she wondered where Ian was, and if she would ever see him again. It was four days since she had heard from him, and for all she knew he might already be dead.

32

'THE ONLY LINK SO far between the two bodies is that they were both killed within around two weeks of each other and they were found only a few miles away from each other. It's a bit tenuous, but we have to consider there could be a connection between them,' Eileen said. 'In the meantime, we have to focus on gathering evidence. So far we've found nothing to connect them while they were alive.'

Geraldine sighed. Once again, it was frustrating that everything seemed so uncertain. Of course it usually was at this early stage in an investigation, but she was finding it harder than usual to cope with so much that was unresolved at work when her own life was such a mess. She sat at her desk all morning with her head down to avoid looking at Ariadne. At lunchtime, Ariadne stood up and left her desk without inviting Geraldine to join her. She might have had plans to meet someone else, but her abrupt departure felt rather pointed. Geraldine wondered miserably whether it had been a mistake to make friends with a colleague, let alone fall in love with one. She wished she had never set eyes on Ian, and hoped she wouldn't also regret becoming friends with Ariadne.

'You're looking down in the dumps,' Matthew remarked as he caught up with her in the corridor after her solitary lunch. 'Looking about as cheerful as I feel, in fact.'

'Never mind,' she replied, 'we've got a visit to the mortuary to look forward to. That's bound to cheer us up.'

He laughed. 'Oh yes, nothing like a trip to the mortuary to raise the spirits, eh? Are you ready?'

Remembering how Ian used to hate going to the mortuary, Geraldine felt a twinge of nostalgia, but she pulled herself together at once. This was not the time to wallow in self-pity. Thrusting her shoulders back and lifting her head, she forced a smile as she accompanied Matthew to the car. On the way there, they discussed what they knew so far about how Vanessa had died.

'Apart from the bumps on the head, there don't seem to be any similarities that I can see, not in the way they lived or in the way they died,' Matthew said.

Jonah nodded at them as they entered.

'You lot are keeping me far too busy for my liking,' he grumbled. 'Another body. That makes two in as many weeks. Can't you do something about all this killing? You're supposed to be keeping the streets safe, aren't you? Isn't that what you're paid to do?' He held up a bloody scalpel. 'If you lot can't do any better, I'm going to have to start carrying this around with me.'

'What do you suggest we do?' Matthew retorted, clearly stung by the criticism. 'We're doing everything we possibly can, but with all the cutbacks we're down to a skeleton staff as it is.'

'Please don't mention skeletons,' Jonah interrupted him, waving a bloody hand in the air and rolling his eyes. 'You know how squeamish I am.'

Geraldine burst out laughing. 'Don't take any notice of anything Jonah says. He's just trying to wind us up. Now, Jonah, be serious. What have you got for us? And it had better be good, after you upset Matthew like that.'

'Oh, I'm sorry,' Jonah replied. 'Let's make up. Shake?' He held out his bloody hand and Matthew started back, laughing.

'All right, let's take a look at this, shall we?' Jonah said, turning to the body lying on the table. 'She's been waiting patiently for some attention. Unusual in a woman, eh?' He looked up at Matthew and winked. 'Here goes. Female, mid to late forties.'

'Forty-one,' Geraldine corrected him.

Jonah raised his eyebrows. 'She hasn't aged well,' he murmured. 'Liver's all shot to pieces so it was probably the drink, and from the state of her lungs I'd say she was a heavy smoker. That would account for her raddled appearance. So, a forty-one-year-old, but not a healthy one,' he added, glancing at Geraldine with a mischievous glint in his eyes.

'Go on,' she said, ignoring his teasing. 'Let's get to how she died.'

'We're in a hurry today,' Jonah replied, but he turned back to the body and pointed to a neatly sewn-up bald patch just behind her temple. 'She hit the side of her head here. Given the bits of bark we picked out of her hair, she must have fallen against a tree of some sort.'

'Yes, well done. We've all seen the photos of the crime scene,' Geraldine said. 'In fact, I went there and saw the tree for myself. Was it the blow that killed her?'

Jonah nodded. 'Yes, ultimately, but she was probably unconscious by the time she hit her head, and she died very soon after.'

'There wasn't much blood,' Geraldine said.

'Most of the bleeding was internal, but she'd been strangled half to death before she hit her head anyway.'

Solemn now, he pointed to a long livid bruise on her throat. 'This injury was inflicted while she was alive. Either she somehow caught her neck in a noose, or else she was attacked from behind, by someone putting a belt or strap of some kind around her neck and pulling on it.'

'They pulled hard enough to bruise her, but not enough to kill her,' Geraldine said, and Jonah nodded. 'Would she have survived the strangulation if she hadn't fallen and suffered the head injury?'

Jonah sighed and shook his head. 'You know I hate to disappoint you by being vague, but it's impossible to say for sure. If you push me, I'd say it was unlikely she would have survived the strangulation, but it's possible. There's really no way of knowing.'

'So she was assaulted, but the attack wasn't necessarily fatal. The attack resulted in her falling and hitting her head and sustaining a fatal head injury. So are we looking at murder or not?'

Jonah shook his head again. 'That's for you to say. But if you ask me, she appears to have fallen over after losing consciousness when she was strangled nearly to death.'

'So it's all a result of the attack,' Matthew said. 'And she was murdered.'

'I wonder if her killer knew she was dead?' Geraldine said.

'What are you talking about? He tried to strangle her, didn't he?'

Geraldine nodded. 'But we don't know whether he actually succeeded in killing her.'

'She's dead, isn't she?' Matthew said.

'He didn't kill her with his bare hands,' Geraldine persisted.

'He was probably wearing gloves,' Jonah pointed out.

Geraldine ignored the interruption. 'He let go of her before she was dead, which means he might not have intended to kill her, only then she slipped and fell and hit her head, and that's what killed her. Her death could have been an accident.'

'And meanwhile her attacker scarpered and left her dying,' Matthew added. 'If he hadn't meant to kill her, why didn't he help her up or call for an ambulance after she fell and hit her head? He ran off and left her lying unconscious, if not dead – lying in the snow, where she would have frozen to death, if she hadn't already been killed. How can you possibly defend him?'

'I'm doing no such thing,' Geraldine protested. 'I'm just trying to understand what happened.'

'A murderer or a mugger killed her, that's what happened, and now we're going to find him and put him behind bars,' Matthew replied. 'Whether or not this was a premeditated murder, or a mugging that went wrong, he killed her.'

Put like that, it sounded perfectly simple.

'Yes, you're right,' she agreed. 'There's no point in overthinking this.'

When they were back at the police station, Eileen was strident in voicing her opinion that Vanessa had been murdered. Geraldine knew her colleagues were right, but she couldn't help wondering what had actually taken place on that empty patch of waste ground, early one freezing morning, when the elusive assailant had encountered his victim.

'I suppose we'll never know what really happened,' she murmured.

Eileen glared irately at Geraldine. 'We will when we find him,' she said.

33

'WHAT'S BEEN GOING ON?' Ian asked Jenny, when they met on their designated bench in a secluded corner of the park.

Her thick make-up was masked by large glasses with tinted lenses, and her hair and outfit were concealed beneath a long hooded grey coat. No one who spotted her walking along the street would recognise her or notice anything remarkable about a woman wearing a winter coat in January.

She sat down at the far end of the bench and shrugged. Taking her phone from the pocket of her coat she spoke quietly, so that Ian had to strain to hear what she said.

'There was some ruck at the club. Nothing out of the ordinary.'

She leaned forward to look at the ground as she spoke, as though afraid someone watching might read her lips.

'You need to be careful. Frank's after you.'

Ian took out his own phone and continued the conversation. With luck, anyone who chanced to see them would assume they were two strangers, both talking on their phones.

'Does he suspect who I am?' Ian asked, not daring to glance at Jenny.

'I don't think so. He would have said. And anyway, he's not clever enough to be discreet.' She paused. 'He's warned me about you, but he's never said anything specific. He just goes on and on about how he doesn't trust you, and I shouldn't trust you, and stuff like that. If he knew who you really were, he'd tell me straight away.' She paused again. 'He's a bit sweet on me, you know.'

There was another pause while they both considered Jenny's warning.

'He thinks I killed Nick,' Ian said. 'He's scared of me.'

'And he's jealous because Tod trusts you and took you on against his advice.' She paused again. 'Frank thinks he's Tod's number one man. You need to be careful. Frank takes his duties as Tod's bodyguard very seriously. He beat someone up really badly – broke his jaw in two places – just for pissing Tod off.'

Ian whistled. 'And there was me thinking he wouldn't hurt a fly.'

'Tod likes to keep his employees at loggerheads with each other,' Jenny went on. 'He deliberately sews seeds of discord among them.'

'Divide and rule?'

'I don't know. I think he just enjoys watching the strife,' she replied. 'And if there's a brawl, he looks on from a safe distance and laughs.'

'It probably makes him feel safe. His thugs are all kept busy vying with each other so they won't turn on him,' Ian said.

Jenny nodded. 'You could be right about that.'

A man entered the park with a small dog on a lead. As he passed them, Jenny continued her charade, pretending to be listening.

'Uh huh,' she said. 'Uh huh.'

Ian tapped at his phone as though he was texting while the stranger walked by. The man did a circuit of the small park and left by the gate he had entered through.

'What does Jack want me to do?' Ian asked, lifting his phone to his ear again.

'Just stay where you are and whatever you do don't blow your cover.' Jenny paused. 'I think Frank's been tailing me. I've thought so for a while. To be honest, it was bothering me quite a lot. I didn't know whether to mention it to Tod, but now I suspect it could be to do with you.' She turned and glanced at Ian. 'We're supposed to be together. I think you'd better come home with me tonight.'

'Is that a good idea? With Frank being keen on you, wouldn't it provoke him?'

'Damn it,' she replied, 'we're supposed to be an item, aren't we? It's one thing our not being all loved-up at the club – I'm still working the punters, don't forget – but if Frank sees we're never together he's going to smell a rat.'

'What's the address?'

'Never mind that. We'll leave together tonight.'

Jenny stood up and left without a backward glance. Ian waited half an hour before doing a circuit of the park and leaving by a different gate. That night, he left the club with Jenny.

'Put your arm round me,' she muttered as they saw Frank hovering in the doorway.

Frank scowled at them when they approached him.

'Night, Frank,' Jenny called out, blowing him a kiss.

Ian ignored him. The less attention he paid to the bouncer, the less reason Frank would have to suspect he was nervous when, in reality, he was terrified of him.

Jenny lived on the ground floor of a run-down old house not far from Archway station. The paintwork outside was peeling, the timber window frames were rotten, and there was a faint stench of drains in the tiny front yard where scraggy looking weeds poked up between the paving stones. A large plastic refuse bin dominated the area, overflowing with garbage. Jenny drew a brass key from her bag and opened the grimy blue door which led to a narrow hallway with stairs straight ahead and a door off to the left. A rusty bicycle all but blocked the access to the stairs, together with a pile of newspapers and magazines and a dreary looking rubber plant with only a few leaves sprouting from its woody stem. The dry earth in the pot was covered in cigarette butts and there was a stink of stale cigarette smoke in the hall. Selecting a second key from her ring, Jenny opened the internal door on the ground floor. Not until they were inside, with the door locked and bolted, did she speak.

'So far so good,' she said. 'I don't know what Frank suspects, but he's a moron and no one listens to him, so I wouldn't worry too much. I don't think Tod suspects a thing. It's not difficult to pull the wool over his eyes. I've been doing it for the best part of a year. But you do need to be careful. At the first sign that Tod seems to suspect anything, you'll need to make yourself scarce. Don't hang about if you think he could be on to you. Go and don't look back.'

'What about you?'

'What about me? I'll be all right. Tod has no idea who I am.'

'I wouldn't want to put you at risk for introducing me to Tod,' Ian replied. 'If Frank persuades him I'm dodgy, it might put you at risk.'

Jenny's expression softened unexpectedly. 'I can take care of myself,' she said. 'Come on in and make yourself comfortable while I get out of this gear.'

While she disappeared he took the opportunity to look around her living room. It was tastefully furnished with an expensive looking leather settee and matching armchairs, each with its own footstool. Along one wall, white shelves were filled with books, CDs and DVDs, all neatly arranged, and interspersed with small pot plants which appeared to be thriving. The decor was restful, pale blue and white, with thick blue velvet curtains at the window. It was the sort of room that might suit Jenny but would never be right for Tallulah. Ian smiled. Clearly Jenny hadn't brought any of her other contacts from the club home with her. He heard a shower running and shortly afterwards Jenny returned, her face clean of make-up, her hair loose, still with the colourful strands which he guessed were a permanent feature. She was wearing jeans and a T-shirt which wasn't loose enough to conceal her curves. She came over and sat on his lap.

'Working undercover, we have to do whatever we can to make it feel as realistic as possible. Just say the word if there's someone waiting for you and I'll back off. But if not...'

Leaning forward, she brushed his lips with hers. Ian hesitated before responding. Her body felt warm and firm against his, and Geraldine had decisively rejected him. He could continue to wait and hope she would change her mind, or he could throw himself into his new role with Jenny, who was offering him the comfort he craved. She pressed her lips more firmly against his and he didn't draw away.

Later on, when they were lying in bed together, he nuzzled her ear and told her he hadn't felt this comfortable for a long time.

'I mean it, Jenny,' he said. 'This is nice.'

She half sat up, leaning on one elbow, and gazed down at him, a serious expression on her face.

'I like you, Ian,' she said. 'I like you a lot. But we can't do this.'

He smiled lazily up at her. 'I thought we just did. And I seem to remember it was your idea I come home with you. Come here and kiss me.'

He started to pull her towards him, but she resisted.

'No,' she said. 'I mean, this is fine for Tallulah and Archie, right? But Jenny and Ian? I can't go there. It's too complicated.'

'So we're only doing this to stay in character?' he asked. 'Like method acting?'

'Something like that. It's not that I wouldn't want to with Ian, but it muddies the water if we are actually getting involved. You do see that, don't you? We can't afford to let our guard down for an instant. Frank's already watching you like a hawk, and we know he's been following me around. We have to stay alert.'

'It's all right,' he told her. 'I understand. This is fine, but it's just for now. For Tallulah and Archie. Now come here, Archie doesn't like to be kept waiting, and he's not a man to cross.'

She smiled and bent down to kiss him. 'Tallulah likes to keep Archie happy,' she said.

It struck Ian that this relationship with Jenny was more than a little strange, but it didn't really matter. He had no intention of becoming seriously involved with anyone other than Geraldine. He didn't think he could. In the meantime there was no harm in seeking fleeting comfort elsewhere. After all, this was Archie, not Ian. Although Archie had only come into existence for Geraldine's sake, he had no relationship with her and owed her nothing. Nevertheless, it felt strange lying in bed with Tallulah.

'Is this a bit weird?' he muttered, more to himself than to her,

She didn't answer.

34

VANESSA'S FACE HAD BEEN virtually undamaged in the attack, which made it easier for her next of kin to view her body and make a formal identification. There were times when a murder victim's features were damaged beyond recognition, making the process far more difficult for everyone concerned, and almost unbearable for the bereaved. Even though that was not the case with Vanessa, Geraldine was still dreading her next trip to see Louise. Asking people to identify the body of their loved one was one of the most troubling aspects of Geraldine's job, almost as painful as sharing the news of the death. People's reactions were impossible to predict. Some of them handled it with surprising equanimity, while others went completely to pieces.

Louise opened the door and scowled at Geraldine. 'When can we have her back?' she asked, as though she had been waiting for someone to call so that she could pose that question. 'We want her back right now,' she added.

'I'm afraid we can't release the body yet,' Geraldine replied quietly.

Louise's face reddened and her voice rose in pitch as she spoke. 'Not release the body? What do you mean, you can't release the body? You have no right to keep hold of her. She's my sister. We have to bury her. It's common decency, for Christ's sake. You let us notify the undertaker straight away, and bring her home, or I'm making a complaint. I'll take this up with the chief of police. The newspapers are going to hear of this. It will be all over the internet by tomorrow. You have no right to hang on to her any longer.'

'I'm sorry, but as I've already intimated, we're investigating the circumstances surrounding your sister's death,' Geraldine explained gently.

'Investigating the circumstances? What the hell is that supposed to mean? Oh my God,' Louise gasped, breaking off suddenly, her eyes widening in shock. 'Are you saying – was she – was she murdered?'

'That's what we're trying to ascertain. In the meantime, we need you to come and identify the body.'

'Identify the body?' Louise's eyes narrowed accusingly, and her voice rose even higher. 'Do you mean to tell me you're not sure it's Vanessa? You've put me through all this, and the body might not be her at all? I can't believe this. No, seriously, I just can't believe it.'

'I'm afraid we're certain it is your sister, but we would still like you to come along to the mortuary and formally identify her, as her next of kin.'

Louise was pale and shaking, and clearly on the point of bursting into tears.

'My sister–' Louise stammered helplessly. 'It can't be her. She's my sister.'

'I'm sorry,' Geraldine repeated, equally helpless.

Having faced other people's grief many times, she had learned that nothing she might say could help alleviate their distress. As an inexperienced officer, she used to try and comfort the bereaved, but however strong her own need to ease other people's suffering, she now understood that the recently bereaved were often beyond consolation. All she could do was speak kindly and gently as she guided them through the necessary procedure that followed a violent death.

They drove in silence to the mortuary where Geraldine led Louise along quiet corridors, past bustling medical and ancillary staff with their clipboards and trolleys, all busy tending to the sick and the living. When they arrived at the waiting room, she offered Louise a drink of water, and gestured to her to take a seat on the sofa. Pushing a box of tissues across the table so Louise could reach it, Geraldine sat down to wait. Before long, a mortuary assistant appeared and ushered them across the corridor to the room where Vanessa's body lay waiting. The dead woman's hair had been carefully combed across the bald patch on the side of her head, and the bruising on her neck had been skilfully concealed. She could have been asleep.

'She looks so peaceful,' Louise whispered, gazing down at her sister's white face.

'Can you confirm this is Vanessa?' Geraldine asked gently.

'Yes, yes, it's her,' Louise muttered, and burst into tears.

Recovering from her bout of weeping, Louise wiped her eyes and blew her nose vigorously as she followed Geraldine back to the waiting room.

'What happened to her?'

'We're trying to find out. Are you aware of anyone who might have wanted to hurt your sister, or been angry with her?'

'Hurt Vanessa? No, no. Are you saying she was attacked?'

'Did she have a boyfriend?'

Louise hesitated. 'There was a bloke, but it was a while ago, and they had a huge bust-up. She was really cut up about it.' She paused. 'I'm not sure which of them ended it, to be honest. They were only together for a few months, but she was talking about moving in with him before it all went pear-shaped. I never really did understand why. All she would say was that he was a bastard, and she never thought he would be so brutal, and a lot more along those lines. But she was just upset and I thought it was her anger and disappointment talking. You know how you get when you break up with someone? All bitchy and vindictive.'

The word 'brutal' interested Geraldine. The sight of the body seemed to have loosened Louise's tongue, and she seemed more inclined to talk about her sister. A few more questions revealed that her ex-boyfriend was called Gerry and he lived in York.

'That's as much as I know about him,' Louise said. 'We only met him the once, and he seemed like a nice enough bloke, but maybe there was more to him than I realised. I never actually asked her why it all went wrong between them. She was so upset, I didn't like to bring it up, and now–' She broke off, overcome with emotion again.

Geraldine made a note of Vanessa's ex-boyfriend's name. Having ascertained that Louise couldn't think of anyone else who might have been involved with Vanessa, Geraldine drove her home. It didn't take long to find the name Gerry stored on Vanessa's mobile, or to see from her records that she had called him numerous times over a period of about three months. Then, quite abruptly, the calls had ceased a month before she died.

'Well, that is interesting,' Eileen said. 'I think it's time we paid this ex-boyfriend a visit.'

35

GERRY HARRIS LIVED IN York, where he worked as a self-employed plumber. Geraldine and Matthew drove straight to his address off the Holgate Road, where he shared a house with his brother. They went there in the evening, and a swarthy thickset man with a mane of dark hair and shaggy eyebrows answered the door.

'We're looking for Gerry Harris,' Matthew said.

'Oi! Gerry!' the man called out over his shoulder. 'There's someone here with a job!'

A wiry version of the man who had opened the door appeared behind him.

'I'm sorry,' he said, stepping forward. 'Have I done some work for you? I'm usually very good with faces.'

He gazed from Matthew to Geraldine and back again with a faintly puzzled frown.

'No, you haven't done any work for us, and we're not here about a plumbing job,' Matthew said.

'How do you know where I live?' Gerry asked, glancing at his brother.

Geraldine held out her identity card. 'We think you might be able to help us with an enquiry.'

Gerry frowned. 'Oh, I see. Well,' he looked uncertain. 'I suppose you'd better come in then.'

Once they were seated in the kitchen with Gerry, Matthew enquired about his relationship with Vanessa.

'Vanessa? Don't tell me she's in trouble with the law?'

Gerry asked with a grimace. 'That's terrible, although I can't say I'm completely surprised. What's she gone and done? Robbed a bank? I wouldn't put it past her.' He gave a little laugh. 'And how can I help you? I haven't seen her in – oh, it must be about three months – so I'm not sure I'll be able to tell you anything you don't already know.'

'Why did you split up?' Geraldine enquired gently.

If Gerry was taken aback by the intrusive nature of the question into something so personal, he didn't show it.

'Vanessa's a lovely girl,' he said. 'A beautiful girl. I was very fond of her.' He sighed. 'But I couldn't cope with her problem.'

'What problem?' Geraldine asked.

Gerry gave another little laugh. 'You're right there. Take your pick. The drinking got bad, but it wasn't that. No, it was the gambling I couldn't take. Vanessa lost a lot of money, I mean a serious amount of money, enough to make your eyes water. And the trouble was she wouldn't stop. I mean, we can all let things get out of control, but she refused to accept she had a problem. She went through money like water. My money. Oh, you wouldn't think it to look at her. She looks the picture of respectability and good sense, doesn't she? But it's like she's obsessed. You know, they're right to call it an addiction. It's a bloody outrage, all that online gambling. In the privacy of their own homes, people can get sucked in, with no one there to regulate what's going on. Those adverts make me laugh,' he added, with a sudden burst of irritation. 'What is it they say? "When the fun stops, stop." That's a joke. To an addict it's not "fun", it's a compulsion. They can't stop. That's the whole point. And losing money's no fun. I hated it and I'm sure she did too. But she couldn't stop. It's a kind of wilful blindness.'

'There is help available–' Geraldine began.

'I know, I know. I tried to stop her. I did my best to be

sympathetic, listen to her, you know. And when that didn't make a blind bit of difference, I encouraged her to join a support group, Gamblers Anonymous they call themselves. But she flatly refused to admit she needed help. She thought she could control her habit. It got to the point that if I even mentioned helping her, she would fly into a rage. "If you loved me you'd support me," she used to say. It was as plain as the nose on your face she was addicted, yet she insisted she could stop whenever she wanted. She never accepted she had a problem. She kept telling me she would stop, but there was always going to be one last throw of the dice, one last game before she packed it in. If I heard that once, I must have heard it a thousand times. I'm telling you, she cost me a packet. I loaned her two grand which I'll never see again, but that wasn't enough. She was on at me all the time to bail her out.' He raised his hands in a gesture of despair. 'I mean, I do all right, but I'm not made of money. Eventually I had to say enough was enough. I told her if she couldn't stop throwing money away, *my* money, we were through. I wasn't going to give her another penny. We fell out over it, and that was the last I saw of her.'

'And you haven't heard from her for three months?'

'I couldn't give you an exact date, but that sounds about right, yes. She accused me of caring more about my money than her. Honestly, I wanted both, but she was bankrupting me. Once all my money had gone, I suspect she would have dumped me anyway,' he added sadly. 'If she'd made an effort, I would have been there for her. Honestly, I would. I wanted to help her. But she wouldn't even try to stop. There are people who can help gambling addicts like Vanessa, but she just didn't want to know. You have to understand it was an impossible situation. I had to end it. So, what's she done to get herself in trouble with the law?'

'I'm afraid Vanessa's been murdered.'

'Murdered? You mean she's dead? Vanessa's dead?'

'I'm afraid so.'

Gerry looked genuinely distressed by the news.

'What happened?'

'That's what we're trying to find out,' Geraldine said. 'Can you think of anyone who might have wanted to harm her?'

Gerry shook his head. 'I didn't actually know her for very long. We were together for less than six months, and I never met any of her friends. I met her sister once, but that was it. I don't think she had many friends. People probably got fed up with her borrowing money and never paying it back, but that's just supposition.'

There was nothing more Gerry could – or would – tell them and they left soon after. A little research confirmed Gerry had transferred sums of money totalling more than two thousand pounds to Vanessa's account, in the three months when he had been seeing her.

'I wonder if Vanessa owed someone else money, someone who wasn't as patient or as understanding as Gerry,' Eileen said thoughtfully.

There was no new activity in Vanessa's bank account to support such a theory, but they couldn't rule it out. Vanessa's sister told them Gerry was the last man Vanessa had been in a serious relationship with, but she might not have known everything her sister did. Certainly Gerry did not seem to be the vicious character Louise had made him out to be. The investigating team had gone from a possible suspect with no clear motive, to an obvious motive with no suspect.

'We need to find out who else Vanessa was associating with before she died,' Eileen said.

'Yes, let's just find out who she was with when she was attacked and killed,' Ariadne muttered to Geraldine. 'That would help. Why didn't we think of that before?'

36

THERE WAS SOME DISCUSSION at the police station concerning Vanessa's ex-boyfriend, Gerry, and more focusing on her sister, Louise. Some of the officers found it strange that Louise had no idea whether her sister was seeing other men. Others were surprised that anyone would find that hard to believe.

'I get on very well with both my sisters,' Susan said, 'but I have no idea what they're getting up to most of the time, particularly my younger sister. Although, to be fair, I have a pretty good idea and, to be honest, I'd rather not know.'

'But Louise knew all about Gerry,' Ariadne pointed out.

'I wouldn't say that,' Geraldine said. 'Gerry told us he was seeing Vanessa for about three months, and in all that time he only met Louise once.'

Back at home that evening, Geraldine reviewed everything they knew so far about Vanessa. It wasn't much. She wondered why Louise hadn't mentioned her sister's gambling problem. It was quite likely she hadn't known about it. Geraldine resolved to speak to Louise again the next morning. For now, she was determined to relax and unwind. Too tired to cook, she opened a can of beans and put a couple of slices of sourdough bread in the toaster. Deciding against wine, she brewed a pot of Earl Grey tea and sat down in front of the television. Her simple meal reminded her how Ian used to cook for her. She wondered what he was doing, and whether he was grilling himself a steak, or making do with something far humbler, as she was.

He might even be cooking for someone else, although she doubted it. He wasn't the kind of man who would flit straight into another relationship after a break up. Knowing Ian, he was more likely to be thinking about her.

For the first time since Ian had left York, she genuinely regretted having sent him away. Somehow she had believed they would get back together before long. For the first time it struck her that she didn't know if he would ever return. The possibility that she might really never see him again hit her like a blow to the stomach and she felt physically sick. They had been friends for so long before finally becoming lovers, life without him was unthinkable. She wanted to feel angry with him for abandoning her, but she knew she had only herself to blame. With renewed energy she threw herself into the investigation, rereading everything she could find about Vanessa. She didn't discover anything new, but it helped to take her mind off her own troubles.

She drove to Louise's house early the following morning, hoping to catch her at home, and Louise answered the door in a white towelling dressing gown.

'Oh, it's you,' she said, starting forward and asking a series of questions. 'Is it over? Can we have the body? Do you know who did it?'

'No, I'm afraid we've not concluded our investigation, and we can't release the body just yet. We don't yet know what happened to her. I would like to ask you a few more questions.'

Seeing Louise's disappointment, Geraldine reiterated her condolences.

'I have a sister,' she added. 'We don't get on all the time, but if I were in your situation, and it was my sister who had been murdered, I'd want to do everything in my power to help the police find out who did it and bring him to justice.'

'Do you think I don't want to see him arrested and locked up?' Louise burst out angrily.

'Help us find him, then. Please. We want to find out who did this and put him behind bars before he attacks anyone else.'

Louise sighed and hung her head. 'You'd better come in then.'

When they were standing in the hall, Louise stared levelly at Geraldine without inviting her further into the house.

'Go on, then, what do you want to know?'

'Your sister didn't have a job, did she?'

'No, but...'

'What did she live on? She had rent to pay. How did she pay her bills?'

'We each receive a modest annuity from our parents' estate. They died in a car accident twenty-five years ago,' Louise added, by way of explanation.

'I'm sorry. That must have been terrible, losing both your parents at the same time like that.'

Louise nodded. 'For a while afterwards, Vanessa and I were inseparable. She was only sixteen and it hit her hard. What am I saying? It hit both of us really hard. You never really recover from something like that.'

'Was that when she started gambling?'

Louise's astonishment appeared genuine. 'Gambling? What do you mean? Vanessa didn't gamble.'

'Gerry told us Vanessa was addicted to gambling.'

'Nonsense. I would have known.' Louise hesitated, as though she had just remembered something.

'Please, Louise, no one wants to sit in judgement over Vanessa. We simply want to find out who killed her. Is there anything more you can tell us about her? '

'My sister didn't gamble,' Louise repeated doggedly, but she no longer sounded sure.

'Did you ever lend her any money?'

Louise fidgeted with the belt of her robe.

'Well, yes. From time to time. I didn't mind. We were sisters. We always had each other's backs.'

'And did she pay you back?'

'It didn't matter,' Louise muttered, lowering her eyes to stare at the floor.

'Did she borrow money from anyone else?'

Louise shook her head helplessly. 'How should I know? Presumably Gerry lent her money or you wouldn't be here asking me about it.'

'Thank you. That's been helpful.'

If Vanessa had been addicted to gambling, either she had been in denial about her problem, or else she had been too ashamed to admit to it.

'Was she killed by someone she had borrowed money from?' Louise asked, indignation briefly eclipsing her grief.

'It's possible. Can you think of anyone who might have lent her money and then become angry when she didn't pay her debt?'

'Apart from me, you mean?' Louise said, with a fleeting grin. Her face fell when Geraldine didn't return her smile. 'That was a joke,' she said hurriedly. 'I never asked her to pay me back. I didn't mind giving her money. It wasn't much, just a little to help her out every now and again. Hardly anything, really. She always seemed to be strapped for cash.' She frowned. 'She was repeatedly short for the rent, or she needed a new pair of shoes. There was always a reason why she needed a loan, never very much, and never repaid. I knew whenever I lent her money, I'd never see it again, but she was my sister. What else could I have done when she needed money? But I never knew she was gambling her money away. Gambling *my* money away, I should say. That's why she never had any money, isn't it? I never imagined...' She sighed. 'You think you know someone but it turns out in the end you never really knew them at all.'

With a pang, Geraldine wondered what Ian was doing and when he was planning to return. Returning to the police station, she caught up with the latest developments. The team was buzzing with the news that a trace of male DNA found on Vanessa matched the DNA found on Pansy. Geraldine learned that a frozen globule from a mist of human breath had been detected on Vanessa's freezing cold face. They were unable to identify the owner of the DNA, but they now had evidence to show the same man had been present at both killings. This was turning into a more serious case than they had first suspected. The new evidence suggested that Vanessa's death had not resulted from a chance mugging that had gone wrong, but from an attack by a man who had already killed, and might do so again.

37

JENNY TOLD IAN THAT she often caught sight of Frank parked outside her apartment. Frank stalking Jenny gave Ian a germ of an idea for how to undermine Tod's trust in his bodyguard. But that was for the future. Right now, Ian had a more immediate problem to deal with. He needed to make his way from Jenny's apartment to the park without being spotted. Jenny lent him a black beanie hat, a grey scarf, and an old coat. Baggy on her, it just about fitted Ian. Any man leaving Jenny's block was likely to attract Frank's attention and, despite his crude camouflage, Ian would almost certainly be recognised. He could do nothing to disguise his height or his build from someone looking out for him. He hung about in the entrance hall until a thin middle-aged Asian woman came scurrying down the stairs.

'Excuse me,' Ian accosted her.

'What? What?' the woman replied, backing away with an expression of alarm. 'What do you want with me?'

'I'm sorry, I didn't mean to startle you,' Ian said gently. He considered disclosing his real identity but decided against it. Instead he said, 'I don't know London at all. I'm here visiting my sister, and she's run out of milk. I'm not surprised, to be honest. It's typical of her.'

The woman looked at him suspiciously, but she didn't move away and he carried on.

'I thought I'd pop out to the shops before she wakes up, and surprise her with it. The only trouble is I've no idea where the nearest shop is. I wonder if you would be kind enough to point me in the right direction?'

If this ruse failed, Ian would have to wait for someone else to come along, and he didn't know how much time he could afford to waste. To his relief, the woman was as obliging as Ian had hoped she might be.

'There's a corner shop by the station where you can get milk, and other groceries,' she said.

'Thank you. And which way is the station from here?' Ian pointed vaguely in the wrong direction.

'Come along, I'm going to the station myself. I'll show you the way. It's quite straightforward really.'

'If you're sure you don't mind my walking with you?'

The woman had not actually invited him to accompany her, but she nodded uncertainly.

'No, that's okay.'

Ian thanked her, and together they left the building. He positioned himself furthest from the kerb, so that the woman was between him and Frank's car, shielding him from view. Side by side they walked along the street to the station where they parted. Although Ian wanted to go to the station as well, he went into the small grocery shop instead, and looked around there for a while. Once he was confident the woman would have caught her train, he slipped out of the shop and into the station, leaving Frank still sitting in his car outside Jenny's block. Safely on the platform, Ian called Jack to let him know he was on his way. Half an hour later, they were sitting on the park bench, a foot apart, holding their phones to their ears as they discussed the situation.

'It sounds like you've gained Tod's trust,' Jack said.

'Yes, I think so,' Ian replied, conscious that he was playing a dangerous double game.

If Jack discovered that he had conducted a private deal of his own with Tod, the Anti-Corruption Unit would be at Ian like a ferret on a rat and he would not only be immediately suspended, he would probably end up behind bars himself.

'The thing is,' Ian went on, 'he thinks I bumped Nick off and that's what got me in with him. As long as Nick never resurfaces, with any luck there shouldn't be a problem.'

Jack grunted. 'Maybe. Even so, don't let your guard down even for a second. He's a tricky bastard and you can't afford to let anything slip.'

'I know that.'

'What about Jenny?'

'What about her?' Ian answered with a question, looking away to conceal his unease.

He wondered whether Jenny had told Jack that he had spent the night in her bed. With a cold feeling down his spine, he realised it was even possible it had been Jack's idea for her to sleep with him. Perhaps Jack didn't trust Ian, and had asked Jenny to keep a watchful eye on him. What better way was there for her to observe him than by inviting him to share her bed? Ian shivered. His undercover role and his own subterfuge within that framework were making him paranoid. He hated the way the work was changing him. He was shaken by a sudden longing to see Geraldine's face, and hold her in his arms again. She had pushed him away, and hurt him so deeply he still ached whenever he thought of her, but he had never for one moment doubted her honesty.

His new set of colleagues and associates were very different. He didn't know who he could trust. Probably no one. He himself had become the most duplicitous of all, and he had slipped into it so easily. Now he didn't know how he was ever going to be able to return to his former life. He had no idea where his relationship with Jenny was heading, if they were even in a relationship. He wasn't in love with her, and she had given no indication that she had any serious feelings for him. On the contrary, she had made it quite clear that the affair was between Tallulah and Archie, and it needed to stay that way. The truth was, as Ian and Jenny they hardly knew anything about one another. He rather thought he was just a passing fancy for her, as she was for him, but thinking about her now, he was uncomfortable with that idea and resolved to try and avoid her. Perhaps they could say they had split up now that Jenny had done her job and introduced Ian into Tod's circle. If she was becoming emotionally attached to him, that might be unkind, but it would surely be better for her than if he allowed her to believe he was beginning to care for her. He sighed. It was just the kind of emotional problem he would once have been able to discuss with Geraldine, only of course that was out of the question.

'You don't think there's any chance Tod might suspect her?' Jack asked.

Once again Ian hesitated. He didn't know whether Jenny had told Jack about Frank's surveillance on her, and wished he had thought to ask her. On balance, he decided it was best to say nothing. Even if Jenny had spoken to Jack about it, he wouldn't know that Ian was aware of the problem. In any case, like Jenny said, she could look after herself. She had done before Ian turned up and there was no reason to suppose that would change. But he felt uneasy, afraid his actions might have compromised her safety.

'I don't see why he should be on to her,' he replied cautiously. 'She seems to be very well established at the club.'

'Yes, she said it's helping a lot having you there to shield her from unwelcome attention.'

Ian squirmed on the bench and gave a feeble smile, wondering what else Jenny had told Jack.

'I'm glad to know our fake relationship's helping her,' he muttered.

'Now,' Jack went on, 'what are we going to do about Tod? You know we've been watching him for a while. Jenny's been there, keeping her ear to the ground for nearly a year, and we know he's running a pretty sizeable drug ring. But we don't think he's at the top of the tree, not by any means. No, there's someone else receiving the drugs into the country and we want to find out who. It's no good constantly shaking the tree and watching the small fry drop out, we want to fell the whole bloody tree, and wipe out the lot of them. Get back in there, Ian. You need to become his right-hand man and make sure he takes you into his confidence.'

Ian nodded. 'I think I can see a way,' he said. 'If I can persuade Tod to suspect Frank of being disloyal, then he might promote me to the position of personal bodyguard, meaning I'll be at his side far more. At the moment it's not easy to get anywhere near him without Frank turning up to elbow me aside. I've only been in the room alone with Tod briefly on a couple of occasions.'

There was no need to explain how that had come about.

'Go for it,' Jack said. 'And if you need us to pick Frank up and take him off your hands, just give us enough rope to hang him with and we'll do the rest. It will be one less drug-pedalling thug on the streets.'

38

JACK WAS RELYING ON Ian to position himself between Frank and Tod but that wasn't going to be easy.

'It seems to me you got two options,' Jack was saying. 'You could try and drive a wedge between them. Force Tod to distrust Frank sufficiently to want to distance himself from him, and that will allow you to step neatly into the vacuum.'

Glancing casually around with a sweep of his eyes, Ian saw Jack grin at the neatness of the scheme he himself had just proposed. What Jack didn't know was that Tod knew exactly who he was dealing with, and Ian was the last person he was ever likely to trust with information pertaining to his drug ring.

'The other possibility would be to enlist our help in removing Frank from the club. You would have to work out some way to have Frank arrested so that we can keep him under lock and key for a while, without arousing Tod's suspicion.'

Ian hesitated. Either of those plans would be more difficult to implement than Jack realised now that Tod knew Ian was a cop. He was hardly likely to trust anything Ian said to discredit Frank. On the other hand, if Frank was arrested, Tod was bound to realise that Ian had something to do with it.

'Funny that,' he might say, rubbing his long fingers together and staring at Ian across his desk. 'You turn up randomly and Frank gets nicked. And now you think you can step into his shoes, just like that? Like he was never here? Well, you can piss right off if that's what you think.'

Frank had been working for Tod for years. Somehow Ian would have to find a way to discredit Frank that didn't appear to involve Ian at all, so that Tod felt he had sacked Frank on his own initiative. That wasn't without its risks. Possessed of a certain low cunning, Frank was almost certain to realise what was going on and retaliate.

'What about Jenny?' Jack enquired. 'Surely she must have something on Frank?'

Ian hesitated again, but he couldn't explain to anyone, least of all Jack, that it would be dangerous for Jenny if she were to cause any hint of dissent or trouble at the club. Now she had introduced Ian to Tod, she needed to keep her head down or Tod might suspect the truth that Ian was only posing as her boyfriend, and she was in on the deception. So far, there was no reason to think that Tod might suspect Jenny knew about Ian's true identity. But it was impossible to discern what anyone was really thinking in this strange world of double lives. Tod must already be wondering if she was an undercover cop too. Ian couldn't do anything that might risk blowing her cover. He had tried to salvage his relationship with Geraldine by enabling her to see her twin sister again, but in his zeal he had overlooked Jack and his plans. Now he could only hope he hadn't endangered Jenny's life in the execution of a plan that had seemed foolproof.

'Let me have a think,' Ian said. 'I'll come up with something.'

He had no idea what to do, but somehow he had to discredit Frank without anyone discovering who was behind it. With Frank out of the way, he would somehow have to convince Tod that he had switched allegiance and was now genuinely loyal to Tod. Gradually, a plan began to form in his mind that wouldn't have to rely on involving Jenny, or anyone else. All it needed was for Jack to put in place a false trail to establish Ian as an inveterate gambler. Heavy debt could explain his eagerness to switch his loyalty from the police to Tod. And after that, Frank could be discredited.

That evening, Ian called on Tod.

'I need to speak to you alone,' he said.

'Get your arse in here,' Tod replied.

Frank opened the door and growled when Tod dismissed him, muttering under his breath as he left.

'I need an advance,' Ian said quickly, before anyone could come along and disturb them.

Tod looked up from his desk in surprise. 'What?'

A sarcastic grin creased his left eye half closed, while his jagged scar pulled at the skin on his right cheek so that eye remained wide open, giving his face a lopsided appearance, like a villain in a Bond movie. The scar had obviously been made by a broken bottle. Ian didn't like to ask the fate of the man who had inflicted that injury.

'Two fat pay rolls not enough for you?' Tod went on, his grin fading. 'What the fuck you doing? You burning notes? You got your dosh from the filth, and you got your dosh from me. What the fuck, Archie?'

Ian shook his head. 'I'm not as well off as you think. A policeman's salary is a joke.' He did his best to sound aggrieved. 'It doesn't even begin to cover my debts. That's how I ended up here in the first place. I had to find another source of income somewhere before the whole thing blew up in my face. When I met Tallulah and she told me she worked here and knew the big boss, it was too good an opportunity to miss. Tallulah wasn't keen, but I persuaded her to introduce me to you and, well, you know the rest.'

Ian took a deep breath, and tried to control his shaking. He had so nearly called her Jenny.

'You got the debt hounds after you?' Tod stared at Ian, his black eyes unblinking. 'How come?'

'Just the odd bet,' Ian said, trying to sound as though he was deliberately playing it down. 'It's not like it's serious.

Not like I've got a habit.' He did his best to look abashed yet defiant. 'All I need is a small bung. Maybe a grand. Just enough to get me back in there. The thing is, I had a run of bad luck and now, just as my luck's about to turn, I'm flat broke. It couldn't be worse timing. You've got to help me out. I'll pay you back. But you can't tell anyone. Tallulah would go nuts if she knew. And if my DCI ever found out I'd be in serious shit. This stays between us.' He glared at Tod, his desperation genuine.

If Tod believed Ian was bent, and stood to lose more than his job if his secret gambling habit ever became known, then Tod would trust him, because he would know that Ian couldn't risk exposure. Tod stared at him in silence for a moment, and Ian held his breath. It didn't matter if he looked nervous now. It was ironic. Tod believing Ian had a secret gambling addiction might give him a stronger feeling of power over Ian than his knowledge that Ian had killed Nick. But Nick's body had disappeared without trace. The police would easily have been able to find evidence of Ian's gambling habit, had it actually existed.

Just as Ian was mentally preparing to look disappointed, and plead for money, Tod laughed.

'This boy needs casino juice.'

Ian waited, scarcely able to believe he had succeeded in fooling Tod.

'You're my boy,' Tod crowed.

Ian nodded warily. 'I have to be careful.'

'Forget careful. Dammit all, I have my very own police protection now.' Tod laughed again and slapped himself on the knee. 'I got you now.' He held out a cupped hand. 'Got you where I want you. My very own private policeman.'

Ian wondered if he was being rash in warning Tod straight away that there was a mole in his organisation, but he needed to act quickly. Taking a deep breath, he shared the disturbing news that it was true about there being a police informer working at the club.

The smile vanished from Tod's face. 'You messing with me? It's for real we got a squealer? Who is it?' he demanded, rising to his feet, his face red with anger. Only his scar remained a livid white. 'Tell me. Tell me and I'll rip his balls off with my bare hands.'

'It must be someone very close to you, someone who knows all about you.'

'No fucker knows all about me,' Tod growled, subsiding into his chair. 'You find out who it is, Archie, and you come to me with a name. Do it and do it now! I'll rip his throat out with my bare hands. I'll drop him off the top of the tallest building. Fuck it, Archie, you find out who it is or you're a dead man. But first,' he added, with a sly look at Ian, 'I've gotta see if your story checks out.'

Ian's life depended on Jack having done a good job.

39

GERALDINE'S NEXT TASK WAS to visit Vanessa's last place of work, which she had left six months earlier. She had been employed at a jeweller's shop in town where she had worked for just over two years. The interior was elegantly set out, with a central island displaying women's jewellery, and cabinets of watches and fake crystal household ornaments around the walls. A young girl with long blonde hair stepped forward with a smile when she entered the shop, and Geraldine had the impression the sales girl was sizing her up, calculating how affluent she might be from her clothes and shoes. Geraldine returned the smile, confident that her own appearance gave little away. Plain black jeans, fairly new, a brown leather jacket, slightly faded on the elbows but originally expensive, and sturdy flat black shoes with no designer logo. With her short black hair and minimal make-up she had heard herself described as anything from 'beautiful' and 'classy' to 'butch' and 'fierce'. When she wasn't smiling she gave an impression of severity. One of her colleagues had told her she reminded him of his former headmistress. Geraldine had not been sure whether to take that as a compliment or a criticism. But now she was smiling warmly at the sales girl.

'I'd like to enquire about a former colleague of yours,' she said.

The girl's smile faded slowly as she understood Geraldine was not asking about an item of jewellery.

'Did you want to make a purchase?' she asked, still

hankering after a sale. 'We have a lot of lovely rings massively reduced. And we can do you a special deal, just for today,' she added, reluctant to abandon her sales patter.

'Thank you but I'm here to ask a few questions.'

'What's this? What's this?'

A fussy little man joined them. As he spoke, his pencil moustache twitched like a thin black caterpillar on his upper lip.

'What's this?' he repeated, rubbing his stubby fingers together.

'This customer has a question,' the girl replied, with a sullen glance at Geraldine.

'Yes, yes,' the man said. 'I'm the manager. What seems to be the problem? I'm afraid there's no return on sale items, but if there's a loose setting we can fix it for a minimal charge.'

'I'm not interested in making a purchase today,' Geraldine told him. 'And I've not come here to complain. I want to ask you a few questions about a former employee, Vanessa Slattery.'

The man took a step back. 'Yes, well, Vanessa doesn't work here any longer and I'm not at liberty to give out any details. You understand that, I'm sure.'

Geraldine held up her identity card and the blonde girl drew in a breath. The manager frowned and nodded.

'I can't say I'm surprised,' he murmured.

'What makes you say that?' Geraldine asked.

The manager hesitated and glanced at her identity card again before inviting her to accompany him into the office. Geraldine followed him through an internal door at the back of the shop. The blonde sales assistant watched them curiously. The shop floor was pristine, with sparkling jewellery artistically displayed behind gleaming glass in every display cabinet. In complete contrast, the office at the back of the shop was squalid, with printed documents and empty food wrappers littering the surface of filing cabinets, along with half a dozen cups stained with tea and coffee. On a small desk in the centre of the room, a computer rose like a volcanic island from a sea of folders, papers, pencils, biros, small jewellery boxes and bags, rolls of Sellotape, rubber bands, staplers and paper clips and other random small items of stationery. Two white plastic chairs were covered with more papers and folders.

The manager shrugged apologetically at Geraldine as if to say he would like to invite her to take a seat but it just wasn't possible. With a shrug of her own, she carefully removed a pile of papers from one of the chairs and placed it on the floor before sitting down. The manager cleared the other chair, and sat down facing her.

'You wanted to ask me about Vanessa Slattery?' he said.

'You said that didn't surprise you. Why was that?'

'I'm not sure I feel comfortable breaking a confidence.'

'If it helps you decide whether to withhold information from me, I am very sorry to tell you that Vanessa is dead.'

'Dead?'

The manager looked genuinely startled. He stared at Geraldine, his top lip working as he cast around for a suitable response, while his moustache jiggled comically. In a low voice he asked what had happened.

'How well did you know Vanessa?' Geraldine replied to his question with one of her own.

'We worked together. She was here for about two years, but I can't say we knew one another well. We shared an interest in gemstones. Our collection is quite lovely, as you no doubt noticed as you crossed the shop floor. How did she die?'

'Why did she leave her job here?'

The manager heaved a sigh. 'It didn't work out,' he said, looking at the floor and avoiding Geraldine's gaze.

'In what way did it not work out? I don't want to press you but I really do need to know exactly what happened here.'

'Oh, very well, she was accused– that is, I suspected...'

'Was she stealing money or jewellery?'

'Yes, no, that is, I don't know. Nothing was ever proved. I mean, it was, she confessed, but she paid it all back and left. We agreed to let her go quietly.'

'What about a reference?'

'That was difficult. In the end, I wrote that she was hard working and pleasant, but incompetent with money.'

'Incompetent?'

'Yes, I wanted to warn any future employer that she couldn't be trusted around money. If I'd said she was stealing, she would never have got another job. And she only stole because she needed to pay for her sick mother's care,' he added. 'What other choice did I have, really?'

Geraldine didn't tell him that Vanessa's mother had died around twenty-five years before she started working at the jeweller's shop. Clearly she had taken the money to fund her gambling habit. The truth was even sadder than the manager had believed.

'Do you know if she was in a relationship?'

'A relationship?'

'Was she living with anyone while she worked here?'

'Oh yes, she lived with her mother.'

'And did she have a boyfriend?'

'I really have no idea. We didn't discuss such matters,' he said, as though it was somehow distasteful for anyone to talk about personal matters with their colleagues at work.

'Was the young girl in the shop working here with Vanessa?'

'No, she replaced Vanessa. There are only two of us employed here at any one time. We're a small shop and we have to keep overheads down.'

With a sigh, Geraldine stood up to leave. There was nothing

more to learn from the manager who had worked with Vanessa for two years without knowing anything about her that was true, apart from the fact that she was a thief.

40

WITH TOD'S THREAT RINGING in his ears, Ian hurried out of the office. The situation had developed so rapidly, he had lost control almost before he realised what was happening, and he felt helpless to stop his own inexorable descent into wrongdoing. As a police officer, he of all people should have known better. Having seized the opportunity to land Frank in trouble with Tod, he was shaken by compunction. There was no denying he had as good as signed Frank's death warrant. Admittedly, Frank was a vicious thug and a bully, a psychopath who was doubtless responsible for multiple injuries and 'accidents'. All the same, as a police officer, Ian's duty was to investigate and gather evidence against him so that Frank could be called to account for his crimes in a court of law. It was not for Ian to effectively order a criminal's unofficial execution, but he was trapped in a horrendous situation of his own making and couldn't see a way out.

Ian couldn't refuse to follow Tod's instructions without arousing his suspicions. Given that Ian was double-crossing his new boss, that was a dangerous path to follow. Not only that, but if he failed to gain Tod's trust, he would be letting Jack down. It might be a long time before another police officer managed to get as close to Tod as swiftly and effectively as Ian had done. But the course of action Ian now seemed destined to pursue was almost certain to end another man's life. Even taking into account that Frank was a violent criminal, causing his death went against everything Ian believed in. He had spent his life pursuing killers and seeing them brought to justice. Now he was actually considering setting up just such an unlawful killing himself. Not for the first time, he wished he could discuss his dilemma with Geraldine. He had never felt more alone.

Leaving the office, he found Frank standing guard at the entrance to the club. Ian took up his position ready to check customers' bags as they came in. It was a token inspection. People could easily smuggle drugs on to the premises concealed in their clothes, and everyone was aware they were simply going through the motions. No sooner had Ian taken his place than Jenny turned up and came over to stand close to him.

'I'll see you tonight,' she whispered, putting her arms round his neck. 'Watch out for Frank.'

Ian tensed, wondering how Jenny knew he was going after Frank.

'He's been pursuing me for months,' she added.

Ian sighed. That was a further complication he could manage without, but at least Frank wasn't aware that Ian was about to tell Tod that Frank was a police informer. Peering over Jenny's shoulder, he saw Frank scowling at him and lowered his eyes. Jenny walked off and Ian resumed his post. All this time Frank remained standing by the door, glowering at Ian. Visibly shifting his weight from one foot to another, he appeared to be considering launching himself at Ian. All at once, he strode across the hall and leaned down until he was close enough for Ian to feel warm breath on his neck.

'I know all about you,' Frank murmured hoarsely.

With an effort, Ian held his ground and glared back at his antagonist.

'I've no idea what you're on about,' he snarled, 'so you can fuck off with your empty threats. You think you scare me?'

'I know what you're trying to do,' Frank went on, his cheeks flushed with anger, 'trying to weasel your way in here. Well, the boss might trust you but I don't and I'm going to have you out of here before you see what's coming. If you know what's good for you, you'll piss off right now and never come back. You're not wanted here. No one wants you.'

'Tallulah does,' Ian replied smartly.

Despite his relief at realising Frank didn't appear to know anything about him, he was wary. Frank was burning with resentment.

Frank clenched both his fists. 'You keep your filthy hands off her,' he growled.

A couple of youths entered the club and Frank turned away to check them out. Ian joined in, patting men's pockets and glancing inside girls' bags in a desultory search for weapons and drugs. While he worked, he was thinking. He had been afraid that Frank had tumbled to his true identity. The truth was far more obvious and in some ways more worrying than that. Frank hadn't been tailing Ian at all, he had been stalking Jenny. She claimed she could take care of herself, but Ian didn't know if she was aware of the intensity of Frank's interest in her. As soon as he could, he would have to warn her. In the meantime, Frank's message had crystallised Ian's decision to act. At the first opportunity, he took a break and made his way straight to Tod's office.

'Frank?' Tod repeated, scowling. 'I don't believe it.'

He seemed so shocked, Ian was afraid the accusation would be dismissed.

'Are you sure?' Tod asked.

'I'm afraid so. The evidence is irrefutable.'

'Evidence? What evidence?'

Ian couldn't afford to be seen to hesitate. 'DNA. I got hold of a sample of Frank's DNA and sent it off to be analysed.' He spoke as confidently as he could. 'My colleague just sent me a message confirming Frank's DNA matches the informant's. There's no doubt. Frank's the one. He's been feeding information to the police for months. But he's been cunning. There's no way you could have tumbled to it without inside information. You're lucky you've got me working for you, or you might never have found out.'

To make the accusation sound plausible, Ian made out he was exposing Frank in order to curry favour with Tod.

'I had to tell you, Boss.'

Ian tensed. He had to act fast to get Frank arrested and locked up before Tod had him killed.

'What are you going to do, Boss? Do you want me to take him out?' he asked. 'You can leave him to me. I got rid of Nick for you, didn't I? I know how to work it so no one can trace it back to you.'

'No, you've done enough.' Tod's eyes narrowed. 'Leave him to me. Send him in. I want to talk to him.' Tod's hand moved towards his top drawer.

'But Boss—'

'I said, send him to me. Now!'

Ian hurried from the office, his thoughts whirling. Somehow he had to warn Frank of Tod's intentions, without revealing his own part in the affair. But Frank was not in the entry hall. Ian hurried back inside, looking for Jenny. He saw her behind the bar, flirting with a punter.

'Tallulah, I need to speak to you right now,' he hissed at her.

She blew the customer a kiss. 'Laters, babe. What is it?' she asked, turning to Ian.

'Where's Frank?'

'How should I know?'

'Listen, he's after you—'

'After me?' she giggled. 'What for? Have I been a naughty girl?'

'Stop it, Jenny, this is serious. He's got designs on you and he's trying to warn me off and get me out of the way. So I've told Tod Frank's a snitch.'

'What? Frank? Are you nuts? He's devoted to Tod. He's been working for him for years. Tod's never going to swallow that.'

'Well, he did,' Ian replied, irked by her distrust. 'I convinced him. But now Frank's gone missing.'

'I'm not surprised,' she replied, looking worried. 'Tod isn't one to hang around and wait for a fair hearing. If he believed your story, chances are Frank's already a dead man. But if Frank's still alive, and gets wind of your story, your luck's run out. You'd best watch your back, Archie. Frank will snap you like a twig with his bare hands. And if Tod ever discovers you were spinning him a line, he'll put a bullet in your guts and leave you to bleed to death.'

Ian forced a grin. 'What's a nice girl like you doing in such charming company?' he muttered.

41

THOMAS HAD ALWAYS LIKED to keep up with the news in general, but lately he had only been interested in what was happening in York. He had taken to buying any local papers he could find on his way to work, scanning through them at lunchtime, and checking obsessively online in case there was any mention of the prostitute he had accidentally killed. It didn't take long for the media to seize on the story, and he read several articles with satisfaction, because they indicated the police didn't have a clue who was responsible for killing the woman. All the while his relief was tinged with fear, because it was clear that the police were throwing huge resources into looking for him.

Several newspapers reported the local police had drafted in officers from other areas to help them with the search. He wondered how many of them were working on trying to track him down. Some of the accounts in the media were more dramatic than others. They ranged from a one-line announcement that a woman's body had been discovered in York, to a full-blown article on the front page of a local paper. It was somewhat histrionic and would have been quite worrying had most of the information not been fabricated. The more far-fetched the journalists' claims were, the safer he felt, and it was reassuring that even the most detailed article revealed that the police didn't seem to know anything at all. How could they, he reasoned, when he had left no trace of himself behind. Alone in the living room, he read carefully through the longest report.

A woman has been brutally murdered in York. The mutilated corpse of Pansy Banks, a glamorous twenty-five-year-old exotic dancer and escort was discovered in Acomb Wood, where her body had been dumped. Local resident, fifty-one-year-old Yvonne Miles, who stumbled on the body, said, 'It was horrendous. I've lived in York all my life and I've never seen anything like it.'

The victim leaves behind a young daughter and son, who are now both orphans. The victim's mother, who has been looking after the children, was too upset to speak to us.

The police are working around the clock to find whoever is responsible for this vicious attack. Police officers have been drafted in from the surrounding areas to help with the enquiry and a massive investigation is under way, although so far there has been no arrest.

Anyone who has any information concerning this violent murder is urged to contact the local police without delay.

As he finished the article, Emily came in. Thomas closed his paper with a guilty start, before she could see what he was reading.

'What's that?' she asked.

'Nothing,' he replied, shoving the paper aside. 'Just glancing through the local news to see what's going on in the world.' He smiled at her.

'Anything interesting?'

'No. Nothing much. Just the usual garbage.'

'Well, you're wrong, because there *is* something,' she replied, sitting down beside him on the sofa and half turning in her seat to look at him. Her expression was solemn, but her blue eyes were animated. 'There's been a murder, right here in York.'

'Oh yes, I saw that,' he replied, lowering his gaze. 'No need to worry. The police always catch murderers, don't they? It says in the paper they've got whole teams of officers working on it. I'm sure they have it under control.'

'Under control? If you ask me, they don't seem to know anything and they don't seem to be doing anything at all to find out who's responsible. The body was found right here in York, in Acomb Wood.'

Thomas raised his eyebrows in fake alarm. 'Really? In Acomb Wood? I missed that. Bloody hell, that's a bit too close for comfort. Emily, I don't want you going out alone until they've found this maniac and put him behind bars.'

'I hardly think there's any need to be so melodramatic,' she replied, but she didn't sound very sure of herself. 'I'm hardly going to put myself at risk.'

'Listen,' he said forcefully, 'if there's a killer out there targeting women, I don't want you putting yourself at risk. I mean it. You can go out if you take the car, but you're absolutely not to go out otherwise.'

She laughed. 'Don't be silly, Thomas. Of course I'll be careful. And it's hardly like there's a serial killer out there targeting women, just because one woman got herself killed. She was asking for trouble.'

Thomas frowned. 'What's that supposed to mean?'

'Oh, I'm not victim blaming, nothing like that, but the fact is the victim was a sex worker who got into a car with a stranger. I'm hardly likely to get into a stranger's car, am I?'

'Who told you she was a sex worker?' he asked.

He felt a flicker of fear in case someone had seen him picking up the prostitute in the street. It wasn't the first time the possibility had occurred to him.

'And how do you know she got into a stranger's car?'

'Everyone knows that. It's all over the internet. Everyone's talking about it and everyone says she was a sex worker.'

'Just because everyone's saying it doesn't mean it's true.'

'Well, everyone I've spoken to says she used to solicit on the street, even though it's illegal. She did it to support her drug habit.'

'That's just ridiculous gossip. If she was picked up on the street, no one else would know about it.'

Emily looked at him curiously. 'What do you mean?'

'It just doesn't make sense, that's all.'

'What doesn't?'

'All this stuff about people speculating about how she got into a stranger's car. Murders are usually committed by someone who knows the victim.'

'That's true.'

'Anyway, I don't want you going out on your own until this is over.'

'Now who's being ridiculous? The girls at the book club all think there's a predator targeting sex workers and killing them. No one seems to know anything for certain, but it stands to reason she was killed by one of her customers.'

Thomas wondered how far to push his pretence of concern. Of course Emily was in no danger at all from the man who had killed the prostitute, but no one knew that apart from him. He had to do his best to behave as though he was as ignorant of the killer's identity as everyone else. He wondered how he would have reacted to the situation had he *not* known for certain that Emily was safe. Whatever happened, it was essential that he appear innocent and behave as though he knew nothing about the woman's death, other than what he could read in the paper.

'Well,' he said slowly, as though musing over the situation, 'you be careful, that's all. These are unprecedented circumstances. I don't want you to go wandering around on your own, and whatever you do, don't leave the house after dark, and when you do go out, make sure you stick to busy streets where there are plenty of people around.'

Emily smiled at him. 'I do love you, you know,' she said.

He breathed a sigh of relief, reassured that he had judged it correctly, at least for now.

'I'll be careful,' she said. 'And you be careful too.'

'I'm not at risk from a violent maniac who's been killing women,' he replied, forcing a laugh.

'You can't assume that. We don't know what he might do. He might attack men too.'

'You're right,' Thomas lied, although he knew she was wrong.

'But the chances are this was a one-off. It's highly unlikely to happen again.'

There was a certain perverse satisfaction in being the only person alive who knew what had really happened, but he was aware that made him vulnerable. He had to stay on his guard. Whatever happened, no one else must ever suspect the truth.

42

THE FOLLOWING DAY, THE news was more alarming. Thomas was on his lunch break, sitting at his desk, scanning through local news reports, when he read that a second victim had been killed on the patch of waste ground near his house, early on Saturday morning. While he couldn't be certain the victim was his blackmailer, the details were too close to what had happened to him for it to be anyone else. He had met his blackmailer on the waste ground early on Saturday morning and had left her, seemingly unconscious, lying at the foot of a tall tree. Now a dead woman had been discovered in that exact same place, apparently killed at the same time. A spasm of terror shook him. Not realising she was dead he had made no effort to cover his tracks. With a shock, he realised how near he had come to discovery. Luckily he had grabbed the bag of cash as he ran off. Now he trembled at the realisation that if he had left it behind, the police might already be knocking at his door.

It was hard to believe his blackmailer was dead. In a way, of course, it was a relief to know he was free of her. The thought of her relentlessly pursuing him had been plaguing him ever since he had received her first note. But now it seemed that, somehow, he had managed to inadvertently be present when another woman suffered a fatal injury. The chances of that happening, all within the space of a couple of weeks, seemed almost impossible. He stared in disbelief at the article, struggling to take in what it said.

A second woman has been found murdered in York. The body of Pansy Banks, a sex worker, was discovered abandoned in Acomb Wood two weeks ago. Last Saturday a second victim, who has not yet been named, was violently battered to death. She was discovered on a patch of waste ground off the Holgate Road by a passer-by, Jennifer Seymour, twenty-two.

'She was lying there, sprawled out, at the foot of a tree,' the witness said. 'I thought she had slipped over on the ice and might need help, but when I was close enough to see her eyes, I could tell she was dead. The police came very quickly. It was a really horrible experience.'

The police have not yet been able to confirm whether the two murders are linked.

'We are asking members of the public to be particularly vigilant,' Detective Chief Inspector Eileen Duncan said.

Anyone who has any information about either of these tragic deaths has been urged to contact the police without delay.

There was a further paragraph about police action, the number of officers brought in from other areas to help with the enquiry, and some vague claims about people who were 'helping the police with their enquiries'. He suddenly felt like laughing, because he knew the only person who could assist the police was most definitely not helping them. They were casting around in the dark. Still, the more he thought about it, the more their failure to apprehend him seemed just. The truth was that he hadn't intended to kill those women, but no one was going to believe him if he confessed to having accidentally watched them both die. While he might possibly have been able to get away with a plea of manslaughter for one victim, two was going to stretch any judge and jury's credulity. More than ever it was vital that he avoid capture.

Reviewing everything he had done, he was confident that no one would ever discover his part in the two deaths. On reflection, far from being horrified at what had happened, he realised that he should be relieved his blackmailer had met with a fatal accident. With the only witness to his one crime of moving a corpse now also dead, he was safe. Returning to work, he tried to put the whole nightmarish episode out of his mind.

But staring at his screen, he couldn't stop thinking about the news concerning his second victim. It was all the fault of that crazy sex worker. If he hadn't been forced to dispose of her body in the first place, his blackmailer would still be alive. Both of his victims had been at least as responsible for their premature deaths as he was. More, in fact. He had never set out to kill anyone and he wished it hadn't happened at all. But no one would have much sympathy for him if his connection to the dead women ever came out, because he was alive and they were dead. As though that exonerated them of guilt. If anything, he was the victim in all this. And now, he had to protect himself. The prospect of prison wasn't as terrible as the thought of Emily finding out what he had done. He could hardly imagine her shock and disbelief. She would continue trusting that he was entirely innocent until it became impossible to deny his involvement with the two victims. But even if he could convince her he hadn't killed anyone, his initial transgression would be impossible to hide.

'A prostitute?' She would burst into tears. 'Why?'

He couldn't bear the thought of causing his wife so much pain. No, the whole truth would have to remain buried, whatever the cost. He would single-handedly kill off the entire police force in York rather than let his wife be told her husband was a depraved murderer. In the meantime, no one was on to him, and there was no reason why that should ever change. He was in the clear, and he was going to make sure it stayed that way. Arriving home that evening, he called out cheerily to Emily who came into the hall to greet him. He loved that time of day, when he saw her after a day's work with a whole evening and night stretching out in front of them.

'Something smells good,' he said, brushing her cheek with his lips.

'I picked up some fish and chips on the way home,' she replied. 'I'm keeping it hot in the oven so we can eat whenever you're ready.'

'How about now?'

He followed her into the living room and switched the television on while she clattered about in the kitchen.

'By the way,' she said when they were both seated with their trays, 'what's that old van doing in the garage?'

'Van? What van?' he stammered stupidly, caught off guard by her question.

'The one in the garage. You never told me you'd bought a van. What's it doing there, Thomas?'

43

THE FOLLOWING EVENING TOD summoned Ian as soon as he arrived at the club. Anxiously, Ian hurried to the office. He expected to find Frank there, ready to confront him with a furious denial of any allegation. To his surprise and guarded relief, Ian found Tod in the company of a brawny bodyguard Ian hadn't seen before, a ginger-haired giant of a man whose pink-cheeked head looked tiny on top of his massive shoulders and thick neck.

'Archie, Wills,' Tod said by way of introduction, nodding from one to the other.

The thought flashed across Ian's mind that Tod must have dealt with his suspected police informer by now, and he wondered if this ginger-haired giant had killed Frank. If that were the case, Ian would be responsible for Frank's murder.

'Tod isn't one to hang around and wait for a fair hearing,' Jenny had said. 'If he believed your story, chances are Frank's already a dead man.'

Ian didn't doubt that for a moment.

'You wanted to see me, Boss?'

Tod's answer was both reassuring and concerning. 'I want you to find Frank and bring him here.'

'What happened to him?' Ian asked stupidly.

'I told him what you said and he blew his stack. You should've seen him.' Tod gave a short laugh. 'He was smoking, trust me.'

'Do you have any idea where he went?'

Tod gave a careless shrug, but his sharp eyes never left Ian's face. 'How should I know? I repeated what you told me and he said it was all baloney, and he was going to drag you here to fess up. Said you'd sing like a bird before he slit your throat. Slowly.' He spoke the last word with relish. 'Trust me, he was mad. "Not in here, you won't," I told him. "I don't want blood stains on my carpet, stinking out my room. Stuff that," I said. "You take him out and do your business elsewhere," is what I told him.'

There was silence for a moment when Tod finished speaking.

'I don't know where Frank is,' Ian said at last in a strangled voice. 'You probably gathered we're not exactly best mates.'

'I never said you were besties,' Tod laughed. 'Find him, Archie,' he went on, growing serious. 'I need to know what's going down, capiche? I need to know which of you is lying to me, because one of you is, that's for sure. I'm thinking maybe it's you, because I'm easy with Frank. He's been my boy for years.'

Ian was looking at Tod. At the edge of his vision, he saw the ginger-haired bodyguard stir and take a step forwards.

'But then again,' Tod went on, waving his bodyguard back, 'you're a very useful asset, Archie. I don't know as I want you to book it. Not yet, anyways. So you see what my beef is.' He nodded briskly. 'We need this sorted. Find Frank and bring him here to me.'

Wondering how he was supposed to do that, Ian hesitated.

Tod frowned at him. 'You still here?'

As Wills shuffled forwards once more, Ian ducked his head in a clumsy sort of obeisance and hurried from the room. Reluctant to return to Jenny's flat, where Frank was probably waiting for him, he drove straight to his own lodgings in Archway, taking a roundabout route to avoid being followed. When he reached home, he drove around a few blocks but couldn't see Frank's car parked anywhere nearby. Finding the front door to his block of flats locked he relaxed slightly, but as he went to insert his key in his own front door, it moved a fraction. Someone had been there and left it unlocked. Instantly alert, Ian tensed, and pushed the door gently. As he did so, powerful arms grabbed him from behind, and he realised Frank had been waiting for him, not inside the flat as he had suspected, but outside in the communal entrance hall. Pinning Ian's arms to his sides, Frank kneed him in the back and propelled him forwards with a rough jerk. Ian wriggled furiously, but couldn't break Frank's hold. Once they were across the threshold of the flat, Frank tripped him up and they crashed to the floor together, with Ian underneath. He heard his front door slam shut as his head hit the floor with a thud. Had the hall not been thickly carpeted, he might have cracked his skull open, or at the very least bust his nose. As it was, he was stunned by the impact, and lay still, conscious of nothing but an odour of stale sweat mingled with a horribly cloying aftershave, and a loud pounding somewhere inside his head.

His assailant yanked him up on his feet and swung him round so they were facing one another. Dazed, Ian staggered and would have fallen if strong arms hadn't held him upright.

'You thought you done for me,' Frank snarled, gripping Ian's arms tightly and shaking him as though he was a child. 'Now it's your turn, you fucking retard. I always knew you were grief. Now you're the one who's screwed. You thought you could cop Tallulah, and be the boss's fam, did you? Well you gotta know, Tallulah's my babe, mine. You won't be pounding her again.'

Still gripping Ian's arms, Frank head butted him, making his head jerk violently backwards with a loud crack. For a few seconds Ian was afraid his neck was broken.

'No,' he murmured, when he was able to speak.

He was relieved to discover he could move his head without any spasm of pain, but his vision was blurry. His right eye throbbed agonisingly and he could feel it closing. Gradually, through the fog of pain, he understood that his relief was misplaced. His neck might not be broken but it made no difference. Frank was going to kill him anyway.

'No,' he murmured again. 'No, wait. You have to listen to me. You've got it all wrong. It wasn't you I was talking about. It wasn't you. You've got it all wrong. You have to listen to me. You've got to listen. Tod's making a big mistake. Tod needs you. I know that.'

He was babbling frantically, desperate to get away, but it was no use. He was struggling not only to escape from Frank's grasp, but to remain conscious. He could hardly see his antagonist's face any longer. Frank's eyes bulged from their sockets, staring at him through rippling water. It felt like they were wrestling under the sea. When a huge fist hurtled towards him, Ian had no time to dodge the blow. There was a thunderous crash, and everything went dark.

44

It was over two weeks since Ian had disappeared. Allegedly he had gone to work in London, although that was nothing more than a rumour. Geraldine wasn't actually sure where he was. When she had tried to prise more information out of Eileen, she had only succeeded in irritating the detective chief inspector.

'All I'm able to tell you is that Ian was unexpectedly recruited by another force, and he left us very suddenly. Almost overnight in fact. I am in no position to share any further details with anyone and it's not your place to ask. I thought you'd know better than that.'

'I just want to know he's all right, and when he'll be coming back,' Geraldine muttered. 'He's a friend. That is, we've been colleagues for a long time.'

For all Geraldine knew, Ian could be dead. Worrying about him kept her awake at night, although she did her best to reassure herself that if he had met with a catastrophe, she would have heard about it. But the station gossip had gone quiet about the absent inspector, and no one but Geraldine seemed particularly interested in finding out what had happened to him. It was as though he had never existed.

'People come and go,' Eileen said. 'And Matthew is an experienced officer.'

Geraldine didn't admit that the reason for her enquiry had been personal, not professional, and that Ian had not been answering his phone. In the meantime, it didn't help that

Ariadne was obsessing about her own forthcoming marriage. That evening Geraldine went to the nearby pub for a drink after work, partly to avoid going back to her empty flat. Ariadne was there talking to Matthew and Geraldine joined them.

'There comes a time in your life when you have to take stock,' Ariadne was saying. 'You look at your life and there you are, on your own. What I mean is, you might want to find someone, but after a few years of trying, eventually you resign yourself to accepting that you're going to be on your own for the rest of your life and that's when you realise it's actually not so bad. Apart from other people and their expectations, it's fine. It's just how your life is. Take me. I own a flat, which I've decorated to my own taste. Everything's arranged exactly as I want it, and there's no one to tell me anything has to be different. It suits me perfectly – the decor, the furniture, everything. And now,' she flung her hands in the air in mock horror, 'I'm about to throw it all away. And for what?'

'So you can wear a pretty ring?' Matthew suggested with a smile.

'You can keep your furniture, surely?' Geraldine added seriously.

'No, no, that is yes, of course I can keep my furniture. I didn't mean I'd literally have to throw all my belongings out. That's not the point. What I mean is, I'm giving up my freedom just because everyone is expected to get married and settle down and if I don't get on with it soon, the opportunity to have children will be lost, and I'll regret it for the rest of my life.'

'Will you?' Geraldine asked.

'Will I what?'

'Will you regret not having children?'

Ariadne shrugged. 'I don't know, do I? If I do have children, how do I know I won't regret that? But then it'll be too late.'

Geraldine turned to Matthew. 'You've got two children, haven't you? What do you think?'

'Well, all I can say is that until you have children, you have absolutely no idea what you're letting yourself in for. Sleepless nights, constant worrying, and money disappearing faster than you can earn it. Not that I'd be without them,' he added, smiling.

'You must have some idea whether you want children or not,' Geraldine said to Ariadne.

Again, her friend shrugged. 'Yes, I suppose I want them more than I don't want them. But that's no reason to get married, is it?'

Geraldine considered the question. It was probably why many women married, but she didn't say so. Then again, there was no guarantee Ariadne and Nico would be able to have children. Ariadne was forty, and time must be running out for her. Shifting the subject away from such a difficult issue, she asked Ariadne if she wanted to spend the rest of her life with Nico.

'The rest of my life? How am I supposed to know right now what I'm going to want to do for the rest of my life? Everyone keeps banging on about the rest of my life, but I'm struggling to decide what I want today. Nico knows what he wants. He wants us to get married. But how can anyone be that sure their relationship is going to last? He keeps promising he'll always love me, but no one can know that. It's not possible to be so sure.'

'A lot of people must be sure, or no one would get married.'

'Yes, and look how most marriages end up. No offence, Matthew,' Ariadne added quickly.

'None taken,' he replied breezily.

Geraldine did her best to focus on what Ariadne was saying, but her mind kept wandering. She and Ian had been good friends for years before they had finally confessed their love for one another. Admittedly Ian's freedom had been constrained by his marriage. It wasn't until after his wife had left him that he had revealed his feelings and moved into Geraldine's flat. By then their relationship had felt so right, neither of them had ever questioned it would last. And yet now they were separated and she didn't even know where he was or whether she would ever see him again. If such a considered affair had faltered, how could anyone know for sure that a relationship was going to last?

She switched her attention back to the conversation and heard Matthew saying, 'I guess you just have to give it a go and see what happens. Hope for the best and all that. It's all any of us can do, really, whatever our circumstances. I'm sorry I can't be more helpful but really I'm the last person who should be offering relationship advice. My marriage was a complete failure for no reason that I can fathom. We're both reasonable adults, we get on well, we loved each other enough to have two children and then, pouf, it was all over. I'm still not sure why.'

Matthew spoke carelessly but Geraldine was sure he must be deeply upset about the break-up of his marriage.

'Have you discussed the situation with your wife?' she asked gently.

'Oh yes,' he replied. 'But it turns out we're both better off as we are. We're happier apart.'

'Yes,' Ariadne sighed, 'I know, a lot of people prefer to stay single. I envy you, Geraldine. I wish I could be like you, but my mother's constantly on at me and that gets me worried, because maybe I don't want to end up on my own. It's one thing when you're young and fit, but what's going to happen to me when I'm old and decrepit, and there's no one to look after me or care what happens to me?'

Geraldine suspected Ariadne was repeating her mother's words, but if they had made such a deep impression on

LEIGH RUSSELL

Ariadne, maybe deep down she felt the same. It wasn't Geraldine's place to tell her friend how to live her life.

'You just have to do what feels right for you, weighing everything up and looking at the situation from every angle. Do you love Nico?'

'Love? Is that enough? And how do you know if you love someone?'

'You don't,' Matthew said gloomily. 'Not really. That is, you never know if anyone loves you enough to put up with you for the long haul.'

'Can you imagine spending the rest of your life with him?' Geraldine persisted.

Ariadne nodded. 'The sad thing is I can, even though I don't think I love him, not like that.'

Geraldine and Matthew exchanged a glance but neither of them challenged what Ariadne meant exactly.

'Well, you have to decide for yourself,' Geraldine said. 'Never mind what anyone else says, this is your life and it has to be your decision.'

Geraldine sighed. She knew very well that her advice was flawed. From her own experience she knew only too well that people didn't always make sensible decisions about their own lives.

45

THE FOLLOWING MORNING, THOMAS left the house as usual and stopped the car after a few blocks to call and say he wouldn't be going to the office.

'It's a dratted stomach upset,' he told the office manager. 'It's nothing. I'm sure I'll be fine tomorrow.'

The office manager wished him a speedy recovery and rang off. The first part of Thomas's plan was complete. He waited around the corner until he was sure Emily had left for work, before embarking on the next stage in his plan, which was to look for a suitable place to ditch the van. After driving for nearly an hour, past Heslington and Holtby, he reached Hagg Wood and found a spot where he thought he would be able to drive the van off the track and through the trees until it was out of sight of anyone driving by. It wasn't a very imaginative idea, but by driving right off the road and leaving the van concealed among the trees, he hoped it would remain there undetected for a while. Few people were likely to be walking in the woods in such cold weather and, with any luck, the van would stay hidden out of sight until after the winter, by which time the police would have lost interest in it. Having settled on a location for the van, he returned home.

His next problem was how to move the van safely. He couldn't drive it on the road with its current registration number, because the police might see it and then everything would be over. Somehow they had already spotted the van driving near Acomb Wood on the night he had dumped the prostitute, and they had promptly plastered an image of it all over the papers and the internet. The dead prostitute's DNA must be spread over the van. He couldn't afford to be caught driving it. Once the police requisitioned the van, he had no doubt a forensic team would find traces of the dead woman in his hall. A speck of blood, a skin cell, a fleck of dandruff, was all it would take. He tried not to imagine Emily's shocked expression when she discovered what he had done.

What he needed was fake number plates and, ideally, a paint job, to avoid attracting any unwanted attention, but he didn't know how to go about securing any of that. A seasoned criminal would have contacts who could dispose of the incriminating van. As it was, all Thomas could hope to manage was to change the registration number. With a flash of inspiration, he realised what he could do. He didn't have the right size screwdriver but he thought that could be easily remedied. As it happened, it turned out to be a challenge to find the right tool but he found one in the end, after scouring the shelves of a local hardware shop and spending a small fortune on different sized screwdrivers. Crouching down, he removed the back number plate from his car and fastened it to the front of the van. He turned the car around so that the front faced the garage door, and removed the second number plate which he attached to the back of the van. Now all he had to do was hide his car in the garage while he drove the van to a secluded spot in Hagg Wood, where it wouldn't be found, and leave it there without being seen. It was too far to walk back, but he could catch a bus from Holtby that would take him nearly to his door.

He drove cautiously, terrified his false number plates would fall off. He wasn't sure they were securely attached. He avoided main roads with speed cameras and traffic lights, anywhere he might be spotted on CCTV. He couldn't drive fast in any case because, apart from the danger of ice on the roads, he had purchased, for cash, a pair of wellington boots that were two sizes too large for him, and stuffed them with paper so that he was able to walk in them. They were difficult to drive in, but he was keen to avoid leaving any further clues to his identity when he walked away from the van. It began to snow lightly as he drove, which he hoped would help to make the van more difficult to see clearly on any CCTV he passed unwittingly. It was less than ten miles to his destination, but it seemed to take him hours to drive there. At last he arrived and slowed to a standstill to wait for a moment with his windows open, listening. As far as he could tell, the woods were deserted.

Halfway along the narrow lane that led into the wood, he turned off into a small clearing from where he kept going, forcing his way through the trees. The van jolted between trunks to the sound of horrible screeching of branches scraping along the sides, until it finally came to a halt when it could go no further. With difficulty, Thomas forced his door open, pushing against branches that grew up right beside the path he had forged. Scratched and dented, the van was firmly wedged between the trees. Fortunately, being grey, it was going to be hard to see from a distance. In any case, with the weather turning bitter and heavy snow forecast, he hoped no one would be out walking in the woods for a while. Once the spring came and leaves returned to the trees, the van would be even better hidden. It was difficult to remove the number plates with his fingers half frozen inside his gloves, which had quickly become sodden once he left the shelter of the van. He worked as quickly as he could in the eerie silence of the wood, and eventually managed to prise them both off.

In some ways the bad weather was a blessing. The snow was difficult to walk on, but it served him much better than mud would have done. His footprints in the snow would hopefully have melted away long before the police arrived to survey the scene. With the number plates from his car stowed in his rucksack, he made his way carefully back through the trees, ducking and dodging overhanging bare branches and twigs, and doing his best to avoid touching anything. A trace of his DNA on a broken twig could be enough to alert the police to his presence there. It was possible the police had already succeeded in finding a sample of his DNA from one of the bodies. What he had to be careful of now was to avoid any situation where he might be called on to surrender a sample of his DNA. As long as the police had no match for whatever DNA they might have found on the prostitute or the blackmailer, Thomas was safe. He smiled grimly to himself as he struggled through the trees and back to the path. He walked along the grass verge, which was less slippery than the path, as the snow began to fall more heavily. It was almost a blizzard as he emerged from the woods back on to the road. Once again, the difficulty of traversing the streets was offset by the knowledge that no one was likely to see him clearly through the driving snow, and any trail he left would vanish the moment the snow thawed. Conditions couldn't really have been better for someone wanting to move around without leaving lasting tracks.

46

IAN COULD ONLY MANAGE to open one eye. As if through a mist, he saw that he was lying on the floor beside a familiar settee. It was a while before he remembered that it was the furniture in his living room in London. Shifting his head slightly, he saw Frank seated nearby, watching him. With an effort, Ian recalled being knocked out. Along with the memory came a return of physical sensations. He became aware that his head hurt, and his right eye was throbbing painfully. Even though he had been convinced Frank was after him, Ian had let himself be caught off guard. As a trained detective, he ought to have known better than to let himself be defeated, outmanoeuvred by Tod's imbecile of a bodyguard. He groaned and attempted to raise himself from the floor, but his hands had been tied behind his back with what felt like a coarse rope that chafed his skin viciously whenever he moved his hands.

'So you're not a goner after all,' Frank said when he saw Ian struggling to get up. 'Not yet. And there's me thinking you're laid out for good. I been getting real bored waiting for you to come round. Not such a pretty face now, are you?' He chuckled. 'So, you fixing for some fun?' He slapped his right fist into the palm of his left hand. 'God knows, I been waiting long enough for this.'

Still grinning, he rose to his feet and towered over Ian who lay squirming at his feet, his head twisted round to look up at his captor. Ian was lying on his back, crushing his hands, which were tied behind him. From his position on the floor,

241

Frank looked gigantic. Taking a flick knife from his pocket, Frank squatted down, his enormous knees centimetres from Ian's face, and slowly moved his hand forward, until the tip of the blade touched Ian's cheek. Frank's hand didn't tremble, but Ian flinched and he heard himself whimper with fear. He couldn't help it. With a roar of laughter, Frank withdrew the blade and went and sat down again. Ian drew in a deep breath, his relief physical rather than mental. He knew it was only a matter of time before Frank slashed his face, or worse.

'I don't know about you,' Frank said, 'but I'm having a ball.'

'You think you can scare me?' Ian muttered, moving his lips with difficulty.

Neither of them was taken in by his pathetic attempt at bravado.

'Sure I can,' Frank replied quietly. 'Just looking at me has you shitting your pants.' He chuckled. 'We both know I'm crushing you.' He sniggered and began playing with his knife, flicking the blade in and out.

'What do you want?' Ian whispered, forcing himself to speak even though every movement of his face was painful.

'Just this,' Frank said. 'Me and you here, easy, both of us wondering how it's gonna play out, and how excruciating it's gonna be for you before you croak.' He grinned happily.

'Oh Jesus, this isn't a Bond film,' Ian snapped suddenly, regardless of the effort it cost him to speak. 'If you're going to kill me, let's just get it over with. If you've got the bottle, that is.'

They both knew Ian was trying to goad Frank into losing his temper so it would be over quickly.

'Take it down,' Frank crooned softly. 'I'm in no hurry.'

He stood up suddenly and walked out of Ian's line of vision. If anything, not being able to see where Frank was made Ian even more frightened than he had been before. After a few minutes, Frank came back into view clutching a bottle of Ian's whisky, a lighted cigarette in the corner of his lips. Frank moved his cigarette very slowly towards Ian's eye. Behind the glowing tip, Ian could see his tormentor's huge face grinning down at him. All Ian could do was twist his head to one side and wait for searing pain to rip through him.

From a long way off, there was a sudden crash and the muffled sound of shouting. Frank leaped to his feet, his face contorted in alarm. The whisky bottle fell from his hand. From the strong aroma, Ian guessed that it was silently spilling somewhere out of sight. He turned his head and saw a uniformed officer appear in the doorway, wearing a bullet proof vest and pointing a gun. A second officer appeared, also armed. Ian let out a cry of relief. Noticing a movement beside him, he kicked out and caught Frank on the shin. One of the officers darted forward and grabbed Frank's arm, twisting it up behind his back until his knife fell to the floor.

'He's armed,' Ian croaked. 'Watch out for his other hand.'

'Get off me!' Frank cried out. 'What you doing? What the fuck?'

The policeman released his grip on Frank's arm only to slap handcuffs on his wrists. As he did so, Ian let out an involuntary groan.

'I'm arresting you for assaulting a police officer. And that's just for starters.'

A second pair of uniformed officers entered the room. One of them untied Ian's hands and gently helped him to a chair.

Meanwhile Frank was shaking his head, looking dazed. 'I don't get it. What the fuck? How did you know we were here? Don't you touch me,' he added, glaring at the uniformed police officer who had handcuffed him. 'Fucking filth, you hear me? He's the one you should be taking down, not me. That scum. He's the one you want. You got it all wrong. Arrest him, not me.'

'Oh, give it a rest,' Ian interrupted him as he sank onto

a chair, examining his wrists which had been rubbed raw. 'Can't you see I'm one of them?'

'One of them? What the fuck you blathering about? Get off me!'

Ian stood up and swayed, and had to sit down again to stop himself falling over. Without warning, he threw up on the carpet.

'You need to get to a doctor,' one of his colleagues said.

'I'm fine, it's nothing,' he replied.

'Have you taken a look at yourself?'

Ian felt his eye gingerly and swore at the soreness and the swelling.

'Someone will drive you to the nearest hospital,' his colleague said. 'And let's get this brute behind bars where he can't cause any more damage.'

'Leave me alone,' Frank cried out. 'What the fuck? Get off me.'

Still protesting, he was dragged from the room. As soon as he was able to make a call, Ian spoke to Jack and told him what had happened. They agreed it was essential that Tod believed Frank was dead.

'Leave that to me,' Jack reassured Ian.

Two hours later, Ian was flat on his back again, this time in a hospital bed. Jenny visited him, looking concerned

'How are you feeling?' she asked. 'You look like shit.'

'No serious damage done,' he replied, sitting up. 'I'd offer you a drink but I'm all out.' He glanced disconsolately around the sparse room. 'It seems I owe you for saving my skin. But how did you know Frank would be there, waiting for me?'

Jenny shrugged. 'Call it a hunch. I suspected he might have found out where you're living so I had a team run a check on every vehicle parked within easy walking distance and guess what? A vehicle came up registered to a bloke in Hackney whose car was reported stolen two weeks ago. That was enough to mobilise back-up from the armed response unit.'

Ian nodded. 'I need to get back to Tod. This,' he pointed at his face, 'won't be a problem as far as he's concerned.'

'We'll do this together, Ian. But first you need to rest.'

'No. I need to get back to the club.'

'Frank's down,' Jenny said, smiling grimly. 'But Tod's still out there and he's the one we need to nail.'

Ian nodded. 'Leave him to me,' he said. 'I've got business with him.'

'You and me both,' she replied.

'Tod still thinks I despatched Nick, so he trusts me. And with Frank out of the way, I can step into his shoes. Jack will make sure no one hears from Frank, so I can tell Tod I got rid of him. I've already convinced Tod that Frank was a police informer.'

'How the hell did you manage that?' she asked.

'Never mind. The important thing is he believed me. Now I need to get back to Tod and nail him.'

'No, right now you need to rest,' she replied. 'You can deal with Tod when you're ready and not before.'

'Since when were you my senior officer?' Ian asked, lying back again with a faint groan.

'Since you turned into an idiot,' she replied, smiling.

47

'You could be right,' Eileen said, her tone of voice clearly indicating that she disagreed with Geraldine. 'Now let's crack on, shall we?'

She turned back to the board where images of the recent victims were displayed.

'Two women murdered in two weeks, within two miles of each other,' Geraldine persisted.

Matthew grinned. 'It sounds like a maths puzzle. Wasn't there one very like that, something along the lines of, if two men take two days to build two walls... I've no idea how it goes on.'

A few colleagues sniggered.

'This is no laughing matter,' Eileen snapped. 'Two women have been killed and we seem to be making no headway at all in finding out who's responsible. Yes, they lived within two miles of each other but we've had a team investigating both their histories, and we've found nothing to connect them in any way, and nothing to indicate they ever met, apart from the fact that they lived within a couple of miles of each other. Now, what exactly are you saying, Geraldine, and do you have anything practical to add to the discussion, or is this just more speculation?'

'Pansy and Vanessa lived quite near each other and they were killed within two weeks of each other,' Geraldine replied. 'I just wonder if that was really a coincidence? I mean, granted it could be, but do we really believe that?'

246

Eileen sniffed. 'It's not a question of what seems plausible, it's a question of finding out what happened. We need to have a further look for anything that links the two victims. Widen the net and look for any associates they had in common. It's high time we did some more delving into the two victims' circumstances, and find out if their paths ever crossed. Geraldine, I'm putting you in charge of a team to follow this up. I hardly need to ask you to be thorough.'

She gave Geraldine a tight smile.

'Teacher's pet,' Matthew whispered as they left the major incident room together.

Geraldine was pleased Ariadne was selected as the sergeant leading her team of constables.

'And no being distracted by your wedding plans,' Geraldine said, smiling.

'Of course not. Come on then, let's get started.'

Constables were tasked with finding out where the two victims had gone to school, and any educational establishment they had attended after that, and where they had worked. Pansy Banks's recorded history was brief. She had left home when she was barely sixteen, reappearing twelve years later to give birth to a daughter who lived with Pansy's mother and stepfather. A son born three years after that had been taken into care, when his grandmother had refused to take him in, on the grounds that one child was enough for her.

'Two children and she couldn't manage to take care of either of them herself,' Ariadne said. 'It's shocking really, when you think there are couples desperate to have a child and she's basically thrown them on the scrap heap.'

'One in care, one with her mother,' Geraldine replied.

'And that's just the ones we know about,' Ariadne added sombrely.

The rest of Pansy's adult life had been spent working as

an exotic dancer or strip artist, and illegally soliciting on the street to fund her heroin addiction.

'What a miserable existence,' Ariadne said, shaking her head. 'And we think we've got problems.'

'Speak for yourself,' Geraldine replied. 'No, don't,' she added quickly. 'We can talk about your problems later.'

Ariadne laughed. 'Don't worry, I'm not going off on one again. Not right now, anyway.'

The second victim, Vanessa, had attended university, studying business management, but had dropped out after a year and gone to work in London where she lived for twelve years, during which time she had married and divorced. Returning to York after the failure of her marriage, for a couple of years she had worked at the jeweller's shop Geraldine had already visited. Sifting through all the information the team had been able to gather, at no particular point in their lives did Pansy and Vanessa appear to have crossed paths.

'They could have had acquaintances in common,' Geraldine said. 'Any number of men could have met Pansy and covered their tracks for obvious reasons. We have no way of knowing the identity of all her contacts. It's not like she kept a journal with their names in it. Perhaps the manager of the jewellery shop knew Pansy.'

'It's possible,' Ariadne agreed, 'but it's unlikely we'll ever be able to find out.'

All their work had brought them no closer to finding Pansy and Vanessa's killer, although DNA evidence indicated they had been murdered by the same man.

'We just have to keep looking,' Geraldine said.

It was a depressing end to the day, especially when she went for a drink with Ariadne who was still worried about her forthcoming marriage.

'If you're that bothered by it, maybe you should consider calling it off?' Geraldine suggested.

'Do you think I should?'

Geraldine shook her head. 'It's not for me to say. It's your life and your decision.'

'I know. That's what makes it so hard. I mean, I know we have to use our initiative, or at least our own judgement, at work, but we're operating within a framework and there are clear rules and guidelines governing what we can and can't do. This is different. Having complete freedom to choose is scary. It's like being in a vacuum. There's no right answer. It's entirely up to me, whatever I want to do. I guess that's why we chose to work for the police in the first place, because it saves having to make decisions completely alone.'

Geraldine didn't answer, but she wondered whether that explained her own circumstances. All this time she had believed her reluctance to settle down with Ian had stemmed from her dissatisfaction with his actions. Perhaps, after all, her own personality was responsible for her solitude. She was so used to following rules she was incapable of making a decision for herself. Ariadne had a point. That kind of freedom was daunting.

48

SOONER OR LATER, TOD would learn the truth about Frank when his case went to trial. Frank's physical assault on Ian and his subsequent capture would all come out in court, and it would be clear that Frank was no police informer. But that would not happen for a while. In the meantime, it was possible in the short term to prevent any contact between the two villains with Frank in police custody. But he could not be denied visitors indefinitely, and Ian intended to make the best possible use of the interim. His first and most pressing duty, once he was able to get to his phone, had been to speak to Jack, and impress on him the need to keep Frank out of sight. It was vital he had no contact with the world outside his police cell, and the fewer officers who knew about Frank's arrest the better. Tod's spies and informers could be anywhere, even within the police station.

In the twilight world of double-crossing informants into which Ian had strayed, it seemed no one could be trusted. As Archie, he had betrayed the trust of both Tod and Jack, not to mention Jenny, and he was generally honest. Uncomfortable with his own double-dealing, he tried to convince himself it was the undercover work that had drawn him into the dubious morality of a character like Archie, but he knew that he alone was responsible for his actions. Once he started to make excuses for his own duplicity, he was on shaky ground as an officer upholding the law, and as a human being. But he remained steady in his resolve, determined to do whatever he could to reunite Geraldine and her sister.

After several hours the hospital released him. He had spent most of his time there lying on a hard bed in a grey room, waiting for the results of X-rays, scans and various examinations. At last the consultant in charge of his admission told him his injuries amounted to nothing worse than a black eye and a few nasty bruises, and he was discharged with instructions to be careful, and to hold an ice pack against his face for brief periods until the swelling subsided.

'Take things easy for a few days,' the consultant warned him. 'No vigorous exercise and no contact sports.'

Even nodding his head made Ian's eye throb. He didn't admit that he was almost bound to be drawn into a violent encounter of some kind, or that the threat of physical contact was not only constant, but would probably be the least of his worries. In fact he was more likely to be shot than battered again.

The knowledge that Frank was securely behind bars offered Ian some hope of respite, as well as consolation for the time he had wasted hanging around in hospital. Ian had to pretend that his real identity was unknown to Tod. That meant Tod must continue to believe that Frank had been spirited away under police protection, as an informer. As long as Tod trusted Ian, there was a good chance Jack would be able to nail him. If Tod discovered Ian's ruse, and learned that he was acting first and foremost as a policeman, Ian's life would be over in the time it would take Tod to shoot him.

As soon as Ian left the hospital, he made his way to the main road where he walked quickly, halting every few yards, ostensibly to look in a shop window, but actually to reassure himself he wasn't being followed. Wills was as likely to distrust him as Frank had been. After buying an old anorak from a charity shop he felt a little less anxious, although his black eye was still noticeable. On balance he decided sunglasses would be less conspicuous than the injury he sported, and he purchased a pair with a fairly light tint that could have been prescription glasses. Poorly disguised, he took a cab to the police station, where he was relieved to find Jack in his office.

Jack looked up in surprise when Ian walked in and took off his glasses.

'Don't worry,' Ian assured him. 'I wasn't followed.'

'Should you be in bed?'

'I'm not sick. Everything's fine. I just don't look too great right now.'

Jack grinned. 'And you're usually such a beauty,' he replied.

Ian laughed, although the movement pulled painfully at the swelling around his eye.

'I got your message,' Jack said. 'Frank's been doing his nut, but we haven't let him make a call. Not yet. It's highly irregular of course. We can't hold out much longer.'

Grabbing a chair, Ian sat down and outlined his idea to Jack. The success of the plan depended on Frank's arrest being kept quiet.

Jack nodded. 'We'll use a trusted lawyer,' he replied. 'We're obliged to allow the brute his call, but I'll make sure he doesn't get through to anyone.' He frowned. 'It's not exactly on the level, but I don't see we have any choice, not if you're going to have a chance of coming out of this alive. And in the meantime, that shiner should help you convince Tod that you subdued Frank and removed him.'

'As long as I can convince Tod that Frank was double-crossing him, we're in the clear and he'll trust me.'

'And if he doesn't?'

Ian shrugged. He would have to deal with that situation if it arose. He was going to tell Tod that Frank was dead, and so eliminate any risk of Tod discovering the truth, but the problem with the claim was that, as with Nick, Ian wasn't able to deliver a body. All eventualities considered, his only option was to say he had dumped the body in the river again, because that couldn't be disproved. In the meantime, Frank would remain inaccessible, and Tallulah could confirm that Frank had betrayed Tod to the police. With luck, the disappearance of his former bodyguard would help convince Tod that Frank had been disloyal. It was only a holding measure to give Ian enough time to gather the evidence he needed to put Tod away. If Tod caught even a hint of a suspicion that Ian had really been working for Jack all along, Ian would never leave his office alive. It was all becoming too complicated for comfort.

'You be careful,' Jack called out as Ian walked out of the office.

'I know,' Ian replied, 'I'm a very useful asset.'

Jack was indignant. 'It's not just that.'

'No, no,' Ian replied, 'it's because you love me. Don't. You'll make me cry.'

'I don't like to lose a man,' Jack said sternly. 'You're important to the team.'

'But dispensable,' Ian muttered under his breath.

Leaving the police station, he donned his tinted glasses and pulled up his hood. A light snow was falling, and he wondered what the weather was like in York. Conditions were almost inevitably going to be more severe there than in the capital. Much as he disliked the snow, he felt a wave of homesickness just thinking about York. Dismissing his nostalgia, he hurried back home. By the time he reached his flat, his swollen face ached from the cold, and he was looking forward to putting his feet up for an hour or so before returning to the club to confront Tod. But the solitude he was eagerly anticipating eluded him. Jenny was sitting in an armchair in his flat.

'How did you get in?' he demanded, dropping his wet anorak on the floor.

'Oh, please.'

Ian nodded. It didn't matter whether she had picked the lock or let herself in with a key Jack had given her. He was just annoyed she was there at all.

He flung himself down on an armchair and closed his eyes.

'What are you doing here?'

'Making your tea,' she replied.

Coming over to him, she gently removed his glasses and he found her confidence both liberating and irritating. She simply assumed he would be pleased to see her. She expected to be liked, especially by men, and he realised it was refreshing to be with a woman who had no emotional hang-ups. Life with her seemed so simple. She didn't seem to care about anything much. He wondered whether her experience of working undercover had cut her off from feeling any real emotion, or whether a naturally detached personality had led her to seek out her particular line of work. In a way he envied her. The emotional attachments he had formed with women had not made him happy.

'It must be nice to be so disconnected,' he said, but she had already left the room and didn't hear him.

Jenny returned after a short time, carrying a tray of tea and toast. In spite of his painful face, Ian couldn't help grinning.

'This looks great,' he said.

And it was. When he had finished, he explained his plan to her.

'Sure,' she replied. 'I can do that. We just need to make sure our stories match in every detail in case he's suspicious and grills us. Although I can always plead ignorance, or stupidity,' she smiled. 'We don't want it to sound too rehearsed, but we need to more or less tell the same story.' She smiled again, and reached out to take his hand. 'We can work together, Ian. We make a good team.'

Ian hesitated. 'Jenny, this is just work, isn't it? I mean, we've agreed this isn't going anywhere.'

'This?' she repeated, pretending to be baffled, although she must have understood perfectly well what he meant.

'This relationship, you and me. It's not going anywhere. It won't last. It can't.'

Jenny stared at him, looking faintly troubled. 'You don't know that.'

Ian was on the point of telling her he was already in a relationship, but he held back. Wanting it to be true didn't make it so. He had once believed he and Geraldine were blissfully happy together, but she had thrown him out. He felt a pang of longing for her, not for the cold resentful woman she had become, but for the passionate and bold person he had fallen in love with. But Geraldine had made it clear she no longer wanted to have anything to do with him, while Jenny was warm and ready to welcome him into her bed. Still he hesitated. He liked women, and enjoyed flirting with them. He had even gained something of a reputation as a lady's man when he was younger. Yet in all the years of his long relationship with his wife, whom he had first dated when they were still at school, and throughout his subsequent affair with Geraldine, he had never been unfaithful to either of them. He had started a relationship with his ex-wife when they were both teenagers, his affair with Jenny was the first time in his life he had embarked on a casual affair with a woman. Never having intended it to happen in the first place, he now wanted to extricate himself, but he didn't know how. He wasn't even sure he wanted to. She smiled and began slowly removing her clothes.

'Don't worry,' she said, 'I'll be gentle. We don't want to do anything that might make your eye hurt. You just sit there, and leave everything to me.'

Exhaustion, as much as lust, rendered him compliant. When Jenny aroused him, he found himself thinking not of her but of Geraldine. Nevertheless he sat back and allowed her to continue. More duplicity, he thought miserably.

49

THE NEWS THAT THE van they had been searching for had been spotted hidden among the trees in Hagg Wood was a welcome development in an investigation that had seemed to be stalling for days. The excitement on discovering traces of the same male DNA on both Pansy and Vanessa's bodies had not brought the police any closer to determining the identity of their killer. Questions to neighbours and known associates of both victims had so far yielded no new information. So it was with some relief that everyone attended a briefing where they were shown images of the battered old van which had been driven off the road in the wood. At last they seemed to be making progress. All they had to do now was find the driver of the van.

'That thing's nearly as decrepit as my car,' Ariadne muttered to Geraldine as they stared at the images.

Geraldine smiled.

'This was clearly an attempt to conceal the vehicle,' Eileen said, her eyes gleaming with excitement. 'It was spotted yesterday afternoon by a couple of teenagers who were walking in the woods.'

A few officers chuckled and nodded knowingly.

'Is that what they call it nowadays?' Matthew asked.

'Oh for goodness sake, it's freezing out there,' Geraldine replied.

'They probably went there to smoke a joint,' Ariadne said. 'I wonder why they didn't report seeing the van straight away? They can't have missed our appeals.'

'Probably for the same reason they went to the woods in the first place,' Eileen replied. 'They had other things on their minds. They were just kids. Anyway, whatever they were there in the woods for, the fact is that they saw the van in the afternoon and got around to reporting it yesterday evening. They wasted a few hours, but at least the vehicle's been found, so let's be thankful for small mercies. A forensic team have been there all night, giving it a thorough going over, and we should have some results from them soon. In the meantime, I want a VIIDO team set up straight away to try and track the van's movements before it arrived at Hagg Wood. It must be on CCTV somewhere, if we have to scour the whole of York to find it. If we can find out where it came from...' She shrugged; there was no need to finish the sentence.

While Ariadne organised visual images identifications and detections officers to scrutinise as much CCTV footage as they could gather from the area surrounding Hagg Wood, Geraldine went to the location to talk to the team who were examining the van. There was nothing she could usefully add to their work, but she was impatient to find out what they had discovered, and curious to see the van itself. Somehow she felt it might give her a sense of what the killer had been thinking when he left it there. It was snowing again as she drew up in Hagg Wood, and she shivered as she left the warmth of her car. Standing some distance away from the forensic canopy visible through the trees, she hung around on the narrow roadway until an officer emerged from the trees, carrying a handful of evidence bags. Calling out, she asked him how they were getting on. He made his way over to her, treading carefully on the icy ground, and nodding at her in acknowledgement of her question.

'We have a number of individual black hairs that are straight and quite long, and probably come from a woman, and there could be skin cells as well, we think,' he replied, his breath forming a white cloud in front of his ruddy face. 'But we haven't found anything else inside the vehicle, and we haven't found any hairs or prints that might have come from the driver, not yet anyway. It's been wiped clean inside.'

'He could have been wearing a hat, or a hood,' Geraldine said thoughtfully, rubbing her hands together to warm her fingers.

The scene of crime officer nodded. 'Indeed.' He looked around. 'He must have really forced his way through the trees here. Several branches have been completely broken off, and the van is horribly scratched and dented along both sides. Whoever drove it into the woods was certainly determined to get it off the road.'

Geraldine considered what he was saying before asking her next question. 'Can you tell when it was left here?'

The scene of crime officer shook his head. 'It's difficult to be precise, but there's been no thaw in the last few days and that certainly helps, plus there's only a thin covering of snow on the bonnet, with a deeper layer on the roof. From the depth of the snow on the bonnet of the vehicle, which would have melted while it was being driven, it appears to have been here for no longer than a day or two.' He shrugged. 'I'm sorry if that sounds a bit vague. We might be able to come up with a more precise answer for you once we've checked our exact measurements against the detailed weather reports. In addition to what we can ascertain from the vehicle, there are tyre marks still visible in the snow, with only a thin dusting of flakes covering them so we can still see the indentations. That seems to confirm that it was driven here within the last day or two, no longer.'

Geraldine nodded briskly. 'Can you measure the exact depth of snow that's fallen since the van was left here, and give us a reasonably accurate estimate of the time it was abandoned? If you can, that would be extremely helpful to the VIIDO team searching for it out on the roads.'

'We'll certainly do our best to come up with a more definite time frame.'

No one was surprised when Pansy's DNA was found in the back of the van, nor that male DNA in the interior matched that of the previous owner, Bill Riley. What was more interesting was that they also found traces of DNA from the unidentified male whose DNA had been found on both Pansy and Vanessa's bodies. There was no longer any doubt that the killer had used the van he had purchased from Bill Riley to transport Pansy's body to Acomb Wood three weeks earlier.

'He must have bought the van especially for the purpose of moving the body,' Eileen said. 'But there's a gap of three weeks between the time he purchased the van and used it to move Pansy's body, and the time he abandoned the van in Hagg Wood. So where was he hiding the van all that time?' Eileen asked. 'And more to the point, where has the killer disappeared to now?'

The team were still looking, but so far there had been no sighting of the van entering York by any of the approach roads after it was purchased. It was looking as though it had never left the city again, meaning it had been kept out of sight somewhere in York itself, probably in a garage. The killer must have realised the police would trace the van eventually and try to track its movements, and he had been careful to avoid CCTV on his way to Hagg Wood. All the same, it was strange that no automatic number plate recognition camera around the city had registered the van passing.

'Where the hell is he hiding out?' Eileen repeated, scowling. 'And how has he managed to stay below the radar all this time?'

No one answered. Any man in York who had brown hair and brown eyes could be the killer they were hunting for. So far the odds of finding him were virtually impossible, and the DNA evidence they had gathered was no help as long as they had no match for it on the database. Eileen tasked Geraldine with setting up a press release asking anyone who thought they might have seen an old dirty grey van, with its specific registration number, anywhere in York. Although it was unlikely anyone would have spotted it, anything was possible, and they had to try every avenue.

'With the trail of DNA he's left behind him, at least he won't be able to evade conviction once we find him,' Geraldine pointed out.

But first they had to find him.

50

THE ROOM WAS ILLUMINATED by an electric chandelier, which Ian had not seen switched on before. In its unforgiving light he saw Tod's large desk was covered with a fine film of dust, and the deep pile carpet was littered with barely visible wisps of fluff, specks of dirt, shreds of paper, flecks of cigarette ash and other detritus. Despite its luxurious furnishings, the room had a grimy air, as though everything in it had been contaminated by the sordid scenes played out there. Previously, Ian had felt an urge to shower after spending time in Tod's office. Now his overriding feeling was terror.

The ginger-haired brute, Wills, was there again, standing guard by the desk. Although his gigantic hands hung loosely at his side, his eyes were fixed on Ian. All things being equal, Ian would have had no difficulty subduing him, but he had no doubt Wills was armed, besides which Tod kept a gun in his desk drawer. Muffled by the baize door, a shot wouldn't be heard above the din of music and voices in the club. If one of them plugged him full of bullets, Ian would simply disappear. He might be escorted out of the club by two bouncers, in full view of the punters, his feet dragging on the floor like a man barely conscious after an excess of alcohol or drugs. Alternatively, his body could be smuggled out at night through a back door. Either way, he would doubtless be thrown into a van and driven out to the countryside to be buried, or weighted down with rocks and disposed of in some deserted body of water. Whatever the preferred method of disposal, he would vanish without trace.

He wondered whether Geraldine would try to investigate his disappearance. She was the only person who might care enough to wonder what had happened to him, but perhaps he was fooling himself to believe she would even notice. Jack would instigate a brief investigation which would soon be consigned to a file no one opened again, and the case would become as cold as Ian's vanished corpse. Before long, no one would even remember him.

Wills continued staring fixedly at him, fists now clenched at his sides. Ian wasn't bothered by the other man's aggressive stance. He expected that kind of a welcome from Tod's heavies. He squared up to Wills, returning his glare.

'Chill, Archie, my man,' Tod said. 'Wills, why don't you go fly a kite?'

'But, Boss, I got to stay.'

'You deaf? Sod off. Archie and me, we got business.'

At the periphery of his vision, Ian saw Tod wink at him. He continued staring impassively at Wills. Grumbling under his breath, the ginger-haired bruiser marched out of the room, slamming the door on his way out. A clamour burst fleetingly into the room as Wills opened the door, leaving only the muffled thump thump of music and a distant hum of voices to disturb the silence after he had gone.

'So what's with Frank?' Tod enquired, leaning forward in his chair. 'Tell me he's bought it.'

Ian laughed as easily as he could, given his swollen face. 'Let's put it this way. He won't be bothering you again.'

Tod flushed darkly although his voice remained steady. 'What you blathering about? Either he's kicked off or he hasn't. Don't get slick with me, you cretin. What's the deal with Frank? Tell me straight.'

As he was speaking, Tod's hand drifted behind his desk.

Ian heard the soft creak of a drawer opening and understood that Tod was reaching for his gun. He decided his best option was to appear nonchalant, although inwardly he was shaking. At any moment Tod could shoot him, or summon Wills to do away with him if he didn't fancy doing it himself. Ian had a feeling Wills would enjoy carrying out that particular order. With a dismissive sniff, he sat down and crossed his legs, flicking an imaginary speck of dirt from his jeans. Tod's eyebrows rose ever so slightly, but the movement of his arm indicated that his hand had shifted away from the drawer. A moment later he leaned his elbows on the desk and rested his chin on his clasped hands. He was listening.

'Frank's gone,' Ian said, and was relieved his voice sounded steady. 'But here's the thing. Before I had a chance to neutralise him, he met with one of my colleagues and dropped you right in it. I heard them arranging a raid on the club.'

Tod swore.

'As soon as he walked away from his police contact, I was on to him and I didn't lose sight of him for a second.' Ian sniffed, and winced as his nose hurt. 'At the first opportunity, I dealt with him. You won't be seeing his ugly mug again and nor will his police contact, not unless they dredge the river. But now, we have to act fast. They'll be here soon.' He glanced over his shoulder as though he thought the police might come marching in at any moment. 'We should still have an hour or so before they turn up here. That gives us a window.'

'A window? What the fuck you yapping about?'

'I'm talking about the police,' Ian replied. 'Pay attention, will you? They're preparing to raid the club. I'm telling you, Frank dropped you right in it.'

Hearing that, Tod was on his feet, all pretence at composure gone. 'When's it going to happen?' he cried out in alarm.

'Some time soon. That's why we've got to act fast.'

'What the fuck, Archie! I got to get away.' He took a step

back from his desk, knocking his chair over in his panic.

'Sit down,' Ian replied firmly. 'There's no point in running. What we need to do is remove anything incriminating from the premises. Drugs, records, contact lists, unaccountable wads of cash, anything that could link you to your suppliers. Let the drug squad come here and take the place apart. It's a gift, knowing when they're planning to bust you. Don't you see? You let them come here and find nothing and after that, you're in the clear. They won't come bothering you again. I know those guys. I know the way they think. This has given you the perfect way to get them off your back. All you need to do is remove any evidence before their visit, and they'll never come back. But you can't leave anything incriminating on the premises, so you'd best get moving.'

Tod nodded his head slowly, his eyes wary. 'You're making sense,' he said. 'But how am I going to hide my gear? Where am I going to stow everything? They'll have dogs, won't they? It's no good hiding stuff under the carpet, is it? What the fuck. I should have ripped that fucker apart with my own hands, the snitch. To think I trusted him.' Tod bared his teeth and snarled like a dog. 'Call the boys in. Someone's going to have to stash my gear, and if anyone fingers what's mine, I'll tear them apart.'

'Wait,' Ian said. 'You can't tell your guys to take stuff off the premises. The police are bound to search all of their lodgings. They'll take their rooms apart.'

'I wouldn't trust any of them with an ounce anyway,' Tod growled. 'But what else am I supposed to do? First you tell me I got no time to waste, and now you tell me to wait. What the fuck, Archie? You're messing with me. You gotta help me out here.'

'Calm down, will you? You're forgetting you've got me. All you need to do is gather up anything and everything you don't want the police to find, every last scrap, and I'll take it home with me. They're not going to search my apartment, are they? Remember, they think I'm one of them.' He grinned. 'Your gear will be safe with me until they're done searching every inch of this place. Once it's over, I'll return everything to you, just as it was when you handed it to me. If there's so much as an ounce missing, you can shoot me yourself. How's that? Listen, Tod, you can trust me. You know too much about me for me to drop you in it. And with me on your side, you can't lose. It'll cost you,' he added, 'but we have to act fast.'

Tod nodded. 'You're my boy,' he said. Suddenly brisk, he went on, 'Let's do it. Call in my boys and we'll gather everything up. You'll need bags. No, a case. A large one. What do you think?'

'Whatever it takes. And don't forget to include all the lists of contacts you have. You'll need to print them out or write them down and then delete them from your computer and your phone or they'll find them.' He paused. 'Anyone who's been in contact with the place needs to be eliminated from all records. All the mules, all the suppliers, all the importers. Everyone in the chain. Especially the importers, the big guys. They're the ones the police will be looking for, not the small-time guys you pass gear on to. But they're dangerous too, because you don't know who might squeal. I know a way of deleting contacts permanently from your hard drive and your sim card so the police can't restore them. And I'll need to do the same for the phones of everyone who works here.'

He hoped Tod wouldn't know he was making this up as he went along. A police technology expert might be able to permanently delete information, but there was no way Ian had the knowledge to access Tod's hard drive, or to wipe every contact from computers and phones within minutes.

'I'll get all the mobiles in here,' Tod said at once. 'I'll have my boys bring them in, and you can wipe them all after you wipe my devices. All of them. And all the lulus too,' he added.

'All their punters, everyone. We won't leave a trace.'

Ian nodded. 'After that, everyone will have to work quickly to restore innocent contacts, like family, and suppliers of drink and whatever, anyone legit. The police will smell a rat if no one has any contacts on their phones. Come on, we'd better get started. We don't have much time and there's a lot to do.'

With Tod on board, the rest was relatively plain sailing. Ian slipped away and sent Jack a preset alert that he was about to receive details of a stream of contacts: drug pushers, dealers, suppliers, mules and everyone else associated with Tod and his drug empire, all the way up to the top of the chain. Once Ian had completed his job, he would let Jack know. The following day, Jack would send in a team to take Tod's club apart. The drug squad wouldn't find anything there but, unknown to Tod and his accomplices, their operations would already be over. The incriminating information would already have reached Jack by the time the drug squad descended on the club. Within a few days, Tod and his contacts would all be behind bars awaiting trial for their illicit activity. Within a few weeks, Ian had achieved what the drug squad had been trying to do for months. As he reached his apartment with a large case of evidence that would see Tod and all his associates behind bars, he felt an overwhelming sense of achievement. His resolve to return to York began to waver. Working for the drug squad was proving more satisfactory than he had expected. A few beatings were a small price to pay for putting so many villains behind bars. Even Geraldine would be proud of him.

51

THOMAS AND EMILY WERE sitting in the living room together watching the local news when a message from the police popped up, asking for information concerning a grey van. Of course he had known the van could not stay hidden forever, but he hadn't expected it to be discovered so quickly. Disappointingly, it had been found in no time at all, a mere twenty-four hours after he had hidden it in the trees. Anyone who might have seen the vehicle recently was encouraged to contact the police urgently. Thomas was vaguely aware of a faint ringing in his ears as he stared at the screen. He had considered Hagg Wood to be a good hiding place, but clearly he had been mistaken.

It might have been better to have stored the van in a lock-up garage where no one could have come across it, but it would have been difficult to organise that without leaving a trail that led back to him if it ever was found. As it was, the police had no way of discovering who had driven the van into the woods. That had been the best place to leave it, after all, even if it had been discovered far sooner than he would have liked. But it didn't really matter. He was not in any danger. No one had seen him. He had made sure of that.

One consequence of its swift discovery was that the tracks he had made walking away from it were probably still visible. He was pleased he had thought to wear wellington boots that were two sizes too large for him. In addition to that, not only had he been careful to avoid being seen in the van, but the man he had bought it from had hardly seen his face, and certainly not clearly, since Thomas had been wearing a hood throughout the entire transaction. Thomas inhaled deeply and concentrated on feeling perfectly calm. It didn't matter that the police had come across the van he had used. He had been too cunning to give himself away.

As he began to relax, reassuring himself that he was in no danger, Emily put down her crocheting and turned to him.

'What happened to that old van you had in the garage?'

'What? Oh, that old thing,' he replied, speaking in as casual a tone as he could muster, and keeping his eyes fixed on the screen.

As he spoke, he flicked rapidly through the channels, searching for something to distract her. He could feel his heart pounding in his chest and his face felt hot. He wiped his brow on his sleeve and realised he was sweating. The room seemed to close in on him and he felt as though he might suffocate.

'Yes, that old thing,' she concurred. 'What happened to it?'

'I returned it to the owner. I only borrowed it briefly to move some stuff for the garden. What do you want to watch?'

But she refused to let the subject drop.

'What stuff are you talking about?'

'Oh, it's nothing. I was planning to buy some bushes for the back garden but in the end I decided against it,' he said, improvising quickly. 'So I took the van back. Why do you ask?'

He cursed himself for having forgotten that she had noticed the old van in the garage. He should have been thoroughly prepared for this conversation. Instead, he was caught off guard, and floundering.

'Thomas, I think you need to speak to the police,' Emily said.

'The police?' Suddenly he felt sick. He struggled to

maintain his composure. 'What are you talking about? What do we want with the police?'

He gazed at the television screen, keeping his face impassive and hiding his consternation. He had a creeping cold feeling, as though he was sitting beside a complete stranger, all connection between them severed by an overwhelming need to protect himself. After all the care he had taken to avoid being seen driving the van, his own wife had noticed it, and was becoming suspicious of him. He tried to ignore what she had said, hoping she would forget about it.

'Didn't you hear what they were saying just now?' she persisted. 'They showed a picture of an old van and they asked if anyone had seen it. But you know what? I could swear it looked exactly like the one that was in our garage.'

Thomas's mouth felt dry, but he managed to force a laugh which sounded almost natural.

'Don't be daft,' he said. 'There must be thousands of vans just like that one knocking about in York.'

'Even so, I think you should call the police and tell them about it, and who you borrowed it from. You could be passing on vital information.'

He laughed again. 'Don't you think you're being a touch melodramatic? Vital information? We're talking about an old van I borrowed from a friend, that's all.'

Emily turned to him, her blue eyes troubled, and it occurred to him that if he refused to contact the police, she might do it herself. Somehow he had to stop her from interfering. With a sigh, he nodded.

'Well, if it means that much to you, I'll phone them now.'

'Here,' she said, passing him a magazine. 'I made a note of the number to call. Can you see it there, at the top of the page?'

With a shiver, he realised that she had been ready to phone the police to report seeing a grey van in their garage. Standing up, he offered her a drink. Then he went into the kitchen to pour himself a cold beer and pretend to call the police. He fiddled with his phone, and held it up to his ear, in case she walked in.

'Hello, hello? I'm calling about the van you mentioned on the news a short while ago,' he said, raising his voice enough to be audible in the living room.

Emily was watching television and probably couldn't hear a word he said.

'Yes,' he went on, as if in reply to a question. 'Yes. Registration number? I can't remember. The thing is, I borrowed an old grey van from a friend and returned it a few days ago and I thought – that is, my wife thought – I ought to report it, after we heard the appeal on the telly.' He paused again. 'His name? Yes.'

Feeling foolish, he mumbled a fictitious name and a non-existent address into his silent phone. When he returned to the living room, Emily was absorbed in her quiz programme, and barely glanced up at him.

'I called and told them about it,' he said. 'They asked me a few questions, but they didn't seem very interested.'

Emily grunted. 'Well done, anyway.'

Thomas sat down with a tremor of relief. Emily was totally oblivious to the danger he had just averted. He took a long gulp of his beer and felt it slither down his gullet, refreshingly cold.

'Are you sure you don't want one?' he asked.

Emily shook her head. 'No thanks. Too cold. America! The answer's America.'

Thomas turned to look at the show on television. It was an innocuous enough quiz with fairly easy questions, but he was too shocked to take anything in. He had a horrible sensation that he had lost his way. Even his wife had abandoned him, leaving him to face his difficulties alone. Well, so be it.

Whatever happened, the police were never going to catch him. They would neither catch up with him, nor catch him out because he would do whatever was necessary to save himself. He glanced at Emily who was absorbed in the quiz show, busily crocheting with her eyes fixed on the screen. He wondered how her fingers could work so fast to produce so neat an outcome without her even looking at what she was doing.

'What are you making there?' he asked.

'A scarf. It's nearly finished,' she replied, without taking her eyes off the screen.

An image flashed across his mind of his blackmailer, the strap of her bag tightening around her neck, and he shuddered.

'I need a refill,' he said.

He stood up and went to the kitchen. Emily didn't even look up as he left the room. Crossing the hall, he did his best to dismiss the image of a dead prostitute lying on the floor, her eyes staring glassily up at him. A gulp of cold beer restored him to his senses, and he began to relax. All of that horror was behind him. He just had to hold his nerve and keep his head down. As long as he was careful not to break the law, he had nothing to worry about. It was possible the police had found traces of his DNA in the old van, but that was of no consequence. They had no way of tracing it back to him. He had never been charged with committing a crime, and so had never been asked to supply a sample of his DNA. Calmly he returned to the living room where Emily was still watching the quiz and doing her crochet as though he had never left the room. With a smile, he sat down and began watching the show.

'Do you think he'll be caught?' Emily asked.

Thomas shook his head. 'No, I think I've got away with it.'

'I hope so. I quite like him.'

With a start, Thomas realised she was talking about the

contestant on the quiz show but he had answered for himself, and he made a mental note to be more careful of what he said in future. He could so easily be fooled into giving himself away. From now on, he resolved to drink less and remain constantly vigilant. He couldn't afford to make any mistakes.

52

IAN SPENT AN ANXIOUS weekend alone in his flat, not daring to go out in case one of Tod's men was watching him. He tried to call Jack several times, but his senior officer didn't pick up, and Ian left more than one cryptic voicemail without hearing back. He checked his messages repeatedly and watched the news online, but could find nothing about the club being searched, nor did he see anything about a drug gang being busted. By the time he was called in to Jack's office on Monday morning, he had begun to suspect something had gone badly wrong at the club, and the raid hadn't happened after all. Taking care not to be seen, he hurried to the police station, satisfied that he had completed his part of the job, and excited to finally have an opportunity to discuss the success of the mission which had so far been kept quiet. Expecting to be greeted with enthusiasm, he was disappointed to be kept waiting in the corridor outside Jack's office, like a school boy in trouble with the headmaster. At last he was summoned and, taking a deep breath, he entered the office.

'How's the eye?' Jack asked, without looking up. 'You all right?'

'It's okay,' Ian replied. 'I'm okay.'

'We've been through all the contacts you sent us,' Jack said, without any further preamble. 'And we've sent samples of the gear off to the lab. Jesus, Ian, there's enough there to supply a small army.'

His next words shocked Ian.

'Now you need to return it all, exactly as it was handed to you.'

'I'm not sure I understand, Guv.'

'It's a simple enough instruction. You're to take the case back to Tod. He thinks you had it stashed in your lodgings, doesn't he?'

Ian nodded. Of course he hadn't been able to tell Jack about his conversation with Tod. No one but Tod knew that Ian had revealed his true identity to him.

'Now we've finished going through every corner of the club, he's going to want it back, isn't he? We've replaced everything exactly as it was and locked the case again, so he won't suspect we've been through it. There's not a tab missing, not a gram. It's all there, at least as far as anyone can tell. He can check through the whole damn lot and not spot any sign that we've been through it all.'

Ian frowned. 'You're telling me you want me to take it back?'

'Yes. I think I made that clear. You can return the case. It's all there.'

'I don't understand what's going on,' Ian protested. 'Aren't we going to arrest them all and be done with it? You've got plenty of evidence. You said so yourself. There's no point dragging it out, and the longer we delay, the greater the risk they're going to smell a rat. I know Tod trusts me – he would never have handed me all that incriminating evidence if he didn't. But guys like that can change their mind on a whim. Believe me, I've spent enough time with Tod to know that he's volatile. No, he's worse than volatile. He's crazy. You can't rely on anything he says. He can change his mind like flipping a switch. One minute you're his best friend, the next he'll have you taken out and shot. Now you've got enough to put him away for a long time, I don't understand why you would want to delay and give him an opportunity to slip through our fingers. As long as he's at large, there's a chance Frank will manage to get a message to him and alert him to what's happened. These people have spies everywhere.'

Jack shook his head. 'I'm sorry, Ian. I understand you're keen we jump in right away and make as many arrests as we can. In your shoes I'd be thinking just the same. But it's not that simple.'

'It seems perfectly simple to me,' Ian replied coldly, feeling increasingly uneasy. 'You've got enough evidence to put the whole lot of them away. What's the problem?'

'Just take the stuff back,' Jack said. 'Those are your instructions. We're not done with Tod yet.'

'What are you talking about? How can I take it back? This is it. We've got them. It's over.'

'It's over when I say it's over. Come on, don't look so down,' Jack said. 'We just want you to keep up the pretence for a while. It won't be for much longer. We'll have them all behind bars soon enough.'

'Why on earth would you want to leave a drug dealer like Tod at liberty when you're in a position to lock him up for life? It makes no sense. It's madness,' Ian blurted out, losing patience and momentarily forgetting the deference due to his senior officer.

Jack stared resolutely at Ian, his eyes sharp. 'All right, you might as well know. I've spoken to Tod, and we've come to an accommodation.'

'An accommodation? What the hell does that mean?'

'There's no need to look so shocked. It's the best possible result. In fact everything's worked out perfectly. Don't you see, with the mass of evidence we've got on him – the evidence you gathered – we've got Tod bang to rights. In exchange for us backing off, he's going to lead us to the really big fish. So far all we have is the chain below him. We want to move higher up the line, and find out who's behind the drugs flooding the city, and where they're coming from. You have no idea how useful Tod's going to be.' He tapped a file on his desk and smiled. 'We've got so much evidence against him, Tod's going to sing like a bird for us until we're ready to haul him in.'

With a shiver, Ian recalled Tod saying Ian would 'sing like a bird' before Frank slit his throat. 'Slowly.'

'You're no better than he is,' he muttered crossly.

'You know that's not true,' Jack replied, clearly stung by the accusation. 'Scum like Tod are in it for profit. Listen, this is the break we've been waiting for, Ian. It's taken us a long time to get to where we are today. Thanks to you, we're in a position to blow the whole damned set-up apart.'

But Ian had heard enough. He was furious to learn about the deal Jack had struck with Tod. After everything Ian had been through, Tod was getting away with it. Not only that, but Jack had used Ian shamelessly, without revealing what he was up to.

'You played me,' Ian said. 'This is what you had in mind all along, isn't it? You never intended to arrest Tod. You wanted to use him to get to someone else, just like you used me to get to Tod.'

'That's the nature of the job,' Jack replied quietly. 'I warned you right from the start, this is a dirty game we're involved in. If you're not tough enough to play, return to your former post and carry on with your duties there. I can take it from here now I have evidence of Tod's involvement.'

'You're involved in the dirt yourself, right up to your neck,' Ian said, fuming. 'Well, do what you like with the evidence I brought you. I quit.'

Jack barely reacted to Ian's outburst. 'That's your choice,' he said quietly. 'This line of work isn't for everyone.'

'It's not for anyone with a shred of decency,' Ian retorted.

'You'd rather we sat back and allowed a few scruples to stop us doing everything possible to stop these drugs flooding our streets?'

'So you're saying the ends justify the means, whatever those means might be?'

Jack nodded curtly. 'And if we step outside the law from time to time, it's for the greater good. Can you honestly claim you never do the same when you're tracking down a murderer?'

Ian stalked out of the room and waited until Jack could no longer hear him before he muttered under his breath. 'Two wrongs don't make anything right, and you know it. Or are you too far gone to remember we're supposed to be on the side of law and order? At least I can tell right from wrong.'

But he wasn't sure that was still true. He had been as disingenuous as Jack in pursuing his own ends. At least Jack's agenda had been professional, while Ian's was purely personal, which made it far worse.

53

GERALDINE SPENT THE ENTIRE weekend poring over CCTV footage with the visual images identifications and detections team, searching for the battered old van in which Pansy's body had been transported to Acomb Wood. Nothing the VIIDO team had watched so far had given them a single sighting of the vehicle they were looking for out on the road, but Geraldine refused to let them relax the search.

'We're not going to give up until we find it,' she said. 'That van has to be out there. It didn't fly into Hagg Wood. Someone drove it there.'

She ignored the looks her colleagues exchanged, and their raised eyebrows. It didn't matter to her if they thought she was crazy, as long as they kept searching until they found what they were looking for.

'It has to be here somewhere,' she insisted. 'No vehicle can travel on the streets of York without passing a single camera anywhere. It's just not possible. It has to be there, and we're going to find it.'

When she and her colleagues failed to come up with anything useful after searching for three days, she broadened the search instructions.

'Show me any grey van at all, even if it looks nothing like the one found in the woods. Isolate any shots of any grey van on the road. I want to see them all, every single one. Don't be selective. Any grey van.'

'There may be an awful lot of them,' one of the constables

objected. He yawned. 'We have to be a bit selective, or we could be at this forever. At least we know the registration number of the van we're looking for. That narrows it down.'

'That's just the problem,' Geraldine replied. 'We've been narrowing it down too much. Now we start again, and this time, don't discount anything.'

'But what if we spot a van with a different registration number?' one of her colleagues asked. 'I mean, if we can see the number plate, surely there's no point in spending hours trying to find out where it comes from.'

'Ignore number plates,' Geraldine said.

'But we know the registration number of the van,' the first constable repeated.

'Never mind that,' Geraldine insisted. 'The number plates could have been changed before the van was driven on the road, and then changed back once it was hidden in the trees.'

The VIIDO officers exchanged another glance, and then set to work again with a will. Geraldine worked with them, studying every frame of every image containing a grey van. After four days, she was seeing grey vans whenever she closed her eyes, and wondering why on earth she had embarked on this futile exercise, when her attention was caught by a detail that looked faintly familiar. Comparing the image of a grey van driving past a sports club near Dunnington with pictures of the van that had been used to transport Pansy's body, she hesitated. The van that had been found in the woods was covered in multiple dents and scratches, and was clearly going to look very different now to when it had first arrived at the woods, before it had been taken on its damaging drive through the trees. But there was one detail that appeared to match in the two images she was comparing.

'Look at this,' she said to one of the VIIDO officers.

He looked at where she was pointing, and nodded silently. A similar dent was visible in the same position on the back bumper in both pictures. The damage was possibly identical if viewed from the same angle. It appeared that a van with that particular dent had arrived at the woods, been driven through the trees, and left there until the police towed it out onto the road again. Geraldine stared at the two images for a long time. The van was scarcely recognisable as the same vehicle, with so many scratches and bumps on the one that had been pulled out of the wood. But the dent in the bumper looked the same.

Images of the two bumpers were rotated and superimposed, and it didn't take an IT expert long to confirm that the two dents were in fact identical. They had found an image of the van on its way to Hagg Wood. What was more they had a shot of the back number plate that appeared on the van as it had driven past the sports club. It wasn't the same as the registration number of the van found among the trees. Geraldine's theory was right. The number plates on the van had been switched for its journey on the road, and then changed back again once it reached its hiding place among the trees. She took her discovery to Eileen and together they stared at the two images and the registration number on the van while it was out on the road.

'So he covered up the real number plate when he was driving the van on the road, because he knew we were looking for him,' Eileen said.

'But once he'd dumped the van, he didn't care if we recognised it as the one seen on the night Pansy was moved,' Geraldine added. 'He left it in the woods with its original number plate and he didn't make much of an effort to hide it in the trees.'

Eileen nodded. 'He knew we'd find the van and then we were bound to discover evidence that Pansy had been transported in it. I wonder why he changed the number plates back again before he abandoned it.'

'He didn't think we'd be able to trace the van back to him because he never registered it in his own name after he bought it, but we may be able to identify him from the false number plates, if they come from a vehicle registered in his name. He has no idea we've identified the same van on the road, with false plates. He thought he could stay one step ahead of us. He was certainly clever,' Geraldine said.

Eileen smiled. 'Not clever enough. You have the registration number he used while he was moving the van. Go and see if you can find him, Geraldine, and let's put this killer behind bars, where he belongs.'

'I'm on my way,' Geraldine replied.

And this time, she was confident the lead they had found would take them to the killer.

'Well done,' Eileen called out as Geraldine left her office, and Geraldine smiled.

54

EMILY SMILED ANXIOUSLY AT Thomas across the breakfast table. Her fair hair was brushed back off her face and she wasn't wearing any make-up, but she was still beautiful. She was nibbling at a slice of toast, while he was toying with a bowl of cereal. He stared morosely back at her over the top of his mug of tea. Emily worked part-time and this wasn't one of her days to go into her office, but he had to leave for work soon.

'Is everything all right?' she enquired for the second time that morning. She put down her toast and stared at him, her pale eyes seeming to glow with curiosity.

'Of course everything's all right,' he replied tersely, replacing his mug on the table. 'Why wouldn't it be?'

He paused to chew a mouthful of cereal, and decided to throw the question back at her. The best form of defence was attack, and in any case he needed to be sure she didn't know more than she was letting on. He wondered fleetingly if she had discovered what he had done, but he couldn't think of any way he might have betrayed his secret. Emily had been away visiting her mother in Manchester when the crazy prostitute had attacked him in his own home. All his wife had seen was one glimpse of a grey van in the garage. There was no way she could have the faintest clue about what had gone on in the house in her absence.

'Is everything all right with you?' he asked.

She nodded uneasily, and he leaned forward across his bowl of cereal.

'Tell me what's wrong,' he said, gazing solicitously into her eyes.

'What do you mean? Why would anything be wrong with me?'

'It's just that you seem to be on edge, and you keep asking me what's wrong for no reason that I can make out.'

She shook her head. 'It's not me that's been acting strangely lately.'

A sliver of fear seemed to crawl down the back of his neck like a touch of icy fingers, and he shivered. He had been trying so hard to behave as though nothing untoward had happened and now, just when he thought his troubles were over, his own wife was starting to ask awkward questions.

'What are you talking about?' he countered, struggling to maintain his outward composure. 'How have I been acting strangely?'

'Oh, I don't know. You've been different lately. Ever since I came back from visiting my mother, you've not been yourself. I'm worried about you. Something's wrong, I can tell.'

'I don't know what you mean.'

'Don't take this the wrong way, but ever since you had that van hidden away in the garage, you've been jumpy. I just wonder if it has anything to do with all the talk in the news about the police looking for a van just like that one.' She gave a helpless shrug. 'I can't help wondering if your friend knows more than he's letting on. Are you sure he wasn't up to no good with that van? Who is he, anyway?'

Thomas hesitated. Emily was asking all sorts of questions, and it was a lot to take in. Clearly she had been thinking and was attempting to join the dots. It was important to stop her speculation before it came dangerously close to the truth. He had to remain calm and answer her questions in a way that both reassured her and put an end to her prying.

'For a start,' he replied, 'I wasn't hiding the van. Where else do you suppose I could have parked it, if not in the garage?'

'You could have left it on the street. You never put the car in the garage. Never.'

'And secondly,' he went on, ignoring her interruption, 'the van that was in our garage has absolutely nothing to do with the van they're banging on about on the news. Listen, you silly thing, the police are always trying to trace some missing vehicle or other. There's nothing for you to worry about. In any case, I returned the van to its owner, and there's an end to it.'

'But did you report it to the police?' she asked.

Thomas scowled. Clearly she wasn't going to let this drop, and he wasn't sure of the best way to fend off her questions.

'Report what to the police?'

It was her turn to frown. 'You said you would tell them about the van in the garage. You told me you'd call the police and tell them about it. You don't know what your friend is up to, do you? How well do you even know him? This could be vital information you're withholding from the police.'

'Don't be so dramatic,' he replied impatiently. 'Now you're just being silly. Anyway, you know I phoned the police and told them I'd had a grey van stored in my garage. They asked for the registration number and then they said they'd be in touch if they had any further questions, and that was that. They never called back. They weren't interested in the van we had in our garage.'

'And you think that's good enough?' Emily asked.

'What do you mean? Don't you believe me?'

She frowned and shook her head. 'Why wouldn't I believe you? No, the point is I'm not convinced the police are being thorough enough. The van they're looking for has something to do with the woman who was murdered, and you can't be sure your friend wasn't involved in that in some way. Think about it, Thomas. He could have changed the number plates on the van. Who is this friend of yours, anyway? You haven't told me anything about him. Where do you know him from?'

Thomas forced a laugh. 'What is this?' he asked. 'The Spanish Inquisition?' He stood up. 'I'm late for work.'

'Well, if you're not going to follow it up, I'll drop into the police station myself and make sure they take this seriously. Just think about it, Thomas. Your friend wanted his van stored out of sight for a few days, and right after that the police are looking for a van just like his. How can you be so sure your friend wasn't using you? All right, I may be jumping to conclusions and barking up the wrong tree, but what if the van you put in our garage is the same one the police are looking for? You don't want to get yourself in trouble. What if I'm right and someone saw you driving the van back to its owner? You have to go to the police, and tell them exactly what happened before they find you. If you come clean, and tell them everything, there's nothing to worry about.'

'There's nothing to worry about anyway, because nothing happened,' he replied firmly. 'Now drop it, Emily. There's nothing to "come clean" about. I don't want you to go bothering the police with this. As if they haven't got enough to do.'

'It'll only take a minute. You can't protect your friend over something so serious.'

'No. You are not going to the police about this.'

He sounded angrier than he had intended, and Emily paused in the act of standing up. She sat down and they stared at one another in silence.

'Isn't it time you left?' she asked at last. Her voice sounded shaky. 'It's really late.'

'I'm not going to work today.' He broke off, not knowing what to say to her. 'Emily, you have to promise me you won't say anything to anyone about the van. Not yet. I have to clear something up first. Trust me, and everything will be all right, I promise you.'

'Thomas,' she whispered, her eyes wide in sudden alarm. 'What have you done?'

In that instant he understood that he couldn't trust her to keep her mouth shut.

55

JENNY STEPPED INTO THE hall and halted abruptly on seeing Ian's cases leaning against the wall. Her expression didn't alter, but he sensed her astonishment in the sudden tension in her stance and the rigidity of her features. She was dressed as Tallulah in a very short, sleek black skirt and black leather jacket, her hair scraped up in a high ponytail that fanned out in a blaze of colourful plumes. Her make-up was brazen as ever, with bold black lines around her eyes and equally striking red lipstick.

'So it's true,' she blurted out. She gazed up at him, her eyes looking enormous in their black circles. 'There's a rumour going around that you're leaving London, and now I see you've been packing. So it's true, then? I can't believe you would make an important decision like this without so much as mentioning it to me.'

Ian hesitated over his reply. He owed her no explanation. As far as he had been aware, their liaison had never been anything other than casual. Neither of them had made any kind of commitment to the other. He had told her outright that their relationship wasn't going to last. When she hadn't remonstrated at the time, he had thought she understood what he was saying, and she had given him the impression that she felt the same. Admittedly she had said they didn't know how their relationship was going to turn out, but he was satisfied he had made his own feelings clear.

'I'm sorry,' he muttered. 'I didn't realise you'd be

disappointed, but I'm not very good at reading women's minds.' He shrugged apologetically. 'It's one of my many failings.'

'Oh poor you,' she snapped. 'So now I'm supposed to feel sorry for you because you're so crap at relationships?' She shook her head and her hair flapped around crazily, like a surreal halo. 'How could you even think of leaving London without telling me? Without saying goodbye? How could you do that, after everything we meant to each other?'

Once again, Ian hesitated. By 'everything' she could only be referring to the few nights they had spent together. He wracked his brains, but he couldn't recall either of them ever hinting their affair was anything other than a casual fling. He should have been flattered that he meant so much to her, but he was appalled.

'Of course I was going to say goodbye to you,' he replied. 'I never had any intention of leaving London without seeing you again. You mean too much to me for me to just disappear, without a word. I'm not that kind of man, Jenny. You know that.'

He paused. She only really knew him as Archie, his undercover alter ego. She didn't know him as Ian at all.

'It seems I don't know the first thing about you,' she replied sullenly, confirming his own thoughts.

'Listen, I never meant to hurt you. I care about you, about your feelings,' he corrected himself quickly. 'But it's time for me to leave London. We both knew it had to happen sooner or later. London isn't my home. I don't live here. I was here on a job, that's all, and now it's time for me to move on. My going away has nothing to do with you. I mean, I'm not going because of you. I'm not saying you're an important part of my life, or that you're not, it's just that my time here is over and I'm going home. I came here to do a particular job and now that's done, I can't stay.' He broke off, aware that he was repeating himself because he could think of nothing else to say. 'I'm sorry, Jenny. I'm really sorry if I gave you the wrong impression. What we had together was very special. I don't sleep with many women – there have only been two others. My wife and I met when we were still at school and I was faithful to her right up until we divorced quite recently. And since then there's been one other woman, apart from you. So you see, I don't sleep with many women, and it means something to me when I do.'

She sniffed and he suspected she didn't believe him, but that was too bad. What she had said was true – they knew nothing about each other. He knew her better as Tallulah than as Jenny, and she had spent more time with Archie than Ian. He was fairly sure she had only slept with him at all because that was what Tallulah and Archie would have been doing. Their whole relationship was based on a fiction. Jenny and Ian had never spent the night in bed together. It had only ever been Tallulah and Archie.

'I'm not Archie,' he said.

'I know that. I'm not an idiot,' she replied crossly. 'So where does this leave us?'

'Us?'

'Yes, us. You and me. I'll be here in London and I don't even know where you're going.'

He sighed. This was becoming complicated, and he wasn't sure how to extricate himself from the situation without upsetting her even more. Yet he was reluctant to reveal that he was going back to York. He had an uneasy feeling she might want to follow him there.

'It's over, Jenny,' he said gently. 'Whatever there was between us, it's over.'

To his surprise, she burst out laughing. 'Oh for fuck's sake, Ian, can't you tell when someone's pulling your leg? Of course we never had a serious relationship. Tallulah and Archie's one thing, but Jenny and Ian? Not in a million years. Christ, I don't even know how old you are, but I can tell you're too old for me. Still, it was fun for a while, wasn't it?' she added, with a slightly wistful smile. 'You have to admit Tallulah and Archie were good together.'

She leaned forward and kissed him on the lips before turning on her heel and strutting out of his flat and out of his life. Ian sighed as he watched her go. With a pang, he wondered what the future held for her, and how long she would survive working at Tod's club. Like Jack had said, Jenny was caught up in a dirty business. Role playing had appealed to him at first and he had welcomed the opportunity to leave his own miserable life behind. But he was glad to quit the pretence and return to his normal life and his own identity. Archie's tempestuous brief existence was over and Ian wasn't sorry.

'Goodbye, Tallulah,' he murmured to the door that had already closed behind his make-believe girlfriend.

He would never know whether her dismay at his departure had been completely fake, but it was gratifying to think she might actually have been a little disappointed that he was leaving. He wondered how Geraldine was going to feel when he returned to York. His absence had given her time to reconsider her own feelings towards him, and he hoped she had forgiven him for what he had done. And now that he had dealt with Jammie, there was nothing to prevent her from seeing her twin sister again. His trepidation tinged with optimism, he set off on his journey back to York.

An irrepressible excitement coursed through him as he rang Geraldine's bell. There was no answer. He tried her phone but she didn't pick up.

'Hello,' he called out cautiously, when her phone went to voicemail. 'It's me, Ian. Can you pick up the phone? I'm at your flat. Hello? Geraldine? Are you in?'

He didn't know where she was and had no idea what to do.

Expecting to find her at home, he had spent the journey back to York rehearsing what he was going to say to her when they saw each other. He had imagined her joy on hearing that she would be able to see Helena again. He was so impatient to see her and tell her the news it hadn't occurred to him that she might not be at home. He tried her mobile but she didn't answer.

'Geraldine,' he said to the messaging service, 'I'm going to let myself in the flat and wait on the sofa. I hope that's all right. I just want to see you and speak to you in person as soon as we can. I have something to tell you and it can't wait.'

Hoping she would not be furious that he had not waited for her outside, he let himself in. He walked through every room. Every inch of the place was filled with memories. In the bedroom he caught a whiff of her perfume and closed his eyes to savour the scent, familiar and haunting. It felt unreal being back in the home where he had been so happy, as though he was dreaming about a distant childhood memory. Yet at the same time he felt as though he had never been away. In some ways he was relieved to be alone in the flat where everything reminded him of Geraldine; her fingers had touched everything he could see.

He was keen to speak to her, but also extremely nervous as he didn't know if she was still angry with him. Whatever her response, he was determined to overcome her resistance. He loved her more than he had ever loved anyone else, and he was sure she felt the same way towards him. She certainly had done, and such strong feelings didn't just disappear in a fit of anger. They couldn't. He tried to rehearse what he was going to say to her, but each time he thought about it, the words came out differently and nothing sounded right. He would just have to play it by ear. If she was adamant that their relationship was over, he would have to accept her decision, but he wasn't prepared to give up yet, not without a fight.

Returning to the living room, he slumped down on the sofa and prepared to wait for her. She would come in, cold and tired after a frustrating day. It was typical of her to be out working, at a time when most people were enjoying their evening. The first thing he would do would be to pour her a glass of wine, and then they would talk. She would give him details about the case she was working on, and they would discuss it. After that, he would no doubt reveal a lot more about his time in London than was strictly allowed. He would tell her what was most important to her, that the drug dealer who had been harassing her twin sister had agreed to leave her alone and Geraldine could see Helena again. No one else knew what Ian had done, but he could trust Geraldine with his dark secret. She was the only person he had ever really been able to trust. With a sigh, he closed his eyes.

56

THOMAS STARED AT EMILY, registering her bewildered expression, and hating himself for upsetting her.

'No,' he muttered under his breath, shaking his head helplessly. 'This isn't how it's meant to be.'

He closed his eyes, but nothing had changed when he opened them again. Emily was still sitting at the kitchen table, her blue eyes staring at him in dismay.

'Thomas, tell me what's going on,' she said.

'What's going on? What do you mean, what's going on? I don't know what you're talking about. Nothing's going on,' he gabbled. 'I just don't want you going to the police. I don't want you going anywhere.'

'What are you talking about? Thomas, what's happened? What have you done?'

He took a deep breath and tried to control his panic.

'I haven't done anything. It's just that the police don't like it when people kick up a fuss unnecessarily,' he explained in what he hoped was a reasonable tone of voice. 'That's all I'm saying.'

'Thomas, you're not making any sense. The police appealed to the public for information. Why would they do that if they didn't want people to respond?'

'Don't you realise, everyone in York who owns a grey van has been phoning the police? And not only that. Everyone who has a friend, or a neighbour, with a grey van, has been calling them? There's no way they'll be able to deal with the volume of calls they're getting. It's a distraction from their real work. And you want to waste police time with yet another pointless call, over something as trivial as telling them I borrowed a van from a friend for a few days? Now let's drop it. I'm not going to the police, Emily, and neither are you, and that's that. I won't hear of it. Once you draw attention to yourself, there's no knowing what might happen. Do you really think you can trust the police?'

Emily stood up and began clearing away the breakfast things. She had barely touched her toast.

'I don't know what you're getting so het up about,' she said. 'I'm just going to tell them there was a van in our garage, and they should talk to you to find out whose it was, and then they can find out exactly why this friend of yours wanted you to look after his van for him. It sounds dodgy to me, whatever you think. I can't believe you don't agree with me. A woman was murdered and her body was moved in a grey van. And just while all that's going on, your friend – whoever he is – lends you his van. The police need to be told about it, and they have to question your friend.'

'The van that was in our garage has nothing to do with the police,' Thomas replied, but he knew it was hopeless. 'If you knew the guy who owns the van, you'd realise straight away how ridiculous you're being.'

'Who is he, then, this friend of yours? You haven't told me who he is. Is he anyone I know?'

'His name's Fred,' Thomas lied, giving her the first name that came into his head. 'He does odd jobs at my office. He's freelance,' he added quickly, realising she could call his office and establish there was no one on the payroll called Fred.

But Emily was unconvinced and she remained set on going to the police.

Helpless to dissuade her, he resorted to pleading with her. 'Please, Emily, be patient. This isn't what you think. I know it all sounds odd, but I'll explain everything to you, I promise. Only don't go to the police.'

She frowned warily. 'I don't understand,' was all she said.

They stared at one another for a moment.

'Go on, then,' she said, breaking the tense silence. 'Explain to me why you don't want me to go to the police.'

Thomas hesitated. He had to give her an answer, but he needed time to work out what to say.

'Neither of us is going to work today, and I've got nothing pressing to deal with. Let's go for a drive and I'll tell you all about it.' He paused. 'It's not something I can explain quickly. It's – it's complicated.'

'Where do you want to go?'

'I'll take you out for a nice pub lunch, somewhere along the river, and we can really talk.'

'Why can't we talk here?'

'I just thought it would be nice to get out.'

'No, let's not go out. I want to listen to what you have to say, right here and now. And I want you to tell me everything, Thomas. Whatever it is you've done, we can get through this together. You know I'll stand by you, but you have to be honest with me. Is there another woman involved? Is that it? You have to tell me.'

Thomas gazed at her, wondering quite how far her loyalty towards him would stretch. She said she would stand by him whatever he had done, but he wasn't convinced she would forgive him if he told her the truth. Clearly she had no idea about what had really happened. She was worried he was seeing another woman. In a way, that was part of the truth, but he was never going to admit that. Instead, he started by telling her how he had tried to be a good Samaritan, but even as he was speaking he could see she was looking puzzled. She sat down and her expression hardened as she listened.

'Let me get this straight,' she interrupted him. 'You're

telling me you brought a total stranger back here to our house, because you saw her in the street and she looked ill? Why didn't you stay with her and call a doctor, or an ambulance?'

Thomas shrugged. 'I probably should have done, but it was freezing outside. With hindsight, I can see that it would have been more sensible to call an ambulance, but I felt sorry for her and wanted to get her in out of the cold as quickly as possible. We were only a few steps from the house. Only when we got back here she collapsed. I think she was on drugs, or alcohol, or both. And she must have been suffering from hypothermia. As she fell, she hit her head on the coat stand and before I knew it, she was dead.'

Emily gasped. 'Dead? She was dead? You brought her here and she died, here in our house?'

'And then I panicked,' he confessed.

That at least was true.

'But why did you bring her here?' Emily demanded. 'Oh my God, Thomas, you're talking about that prostitute who's been in the news, aren't you? You brought a prostitute here into the house.'

He lowered his head. 'Yes, yes, of course I know now that she was a prostitute, but I had no idea of that when I saw her in the street.'

It sounded unlikely, even to his own ears.

'I didn't know who she was at the time,' he went on, more firmly. 'All I knew right then was that she was freezing outside, and ill, and then she was in our hall and she was dead. There was a dead woman in our hall, Emily. What was I supposed to do?'

Having told Emily about the body, he stuck to the truth and described how he had bought a van and moved the body to the woods, while Emily stared at him, horrified.

'I don't understand,' she said when he finished. 'I don't

understand why you didn't call the police straight away. What were you thinking of?'

'I was afraid the police wouldn't believe me,' he replied. 'Don't you understand? I was frightened, Emily. I panicked. It wasn't my fault she was dead. She just collapsed and then she was dead.'

The blackmailer's death hadn't been his fault any more than the prostitute's, but he didn't even get as far as telling Emily about that because she was on her feet, white faced with horror.

'You brought a prostitute to our house while I was away,' she cried out. 'You killed her and tried to get rid of her body. If you'd buried her, she might never have been found, and no one would ever have known what you'd done.'

He wasn't sure if she was angry because she thought he had killed the woman, or because he had left the body where it had been easily found.

'I can see how it must look,' he said, 'but it wasn't like that. I didn't know who she was. And I didn't do anything to her. I never touched her. She just collapsed. I'm telling you the truth, Emily.'

She had her phone in her hand.

'What are you doing?'

'I'm calling the police and you're going to hand yourself in,' she replied, her voice oddly calm. 'You're going to tell them exactly what you told me. You have to tell them the truth, Thomas. Sooner or later they're going to catch up with you, and it'll be better if you go to them.'

If he had only had the prostitute's death to deal with, he might have gone along with Emily's decision. But she didn't know about his blackmailer. Feeling as though he had strayed into some dark fiction, he rushed around the table, snatched her phone and threw it across the room. It landed with a faint clatter on the tiled floor. He stood facing her, physically shaking.

'What are you doing?' she cried out.

LEIGH RUSSELL

Before she could say another word, he clapped his hand over her mouth, his index finger and thumb pressing her nostrils shut. She moaned and struggled, and kicked at his legs, but he held on, pinning her arms to her sides with his free arm. Hours seemed to elapse before she stopped moving and hung heavily in his fierce embrace. He didn't know how long he had been standing there, supporting her inert body in his arms, when he heard knocking at the front door, and the sound of sirens in the street outside his house. With a cry, he dropped to his knees, still clutching Emily in his arms. Leaning forward, he wept over the limp body of the woman he loved.

57

IT WAS MIDDAY BY the time Geraldine knocked at Thomas's door. She knew that neither he nor his wife was at work that day. She had brought several uniformed constables with her, and the back door to the house was being watched as she knocked on the front door.

'Shall I break it down?' a burly constable at her side asked her.

Geraldine gazed up into his broad fleshy face and hesitated. With all the noise of sirens in the street and the hammering on the door, anyone in the house must be aware by now that the police were outside, yet no one had come to the door. She looked around. Several neighbours had appeared on their front doorsteps, and a few people were already gathering in the street, curious to see what was going on.

Geraldine turned back to the constable and shook her head. 'Keep knocking for now.'

Before battering the door down, she wanted to give Thomas time to answer. With the house surrounded, he wasn't going anywhere, so she was in no rush to get inside. Walking back to the street, she approached a woman standing in the front yard of the neighbouring house and asked her whether she had seen Thomas or his wife that morning.

'No, I can't say I have,' the woman replied. 'But I don't see that much of them. We live next door, but we're not really on close terms with them. I mean, we've not fallen out or anything, but you know how it is. Everyone keeps themselves to themselves. Everyone's busy.'

Geraldine didn't point out that the woman was hanging around outside her house, doing nothing but watch what was going on next door. She crossed the road to speak to a woman standing on the front doorstep of the house opposite Thomas and Emily's, and received a similar response. No one could recall having seen anyone come out of Thomas's house that morning. Meanwhile, the constable had continued knocking and calling out in a stentorian voice, but there was no response from inside the house. Since a small crowd had now gathered in the street to watch, Geraldine silenced him before going through the side gate and speaking to one of two constables standing guard at the back of the house. With a nod, he kicked open the back door.

After the wailing sirens and the subdued buzz of chatter from excited neighbours, the interior of the house seemed eerily quiet. Geraldine entered cautiously and some instinct warned her to motion to her colleague to stay back. There was an unnatural quality to the silence in the house. Even the pipework wasn't creaking and the floorboards made no sound beneath her feet. One step at a time, she advanced, hardly daring to breathe for fear of disturbing the silence in the house.

The back door led straight into a living room. There was a faint smell of burnt toast from inside the house as though someone had recently made breakfast. Listening, she thought she heard a sound somewhere ahead of her. She moved further into the room. Behind her, she heard the two constables following her, their footsteps falling almost inaudibly on the floor. She turned and whispered to one of them to remain on guard at the back door in case Thomas tried to run. Leaving the back room, she made her way into the hall. The stairs were on her right. The first door she came to on her left was closed. It swung open with a faint squeal to reveal an empty dining room. The door to the next room was open. From the hall, Geraldine looked into a kitchen at the front of the house where a man was crouching on the floor, his shoulders shaking as he wept softly over a woman who was lying perfectly still in his arms. His head hung forwards, masking the woman's face, but Geraldine could see that her arms hung limply at her sides and she was making no attempt to respond to the man's distress. Aware that the woman might still be alive, Geraldine entered the kitchen, motioning to her uniformed colleague to block the door.

'Thomas,' she called softly. 'Is that your wife? I think she needs help.' She drew closer. 'Is she breathing? Thomas, we need to get your wife some help. Please, you have to let go of her so I can take a look at her.'

With a groan, Thomas laid the woman on the floor and rose to his feet to face Geraldine.

'Who are you?' he asked, glaring wildly at her. 'What are you doing here? What do you want?'

'Right now I want to see if your wife is alive and in need of attention,' she replied evenly.

A second later, she heard the constable who was out of sight in the hall talking quietly on his phone. Clearly he was being careful not to disturb the volatile situation.

'She's fine,' Thomas replied, his voice rising in anger. 'Leave her alone. I can take care of her. I'll take care of everything. Get out of my house. Leave us alone!'

'Thomas, I'm here with the police. We just want to ask you some questions. But first, we need to see to your wife.'

She knelt down and began to examine the woman for any vital signs.

'No,' he replied. 'I can take care of her myself. We don't need you here. Get out of my house! Go away, please, just go away. I need to think.'

'I'm not going away. I'm here with the police and we have

your house surrounded so you're not going anywhere either. We're going to sit down and talk quietly, but first we need to look after your wife.'

'You leave her alone!'

Without warning he lunged sideways and seized a long knife from a magnetic knife holder on the wall. Geraldine hesitated to withdraw, but the woman on the floor was already beyond help. There were police nearby, but Geraldine was within arm's reach of Thomas, who was clearly insane and wielding a knife. She stood up very slowly. As she did so, there was a noise in the hallway behind her and she froze. Thomas heard it too. Her fleeting hesitation had been a mistake. With a wild cry he leapt at Geraldine, slashing at her chest. If she hadn't been wearing a bullet-proof vest, the attack would probably have proved fatal. She seized his arm, but he was strong and managed to wrench it free without dropping the knife which slashed in the air dangerously close to her face.

'If you move, I'll kill you!' he shrieked, his face white with manic determination. 'I'll do it!'

'Thomas, we have the house surrounded,' a voice called out. 'Put down the knife and come out quietly.'

'Think about what you're doing,' Geraldine said, struggling to keep her voice even. 'If you harm me, you won't be able to claim it was an accident, will you? My colleagues are watching. What will it be? Assaulting a police officer? First degree murder? You can't get away, and you'll be locked up for the rest of your life. Is that what you want?'

'Let me go and I won't harm her,' Thomas cried out, his voice shrill with desperation.

'Come out, Thomas,' the voice in the hall urged him.

'Thomas,' Geraldine said gently, eyeing the knife in his hand. 'It's over. You know they'll never let you get away. The moment you set foot outside this room, they'll disarm you.

What can you hope to achieve with a kitchen knife against the police?'

He turned to Geraldine. 'I never meant to do it, you know. I never meant to hurt anyone. It wasn't my fault, the way it all turned out. I didn't mean to kill anyone.'

Geraldine edged towards him, watching the knife shaking in his hand.

'Come along,' she replied. 'Put the knife down and let's go and talk about it quietly and you can tell me everything that happened, right from the beginning.'

'And you'll look after Emily?' he replied, looking down at his wife who lay at his feet. 'You'll see she's taken care of?'

'Yes. She'll be well looked after. Now put the knife down and let's go.'

With something between a sob and a cry, he replaced the knife carefully on the knife rack. As he did so, Geraldine grabbed him by the wrists and handcuffed him.

'Come along,' she said, speaking rather more roughly than before. 'You've got some talking to do.'

'You're hurting me,' he protested as she propelled him towards the door.

'Well, you frightened me,' she replied, angry now that she was no longer afraid for her life.

With an effort, she controlled her response, and by the time they reached the hallway she was outwardly calm.

'He's all yours,' she said to Matthew, who was standing by the door.

'Are you all right?' he asked her, gazing earnestly at her face.

She nodded. 'Nothing a stiff drink won't sort out,' she replied.

'It's a date,' he murmured. 'I'll pick you up at eight.'

Before she could answer, Matthew seized hold of Thomas's

arm and hustled him out of the house. As they left, a paramedic approached Geraldine.

'She's dead,' he said. 'Suffocated by the look of it. It doesn't look like an accident.'

'You would have been next,' a constable added, with a nod at Geraldine. 'You dodged a bullet there, Ma'am. Or at least a knife blade,' he added with a half-hearted grin at his feeble quip.

Geraldine suddenly felt nauseous and turned away to hide her trembling.

58

'TIME FOR THAT DRINK?' Matthew murmured to Geraldine when she had finally finished writing up her report.

Thomas had been locked up in a cell for the night, and they were going to question him in the morning. There was nothing pressing left to do that evening, and it would be better to take a break before returning to work in the morning. Matthew was good company and she could do with a drink to help her relax after her terrifying experience. So she went to the toilets and applied heavier make-up than she usually wore during the day. It was faintly exciting to be driven to a quiet country pub, even though she and Matthew weren't on a date, and there was nothing romantic about their conversation as they had a beer and chatted about the case.

'Say what you like, I couldn't help feeling sorry for him,' Geraldine said.

'After he murdered three women – including his wife – with his bare hands, and threatened you with a knife?' Matthew replied. 'I don't see much to feel sorry for there. The man's a dangerous maniac and he needs to be locked up for life. How can you feel any sympathy for him at all?'

Geraldine shook her head. 'I don't know. I'm not convinced he intended to kill any of those women.'

'We can't let criminals' excuses obscure the facts of their behaviour,' Matthew replied. 'We have to judge people by what they do, not what they say, or no one would ever be convicted of anything.'

'True. But you have to admit it's possible his first two victims died by accident. He was quite insistent about that when we were bringing him in. You should have heard him in the car. And you can't deny intention makes a difference.'

'What about his wife?' Matthew countered. 'Did he inadvertently suffocate her with his bare hands? You saw the report. His legs were bruised from her kicking him. She was resisting for all she was worth. He knew perfectly well what he was doing. I can't see how anyone can feel any sympathy for him at all, and I'm sure any sane juror will see it my way. We all have to accept responsibility for our own actions or no one would ever be found guilty of anything, and our job would be completely pointless.'

'All I'm saying is that it's possible he was telling the truth, and the whole sorry episode started with an accidental death which he stupidly tried to cover up because he didn't want his wife knowing he had taken a sex worker home with him. And everything else followed on from that first incident.'

The menu looked good and they were both hungry, so they ended up staying there for supper and it was past ten by the time Matthew dropped her home.

'That was a lovely evening,' Geraldine said with genuine appreciation as they drew up outside her flat. 'I'm happy to invite you in as long as we're clear I'm not looking for anything more than friendship.'

'Of course,' he replied, smiling easily at her. 'I may be separated but my wife and I are not divorced. I see my two children regularly so I still consider myself a family man, even if my wife and I are no longer living together. To be honest with you, my life is complicated enough right now, living apart from them. There's no way I'd want to do anything to upset my ex, or she might not be so relaxed about my seeing the children. And in any case, after what happened to Thomas, I think I've been put off messing around with other women for quite a while.'

'Are you comparing me to Pansy?' Geraldine asked in mock outrage, and laughed at his mortified expression. 'Why don't you come in for a night cap? Strictly friends or I'll be on the phone to your wife.'

'That sounds almost irresistible, but I think I've had enough to drink for tonight if I'm driving home.'

'Can I tempt you to a cup of cocoa?'

'That sounds perfect. One cocoa and then I'm off home,' he agreed cheerfully.

They were both laughing as they entered Geraldine's flat. She flung open the door to the living room and was startled to see Ian sitting on the sofa. The hesitant smile froze on his lips as he caught sight of Matthew standing in the hall behind Geraldine.

'Ian!' Geraldine cried out in surprise. 'I had no idea you'd be here.'

'Clearly,' he replied coldly.

'Why didn't you call to let me know you were back?'

'I did. If you check your phone you'll see that I left a message.' He stood up. 'I'm sorry, it didn't occur to me that you might have company.'

'No, wait, please.' Flustered by his unexpected appearance, she spoke rapidly, aware that she sounded nervous. 'This isn't what it looks like. That is, I don't know what it looks like, but please don't get the wrong idea. Matthew's a new colleague. He's only recently joined us. We went for a drink, that's all.'

'I'd better go,' Matthew said, glancing from Ian to Geraldine. 'I'll see you tomorrow, Geraldine.'

'There's no need for you to rush off,' Geraldine said politely, although she was finding it hard to think about anything but Ian. All she wanted to do was put her arms around him and hold him close to her. 'Ian, this is Matthew. He was standing in for you while you were away.'

'So I see,' Ian replied curtly. 'Please don't leave on my account, Matthew. I only called round to collect a few things. I can come back at a more convenient time. It's my fault. I should never have turned up unannounced like this, and I had no right to let myself in. This is obviously a mistake.'

'No, Ian, please don't go,' Geraldine said. 'You have every right to be here.'

Hearing the desperation in Geraldine's voice, Ian hesitated.

'Please stay,' she insisted. 'I invited Matthew up for a hot drink. We can all have a cocoa together, can't we?'

'No, really, three's a crowd and all that,' Matthew said cheerfully.

Only Matthew appeared to be taking the situation in his stride. If anything, he looked faintly amused, unlike Ian who was glaring at her.

'Good to meet you, Ian,' Matthew continued breezily. Far from displaying any resentment towards Ian, Matthew extended a hand in friendly greeting. 'I hope we'll be seeing more of each other now I'm working with Geraldine, but I really ought to be getting back. My wife's used to my erratic hours, bless her, but she gets twitchy if I'm home too late.'

Beyond a quick nod, Geraldine barely acknowledged Matthew's departure. She was looking at Ian with a mixture of relief and dismay.

'I can't believe you're really here. But what happened to your face? And where the hell have you been all this time? Why didn't you call? Didn't you think I might be worried sick about you, and with good reason, it seems. Have you had your injuries seen to? For goodness sake, Ian, what happened to you? Did you have a run in with a solid wall?'

'Something like that,' he admitted gruffly. 'A human wall.'

And just like that, they were talking freely, as though their falling-out had never happened. Ian gave her a very brief résumé of his experience in London and she told him about Thomas, but they were both tired and they agreed to leave all explanations, excuses and apologies until the following day.

'There is just one thing I must tell you,' Ian said. 'This can't wait. I managed to sort out your sister's problem. Her ex-dealer won't be troubling her again, so you're free to see her whenever you want.'

'Never mind any of that for now.' She came closer and kissed him gently on his bruised cheek. 'All that matters right now is that you're here. You can tell me everything tomorrow. Let's just go to bed. You look exhausted.'

'Not that exhausted,' he protested, smiling and pulling her into his arms.

59

'YOU DON'T UNDERSTAND,' THOMAS mumbled, shaking his head. 'I never meant it to happen. I never meant any of this to happen.' He broke down in tears again.

Geraldine and Matthew faced him across the table. He was unremarkable to look at, with mousy brown hair and a thin face. As she waited for him to wipe his eyes and regain sufficient self-control to answer more questions, Geraldine glanced at his poker-faced lawyer. A gaunt man with grey hair and pale grey eyes, he looked like a shadow of a man. His low hoarse voice did nothing to breathe life into his presence in the interview room.

'Tell us how you came to kill Pansy,' Geraldine said, pointing to a picture of Thomas's first victim.

'It was an accident. I'm telling you. I never meant to hurt anyone,' Thomas said, not for the first time. He turned to his lawyer. 'Tell them, tell them,' he urged him, 'you know I didn't mean to do it. I never meant to hurt anyone. Tell them, tell them I never meant to do it. She just fell over.'

'We need to hear it from you, in your own words, Thomas,' Geraldine said gently. 'Start right at the beginning.'

'The whole thing started when my wife went to visit her mother and I took a woman home with me. I'm not proud of it, but that's what I did. And that's all I did.'

'This woman?' Geraldine pointed to the picture of Pansy again. 'Pansy?'

'Yes, only she didn't call herself Pansy.' He hung his head.

'She told me her name was Luscious.'

'Had you met this woman before?' Matthew asked.

'No, never. I picked her up outside a bar. She was a whore.' He looked up and raised his voice with an unexpected air of defiance. 'I knew that when I took her home. There, I've said it. I'm not proud of it. And before you ask, no, it wasn't the first time I'd taken a whore home with me while my wife was away. It was just a bit of harmless fun,' he added lamely.

'You found it fun to kill sex workers?' Matthew asked sternly. 'And you think that's harmless?'

'No, no, it wasn't like that. I didn't kill her. It wasn't my fault she died. I never would have hurt her. I'm not like that. I'm not that sort of man.'

'What happened to her?' Geraldine prompted him.

The memory of Thomas's wife hung unspoken in the air between them.

'I took her home and she suddenly went crazy. She attacked me and then she collapsed and hit her head and then she fell down and I could tell she was dead. It was shocking. I was in shock. I couldn't think what to do.'

He began to tremble visibly at the memory.

'Why didn't you call an ambulance when she collapsed?' Matthew asked.

'Why do you think? I didn't want anyone to find out I'd taken a whore home with me. I didn't want my wife to know. The whore was dead and there was nothing more anyone could do for her. If she'd been sick, I would have called an ambulance or driven her to the hospital myself, but she was dead. Are you listening to a word I'm saying? The whore was dead. I couldn't do anything for her, but I could still protect myself. It seemed the most sensible thing to do. So I bought an old van and drove the body to Acomb Wood. But you know that. It might seem stupid, but I couldn't think what else to do. What was I supposed to do? My wife was due home. I didn't want her to know.'

'What about Vanessa Slattery?' Matthew asked, pointing to an image of Thomas's second victim.

'I don't even know who that is. You can't pin that one on me.'

'We all know that's not true,' Geraldine said softly. 'She's the woman you strangled on the waste ground near the railway, round the corner from your house.'

Tearfully, Thomas launched into a rambling account of an anonymous stranger who had tried to blackmail him.

'I was scared she would tell my wife so I got hold of the cash she asked for, or part of it anyway. She was demanding five grand. Where was I supposed to get hold of that kind of money overnight? I managed five hundred and put it by the tree, where she said, but when I saw her with the bag over her shoulder I changed my mind and took it back. It was such a lot of money, I couldn't just let it go like that. So I pulled the bag off her shoulder and ran off. I was behind her all the time, so I didn't think she would see who had taken it. When she contacted me again I was going to tell her I'd left all the money there, all five grand, and someone else must have stolen it so that was that. I couldn't afford to pay her again. I thought I could get away with it, you see. Only then she must have fallen and hit her head as I was running off. She was alive when I left her. It must have been an accident. I never killed her.'

'So a second woman fell and hit her head and died when she met you,' Matthew said. 'You've admitted two women died at your hands in two weeks, yet you seriously expect us to believe both deaths were accidents, and this was all just a horrible coincidence, and you're not to blame?'

'That is for the courts to decide,' the grim-faced lawyer interjected.

'And then there's your wife,' Geraldine said heavily.

Thomas shook his head and tears poured unchecked down his cheeks. It was a while before he could speak.

'I love my wife,' he whispered. 'I love her. But she was going to the police. She'd seen the van in the garage, and she didn't understand. I tried to explain what I'd done, but she just kept yelling about how I'd brought a whore to our house. I knew she would never forgive me. She was threatening to go to the police.'

'So you killed her,' Matthew said.

'It wasn't like that. I never wanted to hurt her, but I was beside myself. I didn't know what I was doing. I never meant to hurt her. I loved her. I never meant to hurt anyone.'

'Temporary loss of control,' the lawyer muttered.

'Three women killed in as many weeks,' Matthew pointed out. 'There seems to be a pattern here.'

'No, no, you don't understand, I never meant it to happen. I never meant any of this to happen. I didn't even know the woman blackmailing me was dead until I read about it in the papers, and even then I couldn't be sure it was her.'

'DNA evidence we found confirms she was the woman you met on the waste ground,' Matthew said promptly. 'So that sorts out any doubts you might have.'

Still insisting that he had never intended to hurt anyone, Thomas was led sobbing back to his cell.

'It's all over for him,' Eileen said when they rejoined her. She beamed around. 'Good job, everyone. And welcome, Ian. It's good to have you back.'

She smiled at Geraldine. Now that Matthew had discovered Ian and Geraldine had been living together, their relationship could no longer remain a secret. Only a few of their colleagues had expressed surprise on learning the truth.

'You could have told me,' Ariadne chided Geraldine, when she joined her for a coffee in the canteen. 'I mean, I knew what was going on, obviously. I'm not blind. But you could have been open about it.'

'I was finding it difficult to be honest with myself about my feelings,' Geraldine replied.

Ariadne sighed. 'I know what you mean. This commitment business, it's hard, isn't it?'

Ian joined them. 'I hear congratulations are in order,' he said to Ariadne.

'Yes,' she replied. 'We've finally fixed a date.'

Geraldine smiled. 'It's good to know where you are in life,' she said, glancing at Ian, who smiled back at her.

Epilogue

THE CASE GERALDINE HAD been working on while Ian was away was all wrapped up. The suspect had made a full confession. He still insisted his victims' deaths had been accidental, but that was for a jury to determine. Geraldine's part in the process was over, leaving her free to concentrate on Ian.

'Until the next case,' he replied, smiling, pulling her towards him and kissing her.

'At least you can be sure no living man will ever take me away from you,' she replied with a grin. 'I'm going to make you breakfast this morning. You stay there and I'll call you when it's ready.'

It was Sunday morning, and Ian lay in bed checking the news on his iPad while Geraldine went to the kitchen. He heard her clattering about and soon after the smell of bacon and toast and fresh coffee wafted out to him, making his mouth water, while he waited impatiently to be summoned to the table. As he scrolled through the news, his eye was caught by a report about an overnight bust of an established drug gang which had been operating in London. An unnamed drug squad officer was quoted in the article, praising the efforts of his undercover team.

'Without their heroic efforts and sacrifices this wouldn't have been possible,' the anonymous officer said. 'Now there are fewer evil parasites pushing drugs on the streets and in the clubs, ruining young lives for their own profit. Many of my officers worked undercover in dangerous circumstances, often risking their own lives. Thanks to their fearless efforts, London is a safer place today than it was yesterday. We're fighting an ongoing war, but we have won a major battle today, and the officers involved in this operation did a magnificent job helping to inflict this blow against the criminal gangs seeking to flood our streets with Class A drugs. Our team endured adversity and danger with silent fortitude. We owe them a debt of gratitude that can never be repaid. For their own safety their identities remain protected, but wherever they are, they should feel justly proud of their contribution to the health and safety of our nation.'

Ian wondered if Jack hoped he would read the tribute, but it didn't matter. He wasn't even angry with Jack any more. He was back where he belonged, in York, working with Geraldine Steel. He was home.

Acknowledgements

I WOULD LIKE TO thank Dr Leonard Russell for his medical advice.

My thanks also go to the team at No Exit Press: Clare Quinlivan for so smoothly organising the online contract signing, Elsa Mathern for her brilliant cover design, Hollie McDevitt and Lisa Gooding for their invaluable marketing and PR, Jayne Lewis for an excellent copy-edit and Steven Mair for his eagle-eyed proofreading, Sarah Stewart-Smith for her efficient bookshop liaison and Andy Webb for his tireless work at Turnaround, and above all to Ion Mills and Claire Watts. I am really fortunate to be working with them and thrilled that there are more books to come in the series.

Geraldine and I have been together for a long time, in the company of my editor, who has been with us from the very beginning. We couldn't have come this far without you, Keshini!

My thanks go to all the wonderful bloggers who have supported Geraldine Steel, and to everyone who has taken the time to review my books. Your support means a lot to me.

Above all, I am grateful to my readers. Thank you for your interest in following Geraldine's career. To those of you who write to me to ask when the next book is out, I can assure you that it is already on its way. Book 17 is currently being edited. I have just started writing Book 18, and there are more to come after that. So I hope you continue to enjoy reading about Geraldine Steel.

Finally, my thanks go to Michael, who is my rock.

A LETTER FROM LEIGH

Dear Reader,

I hope you enjoyed reading this book in my Geraldine Steel series. Readers are the key to the writing process, so I'm thrilled that you've joined me on my writing journey.

You might not want to meet some of my characters on a dark night – I know I wouldn't! – but hopefully you want to read about Geraldine's other investigations. Her work is always her priority because she cares deeply about justice, but she also has her own life. Many readers care about what happens to her. I hope you join them, and become a fan of Geraldine Steel, and her colleague Ian Peterson.

If you follow me on Facebook or Twitter, you'll know that I love to hear from readers. I always respond to comments from fans, and hope you will follow me on **@LeighRussell** and **fb.me/leigh.russell.50** or drop me an email via my website **leighrussell.co.uk**.

That way you can be sure to get news of the latest offers on my books. You might also like to sign up for my newsletter on **leighrussell.co.uk/news** to make sure you're one of the first to know when a new book is coming out. We'll be running competitions, and I'll also notify you of any events where I'll be appearing.

Finally, if you enjoyed this story, I'd be really grateful if you would post a brief review on Amazon or Goodreads. A few sentences to say you enjoyed the book would be wonderful. And of course it would be brilliant if you would consider recommending my books to anyone who is a fan of crime fiction.

I hope to meet you at a literary festival or a book signing soon!

Thank you again for choosing to read my book.

With very best wishes,

Leigh Russell

BECOME A
NO EXIT PRESS MEMBER

BECOME A NO EXIT PRESS MEMBER and you will be joining a club of like-minded literary crime fiction lovers – and supporting an independent publisher and their authors!

AS A MEMBER YOU WILL RECEIVE

- Six books of your choice from No Exit's future publications at a discount off the retail price
- Free UK carriage
- A free eBook copy of each title
- Early pre-publication dispatch of the new books
- First access to No Exit Press Limited Editions
- Exclusive special offers only for our members
- A discount code that can be used on all backlist titles
- The choice of a free book when you first sign up

Gift Membership available too – the perfect present!

FOR MORE INFORMATION AND TO SIGN UP VISIT
noexit.co.uk/members